C000264649

THE GIRL IN THE SMOKE

THE GIRL IN THE SMOKE

Matt Hilton

**SEVERN
HOUSE**

First world edition published in Great Britain and the USA in 2024
by Severn House, an imprint of Canongate Books Ltd,
14 High Street, Edinburgh EH1 1TE.

severnhouse.com

British Library Cataloguing-in-Publication Data
A CIP catalogue record for this title is available from the British Library.

ISBN-13: 978-1-4483-1082-1 (cased)
ISBN-13: 978-1-4483-1083-8 (e-book)

All Severn House titles are printed on acid-free paper.

Typeset by Palimpsest Book Production Ltd.,
Falkirk, Stirlingshire, Scotland.
Printed and bound in Great Britain by
TJ Books, Padstow, Cornwall.

Praise for Matt Hilton

"An action-packed chase thriller"
Library Journal on *Cold Fire*

"Hot conflicts rage in the freezing cold"
Kirkus Reviews on *Cold Fire*

"Just right for the Hammett and Chandler crowd"
Booklist on *Fatal Conflict*

"A riotous action read"
Booklist on *Collision Course*

"Action galore"
Kirkus Reviews on *Collision Course*

"Hilton once again shows he can tell a gripping crime story"
Publishers Weekly on *Rough Justice*

About the author

Matt Hilton worked for 23 years in private security and the police force in Cumbria. He is a 4th Dan blackbelt and coach in Ju-Jitsu. He is the author of thirteen novels in the Joe Hunter series, and ten in the Grey & Villere thrillers.

www.matthiltonbooks.com

This one is for Denise.

PROLOGUE

The stench was the first indication that something very bad had happened ahead. It was a nostril-singeing assault on the olfactory senses: a mélange of burning plastic, overheated metal, molten rubber and blazing fuel. It was carried on a hot thermal wave at odds with the sub-zero mist blanketing the motorway.

It was reckless and potentially dangerous to get out of a vehicle on a motorway, even when the tailback stretched a mile or more behind. People mostly ignore safety advice, especially if there's something to be seen or – these days – recorded on mobile phones. There was little to see. The mist and the smoke obscured all but a faint, flickering glow ahead, but that hadn't stopped dozens from congregating near the front of the traffic jam.

Some of those jostling for a clearer view were ghoulish, wondering at what terrible sights they were missing; others were simply confused and begging answers that others could only offer guesses at. Some considered rushing into the noxious cloud but were torn between doing the right thing and preserving their own lives. Dozens had dialled 999 but there was no sign of the emergency services arriving yet.

Other people had exited their cars ahead, fleeing the choking fumes, and mingling with those lined between their cars and trucks. People coughed and spluttered and were offered steadying hands or shoulders to lean on. Some appeared dazed, others shocked, and there a man was shouting the name of somebody he'd lost sight of. He was prepared to plunge back into the smoke, but others held him back. He struggled with them, until a woman staggered towards him and threw herself into his embrace. The man wept in relief. The woman gestured wildly towards the flickering glow, screaming about people dying, burning in the wreckage of their cars. Some hardier souls heard her cries and started forward, but a billowing cloud of black smoke rolled over them and they retreated, coughing and barking at the toxins invading their lungs, tears streaming from their eyes. Behind the smoke was heat, and sparks rained among those running for cleaner air.

Panic swelled. Others clambered out of their vehicles, some reaching to grab possessions, or for children in the back seats of their cars. They joined the surge of humanity fleeing the spreading flames. The opposite carriageway was deserted, evidence that the pile-up extended across both sides of the motorway, and some people clambered over the central barriers seeking safety on the mist-shrouded embankment on the far side. For the main part, the largest number of fleeing motorists charged between the rows of closely packed vehicles, and others joined them.

There was a momentary lull as people slowed at a perceived safer distance, and they began turning, checking if the fire had progressed. Black smoke formed a bulwark, but was spreading across the fields to the east instead of further along the tarmac ribbon of the motorway. Hacking the fumes from their lungs, some urged the slowest escapees on. The last to emerge from the smoke was a small girl, no more than five years old. She was slight; a tiny thing with blonde hair pulled back in bunches above her sticky-out ears. Her clothing was soiled and there were smears of blood on her cheeks and hands. Her mouth bled profusely. She stumbled and folded to the ground and the smoke engulfed her. She was oblivious to the burly truck driver who ran back and snatched her up like a bundle of dirty laundry. He carried her from the spreading conflagration, the photograph of his sooty features and the tiny bundle in his arms destined to be on the front pages of all the major newspapers the following morning.

DANNI

Danni was tall for her age. Not quite eight years old, some adults mistook her for ten or more, something that left her with mixed feelings. It could sometimes be cool being the tallest girl in her class, except when the other kids laughed behind her back, calling her Giraffe Girl and Lamppost. Sometimes those mistaken adults also thought her immature for her age. She had caught their frowns and sidelong glances when she acted like a normal, everyday seven years and ten months old kid. When she once told one man her real age, he had asked if her parents put manure in her shoes. She was embarrassed, thinking he meant her feet smelled horrid.

Her long limbs accentuated her awkwardness as she ran across the lawn. The ridges in the soles of her trainers were clogged with grass cuttings. Green stains on the knees of her jeans and sweatshirt elbows showed where her ungainly stride had tumbled her to the ground more than once already. She rushed to the ancient cast-iron gate and hung her elbows between the spear-topped railings, breathing heavily as the woman came down the lane. Earlier she'd been too late to pet her dog, and had waited for its owner's return. At the end of the lane was a gate, and Danni had worried that the woman had walked her dog through it, to join the cinder path at the far end that led to the church at the west end of the village. Danni loved dogs; she loved all animals, and wished she could have a puppy of her own.

The dog was a tiny bundle of silky white corkscrew curls, with a button for a nose and sparkly black eyes. It moved like a wind-up toy as it pranced at the end of its lead. Danni giggled at its audacity when it cocked a leg and peed on a bunch of daffodils growing wild at the edge of the path. The woman glanced around, and spotted her audience of one leaning over the gate. She raised a hand in greeting, and turned down her mouth in mock embarrassment at her dog's shamelessness. Danni giggled even more. She was missing her front teeth, and as if the gap was a point of shame, she hid her mouth behind her hands. She didn't take her eyes off the dog for a second, until she grew aware the owner was veering towards her.

Danni withdrew a pace from the gate, and stood with one knee knocking against the other.

Despite the warmth of a spring day, the woman was swaddled under a quilted jacket, woollen hat and scarf, and wore tinted glasses. Her skin was as pale as her dog's coat, in stark contrast to her red-red lips. Danni thought she was beautiful, like an exotic vampire queen who'd dressed to avoid the sun's searing rays. When she smiled hello, Danni surreptitiously checked for fangs, but her teeth were even and white.

'Hello! I didn't see you standing there at first,' the woman said.

It was unsurprising. The hawthorn hedge overhung the unused garden gate on both sides, and Danni thought she was almost as skinny as the iron railings. Danni said nothing. She'd been warned about talking to strangers, and was worried her mum might be watching from the house, and would scold her for answering.

'Do you like my doggie?' asked the woman.

Danni cupped her hands over her mouth, nodding behind the shield. Nodding wasn't really talking, was it?

'He's a naughty rascal,' the woman went on, smiling conspiratorially, 'but he gets away with it because he's so cute. Don't you think he's cute?'

Danni nodded. She wanted to crouch down and reach between the bars to the dog. He watched her expectantly with his teddy-bear eyes, and his little pink tongue lolled with each excitable pant.

Danni patted her thighs and the little dog strained at its lead.

'He doesn't bite.' The woman stepped up to the gate, and the dog jumped up, with its front feet scrambling for purchase on the railings. It yipped in greeting. Watching the woman the entire time, Danni dipped at the knees and offered the back of her right hand for a lick. The dog's tongue tickled and she giggled.

'Told you he doesn't bite,' the woman said with a smile, 'but he might slobber you to death.'

Danni couldn't read the eyes behind the tinted glasses, but the woman's smile was warm. She might have resembled a vampire queen but not an evil one.

Nevertheless, she sneaked a look back at the house. From her perspective, it was almost a mansion, with easily a dozen windows from which her mum might be spying, but she knew her mum couldn't lip-read the back of her head.

She said, 'I love him. I wish I had a puppy.'

'Franklin isn't a puppy, he's fully grown.'

Danni tested the dog's name on her lips and tongue, but without making a sound. She was unsure of it; if he belonged to her she'd give him a name like Button or Snowy, or maybe just shorten it to Frankie. Franklin made him sound like a grumpy old man instead of an excitable doggie. The dog yipped again and danced on its back feet. She gently scruffed between his ears: his hair was so soft she was afraid it would disintegrate like a dandelion in seed if she stroked him any harder. Franklin nuzzled her hand.

'Is he a poodle?'

'Bichon Frisé,' the woman corrected her.

Soundlessly, Danni again tested the breed on her lips. *Beeshon Freeze-ay* she thought of it. She had never heard of that kind of dog before, but she loved it all the same. 'Is he a freeze-ay because he's white like snow?'

The woman laughed at her naivety, but without scorn. 'Frisé means curly in French. Similar to how we'd say frizzy.'

'He looks like a living toy.'

'Which is the point, I suppose. He's one of a toy breed.'

Danni thought the woman was teasing, and forgot to cover her mouth as she said, 'I'm not stupid. He isn't really a toy.'

The woman laughed again at the misunderstanding. '"Toy dogs" is the name for smaller dog breeds like Franklin, and also Shih Tzus and Pomeranians. They're sometimes called lapdogs. Have you heard that name before? A lapdog?'

'Pete says Mum thinks he's her lapdog.'

'Pete?' The woman glanced sharply towards the house. 'Is he your brother, your mum's partner?'

Danni was suddenly guarded. If pressed she wouldn't know how to effectively describe her relationship to Peter Walsh. Her used-to-be-dad, Gary, went to heaven, and then her mum met Pete and he moved in with them. He was like her dad, but wasn't. He was her mum's boyfriend, but they weren't married yet, so she didn't know if he'd be her real dad or not. She said nothing, concentrating instead on Franklin licking her hand.

'What's your mum's name?' asked the woman.

Danni was unsure if she should answer. After all, she shouldn't have talked with this stranger, never mind given out personal details. The woman offered a compromise, naming her mum for her. 'Isn't your mum Josephine Lockwood?' She aimed a nod up the lane, indicating some undetermined location. 'We met a few days ago in the village. She told me she lives here in the old gatehouse.'

Danni had rarely heard her mum referred to as Josephine, only as Josie. Because the woman knew her full name and that their house was once at the entrance to a country estate, there was no reason to believe she was lying or making things up about meeting her. 'Ummm,' she intoned in agreement.

The woman bent forward, peering through the dark lenses of her sunglasses. Danni couldn't help but stare at her scarlet lips. Close up they looked painted on with oils. The mouth opened a sliver, and the woman's tongue ran between her perfect white teeth. 'If Josephine's your mum, then that makes you Daniele, right?'

'Danni,' she stated, taking a little pleasure in correcting the woman this time.

'Aah, yes. Danni.'

There was a distant rapping noise.

The woman straightened, pulling Franklin from the gate. She wiggled slim fingers in a brisk goodbye, and led the dog away. He pranced and tugged at the lead, disappointed to be leaving so soon. The woman picked him up, tucking him under her arm. She offered Danni a final smile. 'Franklin's so happy he's met you at last.'

JOSIE

Josie Lockwood stood with her mobile phone to her ear, barely listening to her sister Grace jabbering on about last night's fall-out from an office party that sounded like the plot of a soap opera. Instead, Josie peered out the kitchen window to where Danni had just galumphed across the garden to the unused gate on to the side lane. Danni was playing with a small dog through the railings, and Josie could only make out vague details of its owner. Her view blocked by the overgrown hedge, she couldn't tell who was talking to her daughter, only that it was a woman, judging by the woolly hat and scarf she wore. Neighbours often used the lane as a shortcut to the far end of the village, or as a route into the adjoining church grounds, but occasionally Josie had spotted an unfamiliar face and wondered what business strangers had in the lane. It wasn't private property, so she had no right saying who could or couldn't walk down the lane, so had warned Danni about talking to anyone she didn't recognize. There was a fine line between being socially polite and keeping her child safe, and for the latter she'd rather come across as downright rude than Danni be coaxed away by a paedophile offering sweets or puppy dogs.

She rapped her knuckles on the kitchen window, but Danni was oblivious as she petted the tiny dog. Perhaps the dog's owner heard, and was conscious of overstepping a boundary, because she abruptly pulled the dog away and bent to lift it. Danni was left crouching at the gate, watching as the stranger walked off. Josie rattled another staccato summons on the window.

'He's too gobby for his own good, and I don't know what he thinks he looks like in those skinny jeans. I've seen more fat on a butcher's apron than on his legs, and those jeans are so tight you can see the veins in his you-know-what, and it's nothing to brag about either. If he's going to wear skinny jeans he should stuff a sock down his underpants . . .' Grace stopped twittering mid-sentence, conscious she was being ignored. 'Josie? Is there something wrong? Josie? *Jo?*'

Grace almost shouted her final question.

'Hang on a mo,' Josie said into the phone. She gestured at Danni to come inside. Unbeknown to her, the sky was reflected on the pane outside, and when Danni guiltily looked in her direction, she didn't see her. Josie knocked on the window a third time, and the old glass shuddered.

'What's going on?' Grace demanded.

'Um, it's nothing. I'm just . . .' Josie knocked on the window again, and this time Danni stood and began a slow walk across the lawn, dragging her feet. Pete had given the lawn its first cut of the year a few days earlier, but hadn't gathered the cuttings. They clogged Danni's trainers. Josie had, only minutes ago, put away the vacuum cleaner, just before her sister called. 'Grace, I'm going to have to go. I need to get Danni in for lunch, and she's about to traipse muck all over the house.'

'Oh, the joys of having kids,' Grace laughed with no sympathy. She was the mother of two boys. 'I did warn you, sis, once you have kids, your house is never the same again.'

'I've just finished cleaning too . . .' Josie watched Danni's slow progress: the girl thought she was in for a rollicking for disobeying the 'no speaking to strangers' rule. Josie didn't intend giving her a hard time, but a reminder wouldn't go amiss. Danni was such a sweet thing it made her vulnerable. 'OK. I'd best go before Danni gets inside. You still coming over this weekend?'

'Yeah. I'll bring the boys over, shall I? Then you'll really see what kind of mess kids can make.'

'Please do. Danni's bored out of her mind, and I can't get anything done for trying to keep her entertained.'

'School holidays. Who needs 'em, eh? I don't remember getting so many days off when we were kids.'

'I'm sure we did. But we had each other for company. Danni hasn't got anyone to play with.'

'The boys won't play with her. Torment her maybe. But at least she won't be bored while she sorts them out, eh?'

If Josie allowed it, Grace would go on and on. 'Love you, sis, but I really have to go.'

'Love you more.'

Josie made a swift bye-bye and pressed the end call button. She intercepted Danni at the kitchen door. Her daughter was kicking off clumps of muddy grass on the back step.

'Don't do that there,' Josie said too snappily, 'or it'll just get trailed in every time you come in the house.'

Sulking, Danni moved away and began dragging her soles on the paving stone path. Josie emitted an audible sigh that meant 'God, give me strength'. Danni stopped scraping and looked for an answer to the dilemma.

'Take your trainers off,' Josie suggested, softening, 'and I'll get you some clean ones. Then you can have some lunch.'

Danni broke down the heels of her trainers in the process, standing first on one with a grassy sole and then the other with her sock. A few cuttings transferred to her socks, but Josie could live with them. She picked Danni up with a grunt, helping her over the mess already on the step, and set her down on safe ground in the kitchen. 'Bloomin' hell! You're getting big,' she said, 'maybe I need to start cutting down your portions, girl.'

'Not yet! I'm starving,' Danni announced chirpily, supposing she'd got away with flaunting the Stranger Danger rule because her mum hadn't mentioned it yet.

Josie patted her tiny backside, ushering her towards the table. Behind Danni she shook her head at the stray cuttings and dirt adhering to her clothes, some of which were bound to end up on the chair she clambered into: apparently her housework chores hadn't ended for the day.

'Who was that you were just speaking to?' Josie asked.

Danni's neck retreated into her shoulders. 'I wasn't talking to anyone, just with Franklin.'

'Franklin? Wasn't that a woman at the gate?'

Danni was animated again. 'Franklin's a doggie. He's a freeze-ay. He's a toy lapdog. Freeze-ay means curly in French.'

'For not speaking with anyone, you seem to have learned a lot about him.'

'I didn't speak to Franklin's mum, not really. She just told me those things when I was stroking him.'

'And what have I warned you about speaking with strangers?'

'I wasn't speaking to her, just listening.'

'It's the same thing, Danni.'

'How?'

'Because.'

'Oh?' She scowled at the table. 'I only wanted to pet Franklin.'

'In future, if you want to pet *anything*, can you please check with me first?'

'OK.' Danni drew out the word glumly. 'I didn't tell the lady anything, because I thought she was a vampire.'

Josie was stuck for a response. Instead she headed for the oven where Danni's lunch was warming.

Danni said, 'She can't have been a vampire, though, because even wrapped up like that she would have still turned to dust in the sunlight. Wouldn't she, Mum?'

'I'm sure you're right, but I'm no expert on vampires. Don't they just twinkle in sunlight these days?'

Danni wasn't old enough to get the movie reference from Josie, but then, Josie hadn't allowed her to watch any movies with vampires yet, definitely not *The Twilight Saga* she herself had loved when she'd read the books. What little Danni would know about supernatural creatures must have been gleaned from cartoons and kids' books.

'You don't have to worry about vampires,' Josie told her. 'We're having chicken Kiev and chips for lunch, and everyone knows vamps can't abide garlic.'

'Mum? Can I have a puppy like Franklin?'

'What? Don't you like chicken Kiev any more?'

It took a moment for the joke to sink in, but then Danni's face brightened and showed her gums in a broad grin. After another moment she touched fingers to the gap in her mouth. 'Mum, if I got bit by a vampire, would I grow fangs?' She was hopeful at the possibility.

'Hmmm.' Josie pretended to mull the notion over. 'I guess you'd have to suck on an ice-lolly instead of on people's necks.'

Her words were meant in jest, but lately Danni's lack of front teeth had become a point of shame for her. When she was younger, her missing teeth had never been an issue, because all her contemporaries were approaching a similar gap-toothed state. But as most of her school friends were now of an age where their adult teeth were growing in, Danni felt like the odd one out. She was already a target for those making fun of her height, and the last thing she needed was to be singled out for the gap in her smile.

'You'll have your big teeth soon,' Josie assured her as she set down a plate of food before her.

'Promise?'

'Promise. They're just taking that little bit longer to grow in because of the way you lost your baby teeth. Don't you remember what the dentist said?'

'He asked me if I'd been kissing boys and that's why my teeth fell out.' Danni wrinkled her nose at the memory. 'His breath smelled like cabbage. Yuk!'

'He told you that because your milk teeth got compressed into your gums; they'd have to grow out first and your second set would take a little longer to follow. Just think on the bright side – when your friends all have braces on, you'll have lovely straight white teeth.'

'I'd rather have fangs,' Danni opined, and her mum picked up two forks, crossing them to ward her off. They laughed and Danni forgot all about her insecurities, and being told off for speaking to Franklin's mum. She tucked into her lunch with gusto, and her missing teeth posed no problem in demolishing it.

CALLUM

Callum Grieves didn't care what people thought of him, or of his bad manners. That obese cow probably believed he should hold the door open for her while she squeezed inside, but to hell with the lazy bitch. Let her get the door herself, and she could claim a minor victory for the feminist movement. He allowed the door to swing in her face, and she slapped the glass with her pudgy fingers to halt it. She glared at his rudeness, her eyes like raisins in sourdough, and he exhaled a spiteful laugh and kept walking. As she struggled inside he could hear her muttering behind his back: something about chivalry being dead and buried. *Here you are*, he thought, *how's about this from the age of chivalry?* He aimed her a two-fingered salute, and in case she didn't get the same message English bowmen allegedly sent their French enemies at Agincourt, he growled, 'Fuck you, lard-arse.'

His crass words carried, and other shoppers in the chain store heard them, attracting frowns and tuts. Nearby a security guard leant an elbow on top of a display counter as he chatted up a sales assistant young enough to be his daughter. The guard's ear was tuned to the F-bomb, and he glowered over his shoulder at the perpetrator. Grieves allowed his mouth to drop open, and he curled his tongue behind his yellow teeth and emitted a string of unintelligible sounds. While the guard frowned harder, he cast the rent-a-monkey a challenging glare. 'What? You got a problem with me?' Before the guard could respond though, he continued on, brushing shoulders unnecessarily to get through the press of customers in the main aisle. He had no interest in the shop's wares, other than using its aisles as a shortcut through to the delicatessen on the next street. He needed food, and quickly. If anyone thought him rude then, just wait until his blood sugar lowered.

He wasn't diabetic; he had one of those metabolisms that burned up everything that passed his lips. The sustenance value of food didn't linger; he was always starving. He was tall and whip-thin. He wasn't skeletal, his muscles were tight and sinewy, and when he used to box had often been referred to as a wiry bastard by his coach. His features were equally tight – pinched even – with deep grooves in his cheeks and brow, while his lips were bloodless horizontal slashes. He wore his dirty blond hair longer on the top, and it stood up, as wiry as the rest of him. One earlobe carried a silver stud and an inverted crucifix. In a dark grey two-piece off-the-peg suit, white shirt open at the collar and loose thin black tie, bottomed off with stained canvas deck shoes, he had the look of a middle-aged man who had never left behind his anarchic punk rocker youth . . . or, judging by his behaviour, was trying too hard to regain it.

Before he exited the store, he swore at two more people who got in his way, and was in no better mood outside. He was set to explode like a rocket when spotting the length of the lunchtime queue at the deli. No way was he going to hold his cool if forced to wait more than a minute. He looked for an alternative and recalled there was a bakery fifty metres up the street. There was probably as much demand for pasties and sausage rolls, but generally the queues moved faster when the goods were simply bunged into a paper bag. He set off, veering among shoppers. Before he reached the baker's his mobile phone rang. He was tempted to ignore it until after he'd fed his face, but he had set this ringtone to a specific number. He pulled the phone from his inside jacket pocket, and found an alcove where he could take the call without fear of eavesdroppers.

'Wotcha, Tobe!'

'That you, Callum?'

'Who else? You rang me, mate.'

'Where are you?'

'In town.'

'Which town?'

'I'm still in Lancaster. But it's a dead end, mate.'

'Yeah, just as I thought it'd be. How soon can you be in Chester?'

'You got a lead?'

Toby Davis didn't immediately answer. After a beat he asked again, 'How soon can you be in Chester?'

'Couple of hours, give or take.'

'Give or take what, Callum? Can you be more specific?'

'Give or take fifteen minutes. It depends, mate. Traffic can be a bit slow on the M6 round this time. Plus, I hav'ta get some grub down me before I hit the road. I was just about to grab a pie when you called.'

'You aren't going to starve to death in the next couple of hours. Get moving now. I'll text you the address where I'll be.'

'Better give me the postcode, Tobe. I don't know my way around Chester.'

'Will do. You'll find me easily enough.'

'So, have you got a lead or what?'

'The best we've had yet.'

''Bout time, mate.' Grieves was about to head for where he'd parked his car, but his stomach gurgled. The bakery beckoned him; he could smell its tasty wares even from where he stood in the piss-stained alcove. He turned and strode in the opposite direction. 'I'll be there as fast as I can.'

JOSIE

When Pete Walsh arrived home from work, he dragged a cloud of annoyance behind him. His dark hair lay flat and listless and stubble shadowed his chin. He almost slumped in the hall as he kicked out of his loafers and hung up his coat.

'Hard day?' Josie asked.

'Don't ask.'

'I just did.'

He exhaled. 'Different day, same old crap.'

After a brief peck on the lips, they moved for the living room and Pete collapsed in an easy chair.

'I was expecting you home an hour ago,' said Josie.

'Yeah, well I was expecting to be home an hour ago too. Bloody Gibson had other ideas though.'

'He made you stay behind again?'

'The miserable git hasn't got a life outside the shop, so he doesn't get it that the rest of us have families to come home to . . . or doesn't care. He ordered us section managers to stay back to get the sale signage up ready for Monday morning.' Pete gingerly loosened his tie and the top button of his shirt. He held out a swollen index finger. The fingernail was livid purple. 'Look at that. I trapped my finger between two racks; I'll probably lose the bloody nail!'

'Looks sore.'

'It's flamin' killing me. The nail might need lancing to release the pressure . . .'

'Maybe you should go to A&E and get it checked.'

Pete shook his hand and the suggestion of going to hospital off. 'I'll wait and see if it gets any worse. Tell you what, though; I made sure I reported it in the accident book. If this gives me any bother I'm going to sue the bollocks off Gibson. He made me shift the racks alone when he knows it's a two-person job.'

'So, if the signage has gone up, does that mean you won't be in work on Sunday now?'

'You've gotta be jokin'. Gibson wants the full sales floor shifted around before the sale.'

Josie scowled: it would have been nice to get a full weekend with Pete at home, but yet again his uncaring manager had wrecked her plans.

Pete threw up his hands. 'It's not my fault, Josie. Gibson just points out that my contract states I must work whenever operational demands require. I'd've been better off signing my soul to the devil.'

'At least with the signage already in place, you might not be at work as long as you originally thought.'

'Don't kid yourself. Gibson won't let me away any earlier; the miserable sod will find something else that needs doing.'

'And you're not even getting paid for overtime?'

'No. I'm *salaried*. I don't get shit for giving up my weekend.'

'You should get time-owed at least.'

'Yeah, I should, but tell me the last time Gibson let me take any I've accrued off. I bet I've a month's worth banked, but the hope of ever getting it off's a bloody pipedream.'

'I'd've liked you at home while Danni's off school.'

'Yeah, I'd like it too, Josie. But we're even more understaffed than usual with other parents taking time off. I was better off when I was on the sales floor than I am as a manager. I bet if we added up all the hours I've worked this year, my hourly rate would be under the minimum wage.'

Different day, same old crap. This wasn't the first occasion they'd lamented the constraints placed on their family time since Pete accepted a promotion to section manager. It probably wouldn't be their last.

'Did you get much work done?' Pete asked.

'Nope. Not a thing.' Josie exhaled sharply. She was a self-employed editor, taking on work for several large publishing houses. Her skills were in demand, therefore her rates were decent, and when time permitted she earned a fair wage. But she had barely found time to get any editing done with Danni under her feet. With Pete home she hoped to squeeze in a couple of hours after dinner, but that wasn't conducive to making their private time together any better. Tomorrow, her sister Grace and the Terrible Trio were due to visit, and although Danni would have kids to play with for a change, she still wouldn't get any work done. She could also say goodbye to working the coming Sunday if Pete was going to be out all day, unless she was more selfish with her time and wilfully neglected her child.

The wilful neglect of my child? What a horrible idea that is. The idea was abhorrent and not one she ever expected to contemplate. Danni deserved better. It was through a mother's wilful neglect that Danni had come to her in the first place, when Josie had pledged she'd never place her personal or career needs before those of her daughter.

Living where they did was expensive. Some of their neighbours were surgeons and entrepreneurs, celebrities and professional sportsmen and -women. Even with their combined salaries they were barely scraping by, and – being honest – if it wasn't for Pete throwing in with her, Josie knew the prospect of keeping the house was unrealistic. One saving grace was that the house was paid for: when a heart attack took her husband Gary, his insurance paid off the mortgage and bequeathed her enough cash to subsist on for a while, but the pot of money had swiftly dwindled. In truth, even without a mortgage to worry about, maintaining the house, and the day-to-day expenditure of living, was far too expensive for her to manage alone, and she'd be lost without Pete's income. She was fortunate that Pete had taken on her baggage, but it made her fearful he'd only do so for so long until real dissatisfaction set in. He took the promotion at work because on paper it gave him a higher salary, but without considering how it'd impact on their lives together. It wouldn't have surprised her if he regretted taking on a single mother and her money pit of a house. She had worried about Pete leaving for months, and whenever he was despondent like this, it didn't help soothe her fears.

'Where's Danni at?' he asked.

'She's up in her bedroom, drawing a picture for you.'

Pete grunted. His forehead creased before rethinking his response and he formed a smile.

She slipped on to his lap, pushed back his limp hair and kissed him fully on the lips. He was tense, in pain, but relaxed into the kiss. After they parted, she continued teasing some life into his locks, drawing her fingernails gently over his scalp as she stared into his eyes. 'I appreciate everything you do for us,' she reassured him in a whisper. 'You do know that, Pete?'

'Yeah. Of course.'

He sounded so earnest she kissed him again.

'What brought that on?' he asked as they again eased apart.

'I only want you to know *how much*.' She was fearful of adding *I don't want to lose you, Pete*, in case it put the idea into his head.

'Hey, just 'cause I'm pissed off with work, it doesn't mean I'm dissatisfied with my life. I know how much you appreciate me, Josie. Hell, I'm the one worried you're going to kick me out because I'm unable to give you the kind of life you'd grown accustomed to. And now you're showing doubt about keeping *me* happy?'

She tried laughing off his words, but wasn't expressing the truth. And she knew that he knew it. She waved a hand, indicating the living room, but more specifically the entire house. 'I've been giving some thought to this place lately. Maybe we should be realistic about our expectations and put the house on the market. If we sold up, downsized, maybe moved out of this area altogether, then we wouldn't have to worry so much about making ends meet, and you could tell Gibson to shove his job where the sun doesn't shine.'

'I'd love to but . . .' Pete shook his head.

'Why not? You forget, Pete, before I married Gary I never lived in a flamin' country house like this. Since moving here I've always felt out of my depth, and my comfort zone. A house this large . . . bloody hell! When you're at work and Danni's at school, I feel like a marble rattling around in an empty box!'

'Now wouldn't be a good time to move house. Not with the poor shape the property market's in. You'd be lucky if you got anywhere close to its true value.'

Josie shrugged off his concern. 'Homes around here are over-priced as it is. If I put it on the market at a reasonable price, it'd sell quickly, and we'd have more than enough to purchase a new home elsewhere. Up in north Cumbria where my parents live, we could buy a full street with what people pay for houses around here.'

'I think that might be a slight exaggeration.'

'Yeah, maybe, but you know what I mean.'

He considered for a few seconds. 'You'd really be prepared to leave this home behind? All the memories you've made here?'

He was referring to her previous relationship with Gary, and perhaps to him that would be a good thing. Josie had good memories, but this was also the place where she'd discovered her husband slumped dead in the bathroom, and she'd happily leave behind any reminders of that horrible day. 'It's only bricks and mortar,' she said without genuine conviction.

'What about Danni? It would mean relocating her again, starting a new school, leaving friends behind. Don't you think she's already had enough of that in the past few years? She has finally got some stability in her life; don't you think that moving her might affect her badly?'

'If there's one thing about Danni, she's resilient. Besides, I get the impression that she's not happy here, and when it comes to school, she's having a bit of a hard time. Moving schools and making new friends might be good for her.'

'She's being bullied?'

'Not so much bullied as excluded.'

'Same thing,' said Pete, and of course he was right. Josie suspected that the realization hit him that he hadn't even said hello to Danni since arriving home, so was also guilty of excluding her. He patted Josie's shoulders, shifting beneath her. She got the message and stood, allowing him to rise.

'Have you thought about dinner yet, Josie?' Before she could answer, he grasped her hand conspiratorially. 'How's about we nip into town and take Danni for a burger? The two of you have been cooped up here for days, going out for something to eat might do you both good.'

'It's almost her bedtime,' Josie said. Also, if they were out for the evening, then she wasn't going to get any work done at all. But then, she wasn't really opposed to the idea of getting out of the house for an hour or two. 'Oh, what the heck? Let's live a little,' she grinned, and took his other hand to lead him out of the room.

'Aaah!' He withdrew his hand. He inspected his throbbing index finger.

Josie sucked air through her teeth. 'That looks sore.'

'It is.' He cupped his other hand protectively around his injury.

'Maybe you should go to A and E while we're in town.'

'That isn't my idea of an evening out,' he replied, 'and I'm not sure a trip to hospital's something Danni will enjoy.'

Immediately the girl galumphed into the room, as if summoned by mention of her name. Josie wondered if she'd been lurking in the hall, eavesdropping on their conversation, and frowned at her daughter. Danni stood, her knees knocking, with a sheet of paper held up so it concealed her mouth.

'Hi, kid,' Pete said.

'Hiya.' The drawing paper muffled Danni's voice. 'Are we going to hospital?'

'Danni,' Josie scolded, 'what have I told you about snooping on adult conversations?'

'Not to,' Danni said, 'but I wasn't really snooping. I only came down to show Pete the drawing I've done for him.'

Josie clucked her tongue. 'Then don't you think you'd better show him it?'

Pete smiled and held out his good hand. Danni passed over the drawing but with slight reluctance. Now it had come time to unveil her artwork, she was nervous about how it would be received. Pete studied it, then briefly aimed it at Josie. 'This is great,' he exclaimed with a tad too much enthusiasm to be sincere. 'Is it a polar bear cub?'

Danni's forehead creased for a second before correcting him. 'It's Franklin. He's a bitch on freeze.'

'Is he now?' Pete chuckled.

Josie interjected. 'She means a Bichon Frisé; a little dog she met today.'

'He looks cute,' Pete said.

'If we move house, can we still have a garden so I can get a doggie like Franklin?' Danni asked in a rush.

She earned a raised eyebrow from Josie who turned to Pete. 'Look at what you've started.'

As an excuse to avoid her mother's frown, Danni was suddenly interested in Pete's swollen finger. Her head rocked as she studied it from various angles. 'Your nail has gone purple,' she stated the obvious.

'Yeah. It's . . . well, it's kinda sore to be honest.' Pete shoved it closer and she shied back, as if the pain or discolouration could transfer to the tip of her nose; she covered a squawk with her hands. He laughed, then again held up her drawing to admire it. 'You're quite a talented artist, Danni. Is it all right if I take this to work with me and pin it up in my office?'

Danni liked the idea, nodding enthusiastically.

'Go and get your coat and shoes on,' Josie instructed. 'And not those dirty trainers you had on earlier. Before we go to the hospital, Pete's going to take us for a burger . . . but you already knew that, didn't you, you little monkey?'

'We can go to the hospital first,' Danni told Pete earnestly. 'I don't mind. When I was little I was in hospital and it isn't a scary place, not like when you go to the dentist's.'

'You remember when you were in hospital?' Pete was surprised. From what Josie had told him, Danni hadn't quite been five years old at the time of her hospitalization: he fully expected that her earlier life would have been a blur to her by now. But then, he was equating the memory of a guy in this thirties trying to recall his childhood; to Danni it might not seem as distant that she still retained some memories.

'Oh, I remember it.' Danni puffed out her chest, as if her capacity for recollection was a point of admiration. 'Just not the stuff before.'

'Funny how you can remember that but not what I told you only a minute ago.' Josie thumbed towards the back of the house. 'Coat. Shoes. If you want that burger, you'd best skedaddle!'

Without replying Danni raced off, making loud, excitable noises that rang throughout the house.

TOBY

A lamppost's wan light fought the gathering gloom. Tree limbs budding with new life cast dappled shadows over the grey Range Rover, dancing on the windscreen when stirred by the mild breeze. Seated behind the steering wheel, Toby Davis was confident he couldn't be seen, but still scrunched down in the seat as Pete Walsh's Ford Focus crawled out between the grand but weathered columns. The tall hawthorn hedges either side of the gateposts had made watching the house difficult from Davis's position, so the emergence of the car was a slight surprise. It was less than twenty minutes since Walsh had arrived home, and Davis wasn't expecting him to leave again so soon. Perhaps Walsh was heading out on an errand, and Josephine and Danni were again alone in the house, but no. The face turned towards him in the front passenger seat was that of Josie Lockwood, and he also made out another figure shifting about in the back of the estate car. Josie looked directly at his Range Rover, and her mouth worked. Davis scrunched lower in the seat, but there was nothing to worry about. She was only giving the all-clear to Pete as he began manoeuvring out of the drive. The Ford went right, heading away from Davis who was parked adjacent to the lane that ran alongside the perimeter of the old country estate. His head rose, neck stretching tortoise-like as he studied the car driving away. Plumes of diesel smoke hung momentarily in the air before being carried away by the breeze.

Davis considered following.

Tailing the car wouldn't serve any purpose, though, other than possibly blowing his cover. It was doubtful that Josie had taken anything more than a fleeting interest in the Range Rover, and had immediately discarded it as unimportant. But the car might stay in her subconscious and attract her attention, and closer scrutiny, if she spotted it again following them through the village and beyond. The last thing Davis wanted was for her to grow guarded.

He took out his phone and dialled.

'Wotcha, Tobe!' Callum Grieves responded. Davis hated being called Tobe, and Grieves knew it, but he would persist.

'Are you still where I left you?'

Earlier, Davis had sent him directions to a gastro-pub situated in the small village on the southwestern side of Chester. As promised, Grieves had liaised with him within the agreed two hours, where they'd gone over an embryonic plan of action. It culminated with Davis instructing Grieves to sit tight while he went ahead and recce'd the location Josephine Lockwood had been traced to.

'Where else would I be, Tobe? It's not as if I've got anywhere better to be, is it?'

'Are you in your car?'

'Yep. I'm waitin' in the car park . . . as you ordered, Tobe.'

'Good. You'll see a blue Ford Focus estate passing any minute. Walsh, Lockwood and the kid are onboard. I want you to follow them, check out what they're up to, but Callum, no contact, right?'

'Not even if an opportunity presents?'

'No. It's too risky. We stick to the plan.'

'We have a plan?'

'Don't be sarcastic. Just do as I ask.'

'Gotcha.'

'Callum.'

'What?'

'Don't allow your impatience to mess this up.'

'Oh ye of little faith. Don't worry, Tobe; I know how to tail somebody without being spotted. It is, after all, what I do for a fuckin' living.'

'Update me with your progress,' Davis went on, 'and if they look as if they're about to return home, I need you to alert me.'

'What you gonna do?'

'Make the most of the opportunity to take a closer look.'

'Gotcha. Hey! Here it comes. Blue piece-of-shit Ford Focus that looks like it's burning oil?'

'That's them,' Davis confirmed, but added the licence-plate number to make certain.

'OK, go and do your stuff, I'm on 'em. Later, Tobe.' Grieves ended the call.

Davis sneered at the phone. He was unhappy about being forced to work with an idiot like Callum Grieves, but he had no choice in the matter. As he had been reminded already, a surly bastard like Grieves had his uses. If Davis had a fault, it was that his nature was sometimes misread as sanguine. He didn't engender the kind of threat that their work sometimes required, whereas there was never any confusion when Grieves made a promise: he had all the subtlety of a blunt axe. If he said he was going to rip off your head, he bloody well meant he was going to try. Davis was then the one who had to calm down the situation, but that could win him more cooperation than if he were the one threatening dire consequences. He was the good cop to Grieves's bad. Sometimes, as he'd also been reminded, it took a blunt axe to crack a tough nut, and then a softer touch to tease the kernel from within.

Davis, though, was nobody's soft touch.

Before getting out, he checked the Range Rover's mirrors. In the last few minutes it had grown darker, and there was no hint of lights other than the lamppost anywhere close by. The nearest neighbouring house was a good two hundred metres away, while behind him a bend in the road followed the contour of the fields adjacent to the River Dee, and the next building, a church, was well out of sight in that direction. A car could approach any second, but he'd have plenty of warning to cross unseen. He got out of the Range Rover and trotted across to stand alongside the gatepost on the right. He checked before entering the drive and saw that a light had been left on inside to deter burglars, and another cast its glow from over the front door. He was certain no one was home, so moved up the drive, feeling the crunch of gravel underfoot. It was a noisy progress, but who was going to hear him? The lawn along-side the drive offered a stealthier approach, but he would make footprints in the grass and he didn't want to leave any clues he'd been there. He didn't approach the front door: these days, even out here in the country, it was common practice for homeowners to lock their doors. He was unconcerned that he might trip a motion sensor; at best it would trigger a floodlight, but with nobody to see him in its glow, so what? He checked for CCTV cameras though, and was confident there weren't any.

At the front window he cupped his hands against the glass to peer inside. A chink left open in the curtains allowed a view of a neat sitting room. Nobody home. He continued around the house, an impressive construction originally erected to show off its owner's wealth and power. It had been built centuries ago as a gatehouse to serve the much larger country mansion at the centre of the estate, now long ago demolished, the estate also sold off in chunks after the family fortune had dwindled. It was amazing, Davis thought, what could be learned from the Internet, but it wasn't enough. He knew its history, but hadn't much of a clue when it came to the internal layout of the property.

At the rear he triggered a sensor. It cast a circle of light around the back door. He was again unconcerned: the lamp was there for the benefit of the occupants coming and going to the side garden during the night, and not necessarily to light up an intruder for the sake of a camera. He checked through a kitchen window before taking a quick look towards the lane that ran alongside the garden. Dog walkers used the lane, and he didn't want to be spotted by anyone who might be alerted by his skulking nature. He couldn't see or hear anyone, so moved to the path and approached the back door steps. There he paused to draw on a pair of gloves fished from his pocket. Once gloved, he tried the handle. It turned, but didn't disengage the latch. All that thwarted him was a simple lever tumbler lock. Unhurriedly he took out a small pouch and opened it. Under the handy glow of the lamp, he selected what was known in the trade as a bump key. It looked like an ordinary key but all the peaks were even and cut down to the lowest groove. It was attached to a short metal rod bossed with a semi-circular steel end that fitted snugly in his palm. He inserted the key, applied torsion, and then thumped his hand sharply with the heel of his opposite thumb. Newton's cradle-esque, the kinetic force shot along the length of the key and moved the driver pins so a gap appeared in the mechanism's sheer line, allowing for the lock's plug to rotate freely. Davis gently pushed the door inward and stepped into a tiny lobby alongside the kitchen. He paused to put away his 'rapping-key' set and took out his phone.

The kitchen retained an aroma of cooking; it smelled faintly of garlic and warm vegetable oil. There was a faint hum from an upright fridge-freezer and the ticking of a wall clock. It was approaching 7.30 p.m. – a bit earlier than Davis had assumed. It was spring, but out there in the country it got darker sooner than in the artificially lit cities he was familiar with. He contemplated using the flash on his phone, but decided against it, and instead went from room to room turning on the overhead lights and snapping shots of each room, before turning off the lights behind him. The activity would be strange to any observer, but less so than the flashing of the camera's flash in an otherwise dark house. Finished with his reconnoitre, he retreated to the kitchen and paused only briefly to check out the laptop on the table and a stack of printed papers next to it. He recalled from what he'd already gleaned about Josephine Lockwood that her editing skills were in high demand but, from the look of things, she hadn't got started on her latest commission. He checked the author's name on the title page and was surprised by its familiarity: he'd read a couple of that guy's action adventures and enjoyed them. He was tempted to sneak a peek through the document to get a taster of the author's upcoming publication, but his ringing phone brought him back to reality.

'Wotcha, Tobe! You finished sniffing Lockwood's dirty underwear yet?'

Grieves's question brought a hard edge to Davis's voice. 'Don't be so fucking disgusting, Callum. Are they on the way back?'

'Nope, so you don't havta rush your hand job.'

'Just tell me where you're at.'

'I'm picking up a cheeseburger and fries in town. D'you want me to get you something?'

'You're still on the family, right?'

'Yeah. I followed them here, and it's a bonus, mate. I'm not gonna miss the opportunity to grab somethin' while I'm in the queue, not after you dragged me away from a pie with my name on it earlier. Don't worry, Tobe, they're all seated at a table munchin' their happy meals: I won't miss them when they leave.'

'You may as well back off for now,' Davis said. 'It sounds as if they just decided to go out for supper and will head home soon. We won't gain anything from having you follow them further now that I'm finished here. Meet me back at the pub car park.'

'Awright,' Grieves replied. 'So, d'you want anythin' then, or not?'

'No.'

'Oh, that's right! You're more into quinoa and tofu and all that healthy bollocks, aren't ya? I could bring you some carrot sticks or one of those little bags of grapes.'

'I don't want anything.'

'You sure?'

'Actually, I want this job done with and to see the back of you, you shit head,' Davis snarled, but only after he had ended the call.

He took a last look around the kitchen, and then exited through the open door. The bump key had caused no lasting damage to the lock, and it snicked into its retainer again as if he had never been inside.

JOSIE

The way in which the man speaking into his phone checked her out sent a worm of unease up her spine. Josie was used to unwelcome attention. She'd never win a modelling contract but she supposed she was attractive enough, and despite a few extra kilos, she carried her weight well on an otherwise athletic, long-legged frame. She often received unsolicited glances or even openly lascivious stares from some men, but the same could be said of many women. It's something she didn't normally get concerned about, but for the briefest of moments, after he quickly averted his gaze, she knew he was still observing her out of the corner of his eye while he finished his call. There was a suggestion of a filthy mind behind the way the tip of his tongue ran over his upper teeth. Seated alongside Danni at the cluttered table, with Pete opposite, blissfully unaware of her discomfort, she watched the man watching her and felt unsettled.

'Oops!' Danni exclaimed, a second before droplets of mustard sprayed across Josie's left hand. 'Sorry, Mum.'

Glancing at the neon-bright yellow goo on her fingers, Josie was only distracted for the briefest of moments, and when she looked back at the man, he was heading for the exit, toting a brown paper bag filled with takeout food. Even angled away from her, she sensed he was still keeping her in his peripheral vision. Josie watched him all the way to the door, where, only very briefly, he turned and snapped a look on her that promised what he'd like to do with her, and it was an ugly image that flashed through her mind. He was momentarily framed in the doorway, a tall man whose grey suit hung on an almost emaciated frame, the trousers baggy at the knees and the pads of the shoulders a few inches too low on his arms. His black Slim Jim tie and collar was loosened, but she suspected it was because if he buttoned his shirt it would only highlight how skinny his neck was within its circle. His face was made up of lines and creases, accentuated by his pale spiky hair, and she couldn't help thinking of a corpse. He might have been recently dug up having spent a few months in his grave, a revenant given new life, but in need of a fresh wardrobe.

'Here.' Pete passed her a couple of napkins, and when she was slow to accept them, he began dabbing at the mustard on her fingers.

'Thanks, love,' she said, accepting the napkins, and wiped more vigorously. Beside her, Danni attempted to open another sachet of mustard, and Josie quickly took it, passing it to Pete before she was sprayed with a second coating. By the time that was done, the man had disappeared, and Josie shivered away the memory of him.

'Can you open my ketchup too?' Danni asked Pete.

He was still struggling with the mustard sachet, his swollen finger making things uncomfortable, and he resorted to nipping the packet with an eye-tooth.

'Here, I'll do it,' said Josie, and accepted a red sachet from Danni. Other open packets littered the table, and grains of salt had got everywhere, not to mention a number of stray French fries that had slipped off Danni's tray. She squeezed tomato ketchup on Danni's disassembled bun, then the girl tucked in, eating with as much gusto as she had at lunch. Ordinarily Josie might tell her to slow down, but she could see Pete wincing in pain, so the sooner they get to A&E, the better.

She reached across for Pete's hand, and he slipped it into her palm. The nail and surrounding tissue of his index finger was now vivid purple, and the skin so taut it looked shiny. 'That's not looking good.'

'It actually feels worse than it looks,' Pete confessed.

'You might lose that nail.'

'I'm worried they might take the end of my finger!'

'Let's not get overdramatic,' Josie cautioned, with a flick of her eyes sideways at Danni. 'But the sooner that's sorted, the better I'll be pleased.'

Pete again cupped his injured digit in his opposite palm. His food had gone untouched.

'Right,' said Josie, coming to a decision, 'let's get this stuff wrapped and we can take it with us. Danni, you can eat your burger and fries in the car, OK?'

'Are we going to hospital now?' Danni was enthused by the idea.

They were out of the door and approaching Pete's car within two minutes, and Josie held out her hands for the keys. 'I think it's best if I drive; it must be painful for you.'

He didn't argue, so Josie got behind the wheel and he settled into the passenger seat. They waited while Danni clipped into her seatbelt and again tucked into her burger, then Josie set off. The car park was small, with room for around twenty vehicles. Most visitors used the drive-through facility, so the car park was rarely full. On this occasion there were only another three vehicles, two of them cars, the last one a works van. Josie was passing one of the cars, speeding up towards the exit gate, when the man sitting inside caught her eye. It was the same creep from inside the burger joint, and again she sensed he was paying her more attention than she was comfortable with. As she pulled on to the slip road back to the main carriageway, she expected him to start his engine and follow. But she kept a discreet watch on her mirrors all the way up the main road, and no car emerged from the car park. Within another handful of minutes, she'd driven off Liverpool Road and forgotten all about the creep as she searched for a parking space outside Chester's general hospital.

For some reason Danni grumbled in discontent.

'What's up?' Josie met her gaze in the rear-view mirror.

'This isn't *my* hospital,' Danni moaned.

'It isn't. The hospital you were in was in another town, before we moved here with Gary.'

'Huh! I wanted us to go to *my* hospital.'

'We're only here to get Pete's finger checked, and then we can go home. You never know, Danni, you might think this hospital's nicer than the other one.'

'Mine had a play room with animals on the walls,' Danni continued, but Josie barely listened to her complaint. Pete nipped his bottom lip between his teeth.

'I'm not looking forward to this,' he said.

'Just think of the relief when they release the pressure,' she said, but he didn't appear reassured. Leaning across to whisper so Danni couldn't hear, she said, 'If you're a good patient I'll help you relieve another pressure when we get home.'

'Come on,' Pete said, 'let's get this done, shall we?'

TOBY

'You're positive you weren't spotted?' asked Toby Davis.

'Gimme a little credit, Tobe.'

'Please don't call me that. My name's Toby, and I don't like it when you shorten it, and you know it, *Cal.*'

'You can call me "Cal" if you think it helps. In fact, you can call me anythin' you like, just don't call me late to dinner.'

Davis didn't answer. He took out his phone, opened the camera app and pulled up the first of the dozen-or-so shots he had taken within the Lockwood house.

They'd convened in Davis's Range Rover, parked at the extreme corner of the car park adjacent to the gastro-pub. Callum Grieves had left his Audi A4 a few bays over, under the hanging branches of a large oak, and hidden from view by an ancient camper van that appeared to have been abandoned: one tyre had deflated, and moss had grown around the window frames. The positioning of the van largely concealed the Range Rover from patrons leaving the pub. Davis was confident they were unobserved. He held the phone so that Grieves could see the screen.

Grieves's harsh features didn't register what was on display. He dipped into a brown paper bag on his lap and stuffed a handful of French fries in his mouth, chewing noisily. 'Could'a done with another burger,' he said, around a ball of half-masticated potato.

'Pay attention, will you?'

'What's the big deal? It's not as if you found what we're lookin' for lyin' in plain sight.'

'Familiarize yourself with the layout.'

'Why?'

'Because you're bloody well being paid to do a job and that's what I want you to do.'

'Send the pics to my phone; I'll go over them later if I've nothing better to do. I don't see what the fuss is, anyway; it's not as if I'm thinkin' of takin' up interior decoratin' as a second career.'

'You're not taking this job seriously.'

'You continue to underestimate me, Tobe. I'm not fully committed to the job, for good reason, but when it comes time to do my stuff, you'll see.' Grieves fed another handful of chips into his mouth. He nodded at the phone. 'You go ahead and plan, see where it gets you. I'm of the old adage that a fight plan only works until you get punched in the face.'

'Pre-warned is pre-armed,' Davis retorted. 'I don't intend getting punched in the face. I want everything to go as smooth as possible, and I'd appreciate it if you actually showed some interest in getting a similar result.'

'Mate, my problem is I'm not gettin' the right kind of motivation.' Grieves rubbed the tips of his fingers together, and not only to shed the grains of salt adhering to them. 'I'd appreciate it if you showed me some cash.'

'You'll get paid when I get paid. And I only get paid when the job's done. You knew the terms when you signed on.'

'There's the issue of my daily expenses; I was told they'd be covered but I haven't seen a fuckin' bean. It's costin' me hundreds. Hotels and food don't come free, you know, and don't get me started on my fuel bill. You any idea how many miles I've put in chasin' down leads?'

'We're all in the same boat. Payment is on completion, and that goes for your bloody expenses too. Besides, we're almost done. I'm convinced we're on the right track here, and if everything goes to plan we should be looking at a fat cheque apiece in a couple of days' time.'

Grieves sniffed at the suggestion. 'I'm not takin' a rubber cheque that's gonna bounce on me. I want hard cash, Tobe, or an immediate cash transfer to my account. I told you that already.'

'It was a figure of speech, Callum. You'll get your cash the minute I do, and something to cover your expenses.'

'You wanna see receipts?'

Davis scowled at him. 'Just round things up to the nearest fuckin' cheeseburger and I'll see you right.' He glanced at the brown bag, noted the grease seeping through it and shuddered. 'How can you put that kind of garbage in your system?'

'It's tasty.'

'Those burgers are made from saturated fat, additives and salt, all moulded into a patty.'

'You're forgetting the cow lips and arseholes . . . they're the tastiest bits.'

Davis turned his face aside and Grieves chuckled.

Grieves crumpled the brown bag.

'Finished?' Davis asked.

Salt was licked from Grieves's fingers. 'You have my undivided attention.'

'Good. I'll text you these photos. Familiarize yourself with them, whether you've something better to do or not. Tomorrow, when we meet Whizzer, we'll go over the plan of action, and I don't want to have to repeat myself.'

'Repeat yourself? Never!'

'Fuck you and your sarcasm, Callum.'

'Anything else, *boss*?'

'Yeah. Set an early alarm; I want you on obs first thing. But like I warned already, you don't do anything until me and Whizzer are in position.'

'Gotcha.'

'I mean it, Callum, I don't want you going rogue on us.'

Grieves reached inside his coat pocket and held something up. He pressed a button and a blade flashed open. He used the sharp tip to probe under a fingernail, then licked whatever he'd excavated off it. He aimed the blade towards Davis, and it wasn't lost on either of them that it was a mild threat. 'Maybe a rogue's exactly what you need. Using this knife, I could have answers in less than a minute.'

Davis's eyes grew diamond-hard, and his voice was a low growl. 'You don't touch anyone with *that* . . . not until I order you to.'

JOSIE

Josie eyed the kitchen floor suspiciously. There were clumps of cut grass here and there, and when she followed the trail, she found they led into the main sitting room. There were more cuttings in the hall and even on the first riser of the stairs. As far as she knew, Danni hadn't left the house that morning so couldn't be guilty of tracking the cuttings everywhere. Not unless . . .

She returned to the kitchen and the small lobby inside the back door. No. The dirty trainers Danni kicked off yesterday were sitting to one side of the mat, the treads still choked with cuttings. The mess wasn't down to her daughter. She reached for the handle and the door clicked open, swinging silently towards her. The door should've been locked: she recalled locking up yesterday evening before going into town. The discovery was far from mystifying. Pete must have gone out into the back yard before heading to work, then trod the cuttings Danni scraped on the back step throughout the house. Maybe, for once, he'd remembered to dump the rubbish outside, but a quick check of the kitchen waste-bin showed the crumpled bags and greasy papers they'd brought with them from the car on their return home from town. She shrugged off the mystery and locked the door.

Grace and her boys were coming over later, and Josie had nothing in the house to feed them. She considered making a trip into Chester to one of the superstores, but Pete had taken the car to work with him, so it would mean calling a taxi, or waiting for the irregular bus service, and she wasn't confident she'd be back in time before her sister's arrival. With nothing else for it, she called Danni down from upstairs and towed her along to the small convenience store at the heart of the village, even though it'd cost twice as much for half of what she could buy from a supermarket. She wasn't stingy, just conscious of overspending, after discussing with Pete last night about selling her home and living somewhere more affordable.

The walk into the village wasn't far. Some outlying houses were new builds, but the centre was primarily made up of centuries-old cottages and reclaimed barns, set around a wedge of greenery

bordered by trees and shrubs. It was one of those villages dominated by holiday and second homes for well-off people who rarely
visited, made unaffordable for the original residents who had mostly
moved away. Her rich neighbours didn't quibble at the over-inflated
prices in the village shop, and it shamed Josie to be thinking that
way. She grabbed various tasty treats, and allowed Danni to choose
a sweetie for on the walk home. It was spring, and pleasantly warm,
but not exactly ice-lolly weather. However, she let Danni have her
orange-flavoured ice-pop of choice. Danni had the paper lid off and
the lolly squeezed half out of its tube before Josie was finished
at the till. She sucked merrily at it, humming a tune, while Josie
followed out the door, lugging her purchases in two carrier bags.

'Look, Mum!' Danni was immediately animated: she jabbed
towards the village green with her lolly. 'It's Franklin!'

A woman was seated on a bench, and at her feet a small white
dog sniffed back and forth. The woman was vaguely familiar; perhaps
someone she had spoken to in passing during previous visits to the
village shop, but Josie couldn't be certain. The woman waved in
greeting and, encumbered by the bags, Josie could only respond
with a nod and smile. Danni, though, hopped off the kerb to cross
the road.

'*Danni!*'

There was no moving traffic, but Danni had bounded out without
checking. The girl's head retreated into her shoulders, and she
backed up to the pavement sharply. 'Sorry, Mum! I just want to
say hello to Franklin.'

'We haven't time. Aunt Grace and your cousins will be arriving
soon.'

'Please, Mum? Can't I . . . just for a minute?' Danni's eyes were
like those of a puppy. Her lips were orange.

Josie felt she'd been a bit tough on Danni lately; her frustration
at getting none of her work completed manifesting as undue intoler-
ance. On the whole Danni was a good kid, and didn't deserve
punishment simply for being a kid. Guilt assailed her. 'OK. But
wait for me. You never cross a road without first checking it's safe,
remember?'

'Sorry, Mum.'

Danni stuck close to Josie's side while she over-exaggeratedly
looked both ways, then glanced up, waiting for permission to
proceed.

'Come on,' Josie said, and they strode across to the opposite pavement. The woman hadn't moved from the bench, but was aware of their approach. She straightened up and drew the dog close to heel, while her smile broadened. She was again muffled in a hat, scarf, gloves, tinted glasses and winter coat. She had exceptionally pale skin and vivid red lips. It was easy to see where Danni's impression of a vampire came from.

'Hi,' said Josie as they approached the bench. 'Would it be OK if my daughter pets your dog? Apparently they met yesterday . . .'

'That's right,' the woman agreed in an accent that Josie couldn't quite place. 'I was walking my dog and your daughter was playing in your garden.' She tilted her head to study the person of interest. 'It's Daniele, isn't it, unless I'm mistaken?'

'Danni,' she was corrected, and immediately Danni's face burned with embarrassment, and she wouldn't dare look at her mum. Not only had she spoken with the woman but also given out her name, two strikes against the Stranger Danger rule in one fell swoop. However, Josie didn't let on.

'Is it OK if she pets him?' Josie asked.

'Of course.' She jiggled the lead. 'Franklin, say hello to Danni again.'

The dog stood on its hind legs as Danni crouched and they met nose to nose. Franklin licked orange syrup off a giggling Danni's chin. Josie smiled at their daft antics. She placed down one bag of groceries to scratch the dog between its ears. Franklin grinned at her, eyes squinting. 'You are absolutely beautiful,' she announced.

'And he knows it,' the woman added.

'Such a cutie,' Josie went on, and Danni nodded in agreement.

'I told you, Mum. Franklin's great. Can I get a doggie like Franklin? Please, Mum, can I get a Freeze-ay and then Franklin can play with him?'

The woman offered Josie a conspiratorial grimace. 'I hope I haven't caused you a problem?'

'Danni loves animals. She'd have an entire menagerie if I allowed it.'

'You've certainly got enough land to house a zoo. Sorry, I didn't mean to be nosy, but I walk Franklin down the side lane beside your home, and it looks lovely and spacious. If only I had a house that large, with those grounds . . . well, I'd most likely have a menagerie of my own.'

'Do you live in the village?'

The woman nodded towards somewhere beyond the green. 'I only recently moved in. Mine's just a tiny cottage, nothing like as grand as your home. I'd love to upgrade, get somewhere bigger, but, well, we'll have to wait and see . . .'

Josie considered mentioning her house might soon come on the market . . . perhaps this woman would be keen to make an offer. But she didn't say a thing: some hard thinking was required, and more discussions with Pete, before announcing her plan to sell. She couldn't help being enigmatic, though. 'Who knows? A property might come up that'll be ideal for you.'

'I live in hope. Money's no object, it's just finding the right place.'

Josie surreptitiously glanced at the woman's left hand. She wore rings, but none that looked like a wedding band. Perhaps she worked from home, or – unmarried – she still had a partner who was the main breadwinner. Her clothing was expensive designer brands, her make-up immaculate, so bankrolling her lifestyle couldn't be cheap. Keeping such a potential buyer on the hook might not be a bad idea.

Danni giggled, and got caught in Franklin's lead as he danced around her. As the woman laughed and untangled the dog, Josie missed her opportunity. In the scrum, Danni's ice-pop slipped from its cardboard holder and hit the ground. Franklin was on it in seconds. Josie expected drama from her daughter, but Danni appeared to think it was one of the funniest things ever and laughed uproariously. 'Now Franklin's going to be a real Freeze-ay, from the inside out!'

The adults exchanged smiles at her glee.

'Hey,' Josie said, coming to a snap decision, 'I'm guessing you don't know many people in the village yet.'

Conspiratorially the woman said, 'Between me and you, I've found most others I've met here very snobby.'

'Yeah,' Josie said. 'How'd you like to come around for a coffee sometime and I'll give you the guided tour? It might give you an idea of what exactly you're looking for.'

'That's very kind of you . . . uh, Josephine, isn't it?'

'Josie.' She held out a hand and the woman accepted it. There was unexpected strength in her slim, gloved fingers.

'I'm Steph.'

'It's nice to meet you, Steph,' said Josie, then bent down to pat the dog, 'and you, too, Franklin.'

Danni stood with her knees crossed, hands clasped at her tummy. 'Please . . . when you come for coffee, will you bring Franklin so we can play in the garden?'

'Of course.' Steph glanced up. 'As long as that's OK with your mum.'

'Yes, please bring him.'

Steph smiled but fell silent. Josie picked up the bags of groceries she'd set aside. 'We'd best get on. Ready, Danni?'

Danni gave a final wave to Franklin and Steph, and they turned to walk away. Josie halted abruptly. The breath caught in her throat.

On the opposite side of the road was a black Audi. While engaged with Steph, she hadn't noticed it arrive, but it had parked near the entrance to the store. The driver hadn't got out; the engine was still running. He sat watching, and it was with the same unhealthy attention he'd given her yesterday evening at the fast-food outlet.

No, she realized, and it was as if a boulder solidified in her chest. She was not the object of his fascination at all! His gaze was set firmly on Danni. Yesterday, when he'd been spying out of the corner of his eye, Josie assumed he was watching her, without realizing that Danni was sitting alongside her. Suddenly his creep factor rose exponentially. He raised a camera and snapped off photos on rapid fire, sounding like subdued machine-gun fire.

'Hey! Stop that!' Josie dropped her bags, enfolded Danni in a hug, and she swung the child off her feet, shielding her behind her. 'You!' she hollered at the man. 'What the bloody hell do you think you're doing?'

He sneered, lowered his camera so he could shift gears. He touched the throttle and the engine growled.

'You've no right taking pictures of her!' Josie ensured Danni was behind her, out of sight.

Beside her, Steph appeared. She stared at the driver and, when Josie snapped a glance toward her, she was almost as furious as Josie.

'What's going on?' Steph demanded. 'Who is that?'

'Another bloody vulture!' Josie snapped, loud enough for the man to hear, and she was certain he'd understand even if Steph were none the wiser. 'Get out of here now, or I'm calling the police.'

'What's happening?' Steph asked. 'Why is that man photographing Danni? Is he some kind of pervert?'

'He's worse!' Josie wanted to rush the car and yank the camera out of his hands, but that would expose Danni again and she didn't dare take the chance.

Suddenly Steph strode forward, Franklin at her heels. She shooed away the driver. 'Go on, get out of here, you dirty rat. Get out of here, or you'll be sorry.'

The driver's sneer switched target, but he was already pulling away from the kerb. Steph had to halt to avoid being sideswiped by the Audi as he swerved across to the left lane and powered off towards the end of the green. Steph glared after him until he took the junction at the end and disappeared from view. She faced Josie, her features a mask of apprehension. She pulled off her sunglasses, her concern obvious. Josie had never seen eyes so pale blue before.

'Thanks,' Josie muttered, as she settled Danni in front of her again, so that she could hug her daughter. Danni was bemused, not alarmed.

'Who was he?' Steph asked. 'A journalist?'

'He has to be. Bloody hell, I thought we'd seen the last of his type.'

Steph eyed Danni. 'What was his interest in a child?'

Josie didn't explain. 'Damn him! How'd he find out where she lives?'

'Journalists can be resourceful.'

'They're like rodents creeping out of the bloody drains. Why can't they just leave her alone?'

Without any idea why the journalist wanted photos of Danni, she couldn't hazard a reply.

'I guess it has something to do with the date,' Josie relented. 'It hadn't occurred to me, but it's almost three years to the day since Danni was hailed a miracle.'

'Really?' Steph again eyed Danni, this time with her scarlet lips in a pout.

'Beyond all odds, she survived a pile-up on the motorway that took ten lives. Maybe you heard about it; it was a terrible tragedy, with Danni's survival being reported as miraculous.'

'Oh, God, yes! I remember!' Steph fisted a hand to her heart. She looked down at Danni with fresh wonder. 'It's really her? The girl the trucker plucked from the flames? What was it the papers dubbed her: "The Girl in the Smoke"?'

Josie was always reluctant about admitting to Danni's true

identity, because it invariably begged other answers she'd rather remained private. She nodded without expounding.

'Oh,' said Steph, and her hand crawled up to her throat. 'Didn't I read something about that poor man getting mugged or something recently? Some thug with a knife attacked him and . . .' She shut up, because Danni was in earshot and unfortunately the girl's saviour had died from his injuries.

'Do you think it could be because of what happened to him that the press have a renewed interest in Danni?'

'I couldn't really say what goes on in their minds,' Steph admitted. She laid her hand on Josie's wrist. 'You look really shaken up. Let me walk you home, and if that guy shows up again I'll see him off. Here, let me carry one of those bags for you.'

Josie dithered for a moment. She should report the man to the police, but knew nothing would come of doing that. Right now, she only wanted to get Danni home and out of range of the creep's camera. She was worried that he might follow them back to the house, so Steph's offer was appreciated. Perhaps Steph could deter the man long enough for her to get Danni safely tucked inside. She juggled up her bags, then held one out to Steph, who was slightly encumbered too.

'Can I walk Franklin?' Danni asked, totally unperturbed by what had happened.

'No, Danni,' Josie explained, 'we must hurry, and there's no time for playing with Franklin just now.'

Danni's bottom lip rolled out, but she nodded: she was more astute than she made out.

Steph eased out an extra few feet play on the lead. 'Why don't you walk alongside Franklin?' she suggested. 'He knows the way and will get you home in no time.'

It must have sounded like a fine plan to Danni, as she set off, Franklin trotting along at her side, his head tilted up, eyes sparkling and tongue lolling. As they followed, Josie explained to her new friend her theory why a journalist had tracked the girl there, and also why it had taken three years.

JOSIE

'Nobody came forward to claim their little girl? Wow! That's unbelievable.' Steph sat at the kitchen table, while Josie prepared coffees for them. The subject of their discussion was upstairs, entertaining her furry guest in her bedroom: the bumps, clatters and giggles filtering down through the house suggested they were having a whale of a time. 'In this day and age, I'm surprised she hasn't been identified.'

'If you mean through a DNA match, they need a viable donor to match it against, but there hasn't been one. Danni has been identified as the daughter of the woman in the car, but their actual identities remain a mystery.'

'They were unable to identify her mother either?'

Josie placed steaming mugs of instant coffee on the table and sat opposite Steph. Her new friend had doffed her hat and scarf, but even indoors kept on her tinted spectacles and tight leather gloves. Her hair was as fine as silk, and as pale as her skin. Josie hadn't asked, but wondered if Steph had albinism or some other similar condition affecting her pigmentation. 'That's the thing,' said Josie, first taking a brief check to ensure Danni wasn't eavesdropping. 'It's horrible to imagine, but her mother was burned so severely it was difficult at first to even determine her gender, and' – Josie visibly shuddered – 'there was no way of making a dental match because her entire skull was crushed to a pulp during the impact with the petrol tanker.'

Steph cupped her mug in her hands but didn't drink, mulling over the shocking image Josie had painted for her.

'One of those facial reconstruction models was made, but with so little to work with, the end result was only ever going to be a facile likeness. It was shown on the news and in the daily papers, but nobody came forward with a name.'

'They couldn't identify her from her belongings, or from her car?'

'That's the thing, the car was allegedly hired, but under false details.'

'But what about Danni, wasn't she able to give the police a name for her mother?'

'The very strange thing about Danni is, she can vividly recall everything from a few weeks after the crash, but nothing before, not even her original name. Daniele Lockwood is the name she took when my husband Gary and I adopted her.'

'She has no memory of before the accident?' Steph asked. 'She has amnesia?'

'It happens sometimes to trauma victims,' Josie said. 'It's a coping mechanism so that the mind isn't overwhelmed by it, so that the victim can heal.'

'Surely the condition isn't permanent?'

'Her doctors said that some of her memories might return, but they might be selective. Interestingly, only last night she spoke about when she was recovering in hospital, describing a playroom on her ward, and to my knowledge it's the first time she's mentioned it. Before that, her first memories seem to have been solely from after Gary and I initially fostered her.'

'Then there's hope that her full memory will come back?'

'I'm unsure if *hope* is the word I'd use. I'd rather she never remembers.'

'Oh, God, no! You're right, and I'm so sorry. That must have sounded so insensitive of me?'

Josie stood, but not to escape the discussion; she delved in the carrier bags, placing some items in the fridge, and others she left on the counter. Grace and her boys were due to arrive any minute. She'd no intention of hurrying Steph, though, and was happy to note Steph sipped her coffee, appearing thoughtful as she sat and scrolled through messages on her mobile phone. She'd slipped open a vent on the fingertip of her gloves to allow her to manipulate the screen while Josie completed her chores. Josie returned and sat opposite.

'That man,' Steph said, 'the journalist? I take it you've noticed him hanging around before?'

Josie nodded. 'Last night, my partner, Peter, had to go to hospital after injuring a finger at work, and we stopped off for burgers for supper beforehand. That creep was in the queue, and took an awful lot of interest in me. Actually, in hindsight, I wasn't the one he had his eye on, it was Danni.'

A grunt escaped Steph. 'Not a nice thought, is it? You're certain he's a journalist, and not a dirty pervert?'

'I can't be positive. He was a little too open about taking those photos to be a paedophile, right? Wouldn't he have been more secretive about it? From my experience, the journalists we came into contact with before were very much in our faces . . . well, if we'd showed our faces, that was. They tried following Gary and me to get snaps of Danni when she first came to us, but the police and social services intervened to ensure all our anonymity. Ha! I felt like a government whistle-blower or something, getting smuggled in and out of courtrooms under blankets.'

'Sorry if I'm prying, and feel free to tell me to back off if I'm being too nosy. You said Gary was your husband; didn't you mention someone called Peter a moment ago?'

'Pete's my current partner. My husband Gary died shortly after we adopted Danni; massive heart attack.'

'Oh, my! I'm sorry to hear that. Josie, you must forgive me. That's twice I've put my foot in my mouth in the last minute.'

'Don't worry. You weren't to know.' Josie sipped from her coffee as she eyed Steph. 'What about you? Do you have a significant other?'

'Only Franklin.' Steph laughed at the absurdity of her comment. 'Oh, I'm coming off the back of a divorce at the moment, and the last thing on my mind's confusing matters with a new love interest. Besides, I'm enjoying the singleton lifestyle, and moved here to make the most of my new-found freedom.'

'Wouldn't a house like this be too big for you?' Josie said, instantly wanting to bite her tongue: she might be putting off a potential sale.

'Oh, being single doesn't mean I won't have *friends* over.' She showed her teeth in a salacious grin to emphasize the type of friends she meant. 'I'm divorced but not dead.'

Josie laughed with her.

'So the courts ensured your anonymity, eh?' Steph asked, getting back on track.

'For Danni's sake, yes. After she survived the pile-up, particularly when there were questions about who she was, the media was full of conjecture and were chasing the story. Social services deemed it necessary to protect mine and Gary's identities in order to protect Danni.'

'I'm surprised you'd trust me with this.'

Josie shrugged. 'If that journalist has found us, it's only a matter of time before the world knows who we are. Still, if you could keep this between us for now, I'd much appreciate it.'

'My lips are sealed.'

'Not too tightly, I hope. Go on. Drink your coffee before it grows cold.' Josie stood again, sorting through groceries. While Steph enjoyed her coffee, she watched Josie shifting food from the refrigerator to a counter-top. Josie approached the table and shifted aside her laptop and the ream of printed papers.

'If I'm in your way, just say,' Steph said.

'You're not, and you're welcome to stay. It's not often I get to speak with a friend.'

'I imagine you don't get too close to many new people, if you've been trying to keep Danni safe from the public eye?'

'Oh, it's not just that. I'm a freelance editor, so most of my work is done right here at this table. Most interaction I get these days is through emails.'

'Isn't it the half-term holiday? It must be nice having Danni at home for a few days then; at least it's some kind of company.'

Josie laughed at the idea. 'I love Danni to bits, but you can probably tell I don't get much work done while she's around.'

'I bet.' From overhead they heard Danni shriek in high spirits. There followed a thunder of feet. 'Maybe you should get her a puppy; they're having a riot together up there.'

'Maybe it isn't a bad idea, but it might have to wait until after we've—' Josie never got to mention selling up and relocating, as she heard the growl of an engine and the crunch of gravel as a car drove up to the front of the house. She held up a finger, as if to say: 'hold that thought', then headed through the hall for the front door just as the doorbell chimed. Grace and the boys had arrived a little before expected.

She opened the door, and her smile of greeting withered to one of mild suspicion.

It wasn't Grace's car on her drive, but a Range Rover, and standing on the front step was a man whose face was turned away, as if surveying the grounds. His hands were clasped behind him, out of sight.

'Hello?' asked Josie.

The man turned and smiled. He was a complete stranger, aged in his late thirties, muscular across the shoulders and arms, with short dark hair and designer stubble. He'd dressed simply, wearing a navy-coloured round-necked sweater, jeans and trainers, but they were of good quality. He was handsome and fit. Briefly, Josie wondered if he was one of the sportsmen or TV stars who lived locally; he had that image. He didn't say a thing.

'Uhm. Can I help you?' Josie prompted.

'Mrs Lockwood?'

She didn't want to answer. This man showing up at her home so soon after the incident with the journalist couldn't possibly be a coincidence. However, it was obvious from the way she straightened up and set herself that he'd found the right place. His smile widened, but again he didn't speak.

'What is it?' Josie was prepared to hear him out, but also to send him packing once he was done.

'You *can* help me,' he said, and without permission stepped up and into the house before Josie could stop him. Her squawk of outrage died as he disclosed a pistol in one leather-gloved hand. 'If you want to live, you'll be quiet and do exactly as I say.'

JOSIE

J osie had never seen a real pistol this close before, and it terrified
her into complete obedience. She held back all the questions
flying from her mind to her lips, and only retreated, with her
hands up. The man matched her steps, advancing into the hallway
and closing the door behind him. His dark eyes were on her, slightly
pinched, but what was that look deep within them? Was it regret?
Pity? More like subdued victory?

'Wh-what do you want?' Josie finally croaked.

'Just do as I say and everything will be fine.' He jerked the barrel
of the gun, directing her towards the kitchen.

It was absurd, but Josie thought this was a *fine* way to introduce
herself to her new friend, Steph, with a gun pointed at them both.
She momentarily halted moving backwards, as if that was going to
remove Steph from the scenario: the woman was sitting in the
kitchen, oblivious to the gunman, but that was bound to change.

'Who else is here?' asked the gunman.

Josie should've lied, kept him there in the hallway until Steph
overheard and realized something was wrong. Josie had seen Steph
playing with her mobile phone while she was putting away her
groceries. Given an opportunity, maybe she'd call the police! But
if Josie claimed to have company, then perhaps this man would cut
his losses and leave. Or he'd hurt them both.

'Just take whatever it is you want and go,' she said.

'Please answer my question.'

'I haven't much money, but you can have it all and—'

'I did not ask for your money.' He cocked an ear. Upstairs, Danni
and Franklin were playing chase, and the drumming of their feet
rumbled through the house. He raised an eyebrow.

'Please, that's only my daughter. She's a little girl and—'

'Call her down.'

'No. Please, leave her alone.'

'She won't be harmed, I only want her where I can see her.'

'No, wait, *please*.'

From the kitchen a squawk rang out and a chair juddered across the floor. Josie turned briefly, but couldn't see very much of the kitchen. Another man growled in anger, and Steph berated him before her mouth was clamped shut. Josie was torn; Steph didn't deserve to be caught up in this – whatever this trouble was – but Danni was her priority. She looked at the gunman, her hands outstretched, pleading.

'Please, I don't know what this is about, but you can't do this.'

'I can, and quite frankly I *am* doing this. Call your daughter down or I will go and fetch her.' He waggled the gun as a reminder he was in charge.

'Leave her alone! She's only a child!'

'I promise she won't be harmed, but she will be more frightened if I have to go and get her. Call her down, Mrs Lockwood. *Now!*'

She really wanted to shout at Danni to run and hide, but what would happen then? The gunman might have to incapacitate her somehow while he went off in search of Danni. And he was right; Danni would be terrified if a stranger with a gun suddenly appeared in her bedroom.

'Danni? Danni!' She peered up the stairs. 'Danni, can you come down and bring Franklin with you?'

'Who's Franklin?' the man whispered.

'He's only my friend's dog. He's only a tiny thing.'

'Your friend's the woman in the kitchen?'

'We only just met. We barely know each other; please, she has nothing to do with any of this.'

'Wrong place, wrong time for her then.' The man checked upstairs as Danni peeped around the top banister. He smiled up at her, holding the gun at his side, out of sight.

'Hi, sweetheart,' he said. 'Why don't you come down and say hello?'

Danni frowned, one hand concealing her mouth.

'Danni,' said Josie, trying to control the tremor in her voice, 'come down please.'

'Is Mrs Steph going already? Awk! I wanted to play with Franklin a bit longer.' Danni wasn't stupid; she knew something was wrong.

'Just do as I say,' Josie commanded, feeling awful, as it was almost verbatim the same order given to her a moment ago by the gunman. Danni waited only a second longer before beginning a slow trudge down the stairs, her eyes huge as she watched the man: she was carrying the little Bichon Frisé against her chest. It was the only one happy to see the new person in the hallway. It grinned, tongue lolling.

The gunman shifted, allowing Danni to rush to her mother. Josie pulled her and the dog into her embrace. Behind them there was another brief scuffle in the kitchen. Something shattered. 'Get off me!' Steph screeched.

A man's voice snapped, 'Quit it, or I'm gonna cut you, bitch.'

'In there, now,' the gunman commanded, and Josie backpedalled with Danni and Franklin to where Steph was being threatened.

Josie halted, staring in dismay at the tableau.

Steph was seated on one of the kitchen chairs; it had been dragged clear of the table towards the back door. From behind her a man clamped long gloved fingers around her chin, forcing back her head so that her throat was open to a flick knife held an inch below it. It was a shocking scene, added to by the man's identity. It was the creep Josie had mistakenly taken for a journalist. He leered; his tongue rolled behind his lower teeth. 'We meet again.'

'Who are you people?' Josie demanded. 'What do you want from me?'

'I want you to sit down and be silent.' The gunman motioned at the chair Josie had vacated only minutes ago.

Josie still hugged Danni. From between them, Franklin squirmed free. The little dog immediately scrambled towards Steph. When she didn't reach for him, Franklin switched his attention to the man crowding her. It yipped excitedly, bouncing on its front feet.

'Gertcha!' The knifeman brusquely kicked the dog aside. Franklin yelped and scurried under the table.

'Touch my dog again and I swear to God I'll kill you,' Steph snarled.

'Is that right?' The severe man lowered his face alongside hers and nipped Steph's earlobe between his teeth. He didn't bite enough to hurt, only to dominate. Steph tried to rear away, but he controlled her chin. He licked her neck then laughed bitterly. 'If there's killing to be done, I'm the one who'll do it.'

Josie stalled, statue-like, and Danni moaned at Franklin's abuse. The gunman nudged Josie. 'Sit down. Danni, you just wait there a moment.'

Tears ran down Danni's face as she checked his instructions with her mum.

Josie refused to release Danni.

'Let's not make this awkward,' said the gunman. 'Danni won't be harmed; you have my word on it. Now please sit down, Mrs Lockwood.'

'What are you going to do?' Josie asked.

'We're going to have a little chat. The sooner I get answers, the sooner this can be over with.'

'Answers about what? I don't know what you want from me!'

'So sit down, and I'll explain.'

Josie aimed a look of sincere apology at Steph for involving her, but the woman's ire was aimed at the gunman, and more particularly at the creep threatening her with the knife. Josie wished she was as brave as Steph, but more so that Steph would stop struggling before the knifeman went through with his threat.

Josie sat, without releasing Danni. The girl sobbed, beyond comforting. The gunman bent at the waist to Danni's level. 'It's going to be OK; you needn't be frightened. I just need you to do as I ask and stand over here.'

'I want to stay with my mum.'

'Your mum's going to be right here, OK?'

Franklin offered a compromise. He shuffled out from under the table, seeking Danni's attention. The little dog rolled its eyes at the severe man dominating Steph and whimpered. Danni sat down on the floor, pulling the dog into her lap. She was alongside her mum, but the gunman could now speak directly to Josie. He seemed satisfied with the arrangement. From his trouser pocket he removed a pre-prepared set of zip-ties, looped together like handcuffs. He gestured for Josie to put her arms behind her back. 'Put your hands through the rungs on the chair,' he said, and as she complied, he set the hoops over her wrists and pulled them tight. She was only partly restricted, because nothing stopped her from standing, forgetting the gun of course. Josie watched the knifeman similarly securing Steph. Steph growled words at her captor unfit for Danni's ears, but Josie agreed with the sentiment. She set her features rigid and stared up at the gunman.

Slightly abashed, he glanced down at the gun, then made a performance of slipping it into his belt at the small of his back. 'There. I don't think I need to motivate you with that for now.'

His partner in crime snorted, making no attempt to put away his knife. He did, however, move away from Steph and set his backside against the worktop, his back to the kitchen window. He cleaned under his fingernails using the tip of his knife, acting nonchalant. Josie feared him capable of extreme violence at a moment's notice.

'Just tell me what you want.' She glanced sharply at the knifeman. 'Why have you been following me?'

The gunman opened his hands, as if to say their attendance explained everything. 'We wished to get you and Danni alone. We didn't expect you to bring home a stray.' He wasn't talking about Franklin, but its owner. He turned his attention to Steph. 'Accept my apologies for involving you like this, but it is unavoidable. You're here now and that's all there is to it. We can't let you go until we've concluded our discussion here.'

'It's what you get for stickin' your beak into our business, you nosey cow,' the knifeman added. The gunman flashed him a look to stay silent, and was rewarded with a sneer. The glare Steph shot at him could have curdled milk.

'Just tell Josie what you want,' Steph snapped.

'Right,' said the gunman, 'let's begin.'

He thought, as if getting his words in order, then raised a finger. 'I'm confident that we've a lot to gain from your full cooperation, so I'm willing to share with you everything I know so that there's no confusion. I'm not really interested in you, Mrs Lockwood, but your adopted daughter and how she came to live with you.'

'Why? This can't possibly be about her surviving the crash?'

He nodded, because her question had just confirmed to him he'd definitely found the girl he was looking for. He flicked a hand towards Josie's laptop and the unedited manuscript. 'You're in the publishing business, Mrs Lockwood. I trust you're able to narrate an interesting story, and are pretty damn good at editing out the bullshit. So go ahead; I'm listening.'

'You obviously already know how I came to adopt Danni.' She checked with her daughter, but Danni had her head down, concentrating on hugging the dog. It had never been a secret that Josie wasn't her biological mum, but Josie didn't want her to think she loved her any less. 'After the pile-up, no relatives came forward to claim her, and she needed a home. My husband and I were already listed with social services, and had shown an interest in adopting an older child.'

'I'm not so much interested in the process as what you were told about her.'

'There was little to tell.'

Steph suddenly chipped in, 'Danni has amnesia, and has absolutely no memory of the crash or what happened before.'

The gunman stared at her, and Steph's lips formed a tight slash. He looked at Josie for confirmation.

'It's true,' Josie said, 'she has no memory of her life before the crash happened. She doesn't even recall her own name!'

'Seriously?' The gunman observed the little girl. 'Danni? Are they telling the truth?'

She snapped distrusting eyes on him, and only answered with a shrug.

'I'm sorry, *Danni*, but I find that hard to believe.'

Josie said, 'Believe it or not, it won't change anything. What the hell do you want from a little girl anyway? You seem to know more about her past than I do – or than Danni does, for that matter.'

'Too convenient,' the gunman said. He again regarded Danni. 'You know it's wrong to lie, don't you?'

Again Danni tilted fearful eyes at him, and he waited her out.

Before she broke, the other man lost patience. He pushed away from the worktop and crouched directly in front of her. He pointed the knife at Franklin. 'I could always loosen *his* tongue to loosen yours. Wanna watch me cut it off?'

While Josie and Steph both reacted vociferously to the threat, Danni bit her bottom lip. She shook, her arms almost crushing the dog in her desire to keep him safe. Sobbing, she said, 'I . . . I remember *some* things.'

DANNI

She had no idea who these horrible men were, or what they wanted from her. At first she was only confused when peering over the banister, but very quickly she could tell her mum was frightened, and that scared her too. The man looked nice, like a movie star, but – even without fully understanding why – she could sense he was nasty. He had made her mum make her come downstairs with Franklin, and then things had only got worse.

The other man scared her more than the first, and it wasn't just because he had a knife and was holding Mrs Steph. He kicked Franklin, and what kind of monster would hurt a little doggie?

She held the dog protectively, watching the corners of the man's lips turn up. His teeth were yellow and his eyes as flat and depthless as black ice: he was like the Halloween lantern her mum helped her carve last year. 'See,' he said, and his breath stank worse than her dentist's had, 'all that's needed is the right kinda motivation.'

He wasn't talking to her. His words were for his friend, but the other man didn't look impressed. He stepped forward and grasped the knifeman's shoulder.

'There's no need to scare the kid,' he growled.

The knifeman stood abruptly. 'Isn't there? I got her to admit to rememberin', didn't I? More than you did with yer pussyfootin' around.'

Neither man spoke for a few seconds. They stared at each other. Danni expected they'd fight. But then the dark-haired one said, 'Stand over there and keep an eye on these two.' He meant her mum and Mrs Steph. 'I'll speak with the kid.'

Danni didn't want to talk with him. She only wanted to get Franklin away from the skinny man, an evil scarecrow who had come to life to eat doggie's tongues. She looked pleadingly at her mum for help, and her mum leaned as far forward in the seat as her bound wrists would allow.

'Stay away from her,' her mum spat. She'd heard her mum angry before, and knew when to take heed of a warning, but she'd never heard her like this. If Danni were the man, she'd definitely take note. The man ignored her mum.

He knelt in front of her, eye to eye. 'Don't worry, Danni. No one is going to hurt the dog, and' – he glanced back at the scarecrow so there was no doubt who his next words were intended for – '*no one* is going to hurt you. We aren't here to hurt anyone. I only need to speak with you, and I need you to tell me some things. Important things that only you might know.'

'She was only five when the crash happened. What of any importance can you expect her to remember from then?' Her mum had half-risen from the seat, the cuffs incapable of holding her down. Danni flinched in anticipation of her mum kicking out.

'Sit yer arse down!' The scarecrow took a warning step. The dark-haired man held out a hand to halt him. Mum sank down again, though, and Danni scooted a few inches closer to touch her. She'd have hugged her mum's legs, but already her hands were filled with Franklin.

'Let's see,' said the dark man, smiling at Danni. 'I bet you can remember stuff from when you were five. It isn't very long ago, is it?'

It seemed like forever since she was five. After the crash, it was as if she'd been reborn, with no memory whatsoever of her former life, but that wasn't exactly true. In her dreams and in reflective moments, when she'd been alone, Danni had experienced recollections from the time before she became Daniele Lockwood.

'I . . . I remember Coal Axe,' said Danni, earning her an exchange of tight-lipped smiles between the two men.

'What about Kolacz do you remember?'

'He was nice. He used to bring me sweets.'

'That's right,' said the dark man. 'He always carried a packet of toffees with him.'

'He never gave me toffee; I liked the rhubarb and custard ones best.'

Familiar tastes and smells, they had come back to her first, and sometimes with the memory of where she'd first experienced them attached. She'd recalled her love of the pink and yellow sweeties before she had recalled the big man who used to give her them. They were always presented in a crumpled white paper bag, and Coal Axe had to untwist the corners so she could delve inside. He was a huge man with a red, pock-marked face and big ears, and he'd spoken funny, sometimes not in English, and the others used to be frightened around him: to Danni he'd been more comical than scary though.

'Who else do you remember?' the man prompted. 'What about Freda?'

Danni frowned. 'I . . . I think so.' She rubbed her nose, then returned to hugging Franklin. 'Yes. Freda. I think I remember her, too.'

'Freda's a bloody fella,' the scarecrow snarled. 'Don't put names into her mouth or she'll only make things up.'

The dark-haired man calmly said, 'Freda was a man.'

Danni nodded emphatically. 'I remember *now*. He had white hair and couldn't get up.'

The corner of his mouth twitched. 'That's right. He needed to use a wheelchair.'

'Fucksake!' snapped the scarecrow. Again his friend had given away details that weren't fully formed in Danni's mind: she could see Freda now, though, seated in a wheelchair – an old black one, not like the wheelchairs people use these days – with another man standing behind him. She couldn't picture Freda's helper.

Ignoring the scarecrow's outburst, the other man smiled. 'You're doing well, Danni, and I knew you would. So if you can remember Kolacz and Freda, you must remember your mum too?'

Danni feared making another admission. Not because the man would get mad at her or anything. She was more concerned how her mum would take it. Admitting to recalling her birth mother might feel like a betrayal to Josie, her real mum in Danni's mind and heart. It was as if her mum knew what was going through her head though, because she softly urged, 'It's OK, Danni. Don't be afraid to say. I'm your mum, and I love you no matter what and will always love you.'

'Sweet,' said the scarecrow, but didn't sound as if he meant it.

Danni stared at the dark-haired man, deciding how much to admit to. For a reason she couldn't explain, she began crying and finally opened her mouth to speak.

Everyone in the room jumped at the blare of a ringtone.

JOSIE

J osie, for all she worked with modern technology, was still 'old school' at heart. Even though she rarely received any communication via it, she'd kept her landline, and an archaic press-button phone still hung on her kitchen wall, a second one in the living room. These days the calls she mostly received on them were from consumer marketing companies and misdials, but occasionally she received calls from others equally old school: her parents, for instance.

The ringing was ear-piercing in the otherwise sudden hush.

Everyone bar none stared at the phone on the wall. The two interlopers exchanged a look, before the gunman directed his question at Josie: 'Who could that be?'

'How should I know?' Josie sneered. 'I'm not a bloody psychic!'

'Are you expecting anyone?'

She exhaled sharply.

'Probably from one of those friggin' call centres,' said the creep.

'You aren't helping. Please be quiet.' The gunman approached the phone, but only stood watching as it continued to ring. There was no caller display.

'They're persistent,' the creep commented.

The ringing stopped.

'Or maybe not.' The creep grinned but nobody found him funny.

The gunman pondered, then reached down to where the phone was wired into a socket. He yanked the cord, ripping the wire free of the jack. Turning to the creep, he said, 'Go and disable the phone in the front room, and find where the broadband router is: I want that disabled too. And don't forget the PC in the kid's room upstairs.'

The creep was slow to move. He eyed both Josie and Steph. The other pulled out his pistol and laid it on the counter-top. 'I've got this covered,' he said, and the creep shrugged. He curled a lip at Danni as he strolled past, laughing when she drew the dog into a tighter hug.

'He's an arsehole,' Steph snarled, and the gunman didn't disagree.

'Where are your mobile phones?' he asked instead.

Neither woman answered.

'Come on. Let's not play around. The longer this takes, the longer you stay tied up.'

Josie said, 'You've been in my house before.'

Now he didn't answer.

'This morning, when I got up, there was grass tracked through the house and the back door was unlocked. That was you, wasn't it? You came inside while we were out last night, and your creepy friend followed us to make sure we weren't about to return.'

He still didn't answer. But it was unnecessary.

'You know where the other phone is, and you even know about Danni's computer.'

'And now I want to know about your mobile. Don't try lying, I know you have one.'

'Are you blind? It's on charge,' Josie said, because she had more to worry about than him discovering a phone she couldn't use while under armed guard. She nodded towards the corner of the room, and he followed the gesture. Her phone was lying on the counter, plugged in. Ironically Josie had forgotten to turn on the socket.

'Battery's flat,' he said after a quick check. He set the phone aside, face down on the worktop, and regarded Steph. 'What about yours?'

'Pocket.'

Josie saw her new friend stiffen as his hand delved in her coat pocket and pulled out a smart phone. He powered it down and set the phone alongside Josie's on the counter. He wasn't finished. He checked Josie's laptop. It was wired up too, so he unhooked both the power and Internet cables. Once his friend had disabled the broadband router, the laptop's Wi-Fi function couldn't be used as a conduit to message the outside world. He placed it on the worktop alongside the phones, well out of reach of the women. He picked up his gun. 'See, if we all stay calm and reasonable, we can get this done much quicker.'

'Fuck you and *reasonable*,' Steph snapped, tugging at her restraints. It wasn't a serious effort at escape, only a display of her outrage. He shook his head and slipped the pistol in his belt.

'OK, settle down.'

Steph strained again. Josie also shook her head at her, pleading silently for her to stop. Fighting her restraints wouldn't get them anywhere, except in deeper trouble. She already had enough to worry her to an early grave, especially the possible identity of the unexpected caller on the landline. Grace and her boys were due, and because Josie's mobile-phone battery was flat, was it Grace who'd called the house phone for some reason? Hopefully her sister was running late, or better still had reason to postpone the visit, because the last thing she wanted was for Grace and her nephews to get caught up in this.

Despite Josie's plea, Steph carried on, 'Let us go. You can't treat us like this!'

'I've treated you well. Trust me, things could be much worse.' The gunman again stood directly before Danni. 'As I said before, I only need answers, and Danni was just about to give me them before we were rudely interrupted. What do you say, Danni? Now you've had some more time to think, what was it you remembered about your mum?'

Danni wouldn't relinquish her hold on Franklin. Somehow she still managed to turn around and bury her head in Josie's lap. Josie desperately wanted to comfort her, but could only lean protectively over her child.

'Mrs Lockwood,' he said. 'Can you please assure Danni everything's going to be OK?'

Josie's face rose, but she could barely see him through a wash of tears. 'How can I? You've invaded our home – thugs with guns and knives – and expect a little girl not to be terrified? Why's it so important Danni remembers who her mother was? For God's sake, leave her alone! Have you no pity?'

He said nothing. If he were a compassionate man, he wouldn't have taken on this task.

'Danni,' Steph said. 'Please look at me.'

Kneeling beside Josie, Danni couldn't see Steph for the table. She craned to peer over the top.

Steph smiled in encouragement. 'If you remember anything at all about your birth mother, just tell this person so that he can leave.'

Danni ducked again, muffling her words against Josie's thigh. 'You're my only mum.'

'I am,' Josie agreed, 'and I always will be. But it's OK to talk about your birth mum, too. I won't be upset.'

'Promise?'

'With all my heart and soul.'

Danni squirmed around but wouldn't meet the gunman's gaze. She concentrated on stroking the traumatized dog.

'What was your mum's name?' the man prompted.

Danni shrugged without raising her head.

'You remember those other names, why not your mum's?'

'I called her Mam.'

'But the others would have had another name for her. Think, Danni. What did they call her?'

DANNI

anni recalled names aimed at her mother that weren't meant for her young ears. Slut. Whore. Bitch. And a name beginning with the letter 'C' that she couldn't even bear to think about. She knew all of those names were awful, and the latter the worst. Her mother wasn't treated with any kindness, and Coal Axe didn't ever give her any of his sweets. She could picture the woman, who was thin and tall, like Danni was now, whose hair was also the colour of straw: she thought that when she grew older she might look just like her birth mother. Hopefully she wouldn't be as sad all the time. She couldn't recall ever seeing a smile on her mother's face, only deep sadness in her green eyes and the way she held her mouth. She'd heard her mam crying a lot, and often she'd shout and swear, but never at Danni. Her frustration was always aimed at the others. One time a horrible man pulled her mam's hair, and made her kneel down: she thought he was called . . . Barker. Yes, Barker, because he reminded her of an angry dog, not like lovely Franklin at all.

'Mel,' she finally said. 'They called her Mel.'

The gunman winked. 'That's right. What's the last thing you remember about being with Mel?'

A snapshot memory of being in a car with Barker and Mel hit her. Danni was in the back, sitting in a child seat, but she wasn't strapped in. Barker braked sharply, and Danni tumbled out into the footwell. Her mam reached to help her, and Barker shoved her roughly with his elbow. Danni remembered crying.

'I didn't like Barker,' she said.

'You remember Barker too? That's good.' The man dipped his head in praise.

'He was horrible to Mam and me.'

'He wasn't the best of father figures,' he admitted, and Danni knew the words were for her real mum's benefit.

'He hit my mam.'

'Sometimes your mam disobeyed,' said the man, and again she felt his words had double meaning and were aimed elsewhere.

She glanced up at her real mum; she was stone-faced. The man swirled a hand. 'You're doing well, Danni. Think back to when you were last with your mam and Barker.'

'We saw a scary flying saucer.' Danni could picture it then; wreathed in mist, it was hovering overhead as they drove towards some buildings. It was grey, with dirty windows, and she couldn't see any aliens inside. But she knew they were there, watching her.

The man didn't seem surprised by her story. Maybe he believed in aliens too, unlike Barker, who'd scoffed at her and growled there was no such thing – he'd also used the naughty F-word to enforce his point. The man squatted once more, nodding in encouragement. 'I saw it too. Later, when I went to pick up Barker. Your mam left him there, didn't she, and drove off in the car with you?'

'Barker needed a pee,' said Danni, in the naïve way that children do. 'I wanted to go for one too, but I was scared the aliens would abduct me.'

'So only Barker went inside?'

Danni nodded. Because he believed her, she lifted her head and eyed him steadily. 'When he was inside, my mam drove us away.'

The man straightened up, smoothing his sweater down at the front where his constant kneeling and rising had rucked it up. 'You're doing really well, Danni. See, remembering isn't so hard if you take your time and think. So Mel drove you away, leaving Barker behind. Think about how you felt at the time, and what happened next.'

'I was happy but Mam was crying.'

'She was upset for leaving Barker behind?'

'No. She was frightened he'd run after us.'

The man nodded again, so Danni didn't explain her mother was so frightened that she was crying out and banging her fists on the steering wheel. Danni had tried to cover her ears, and all she wanted to do was close her eyes and go to sleep, but she had needed to pee too badly. Unexpectedly, Danni began blubbing, and looked to her mum for support. 'Mum, I don't want to say any more . . .'

'Then don't,' Josie told her.

The man scowled at them both. 'We were just starting to get somewhere.'

'I don't care,' said Josie. 'She's had enough for now. Leave her alone, for God's sake.'

Steph echoed Josie, telling the man to give the little girl a break.

He wasn't having it: he stood over Danni, unaffected by her tears. 'Danni, it's important that you tell me. Right now!'

Danni's head shook from side to side; her hair bunches flailed her cheeks.

'Tell me *now!*'

'I couldn't help it!' she squawked.

'Help what?'

'Wetting myself!' Danni was mortified by the admission, her shame manifesting as anger. 'I told Mam I needed to pee but she wouldn't stop. *It wasn't my fault!*'

As Danni howled, the man blinked in astonishment at Josie. Obviously that was not the admission he'd hoped for.

JOSIE

Josie noted the creep's return to the kitchen. He stood at the threshold; his tongue rolled behind his bottom lip. 'What've I missed?'

The gunman threw up both hands.

'Let me have a go at the brat,' said the creep, and stepped into the room, flicking open his knife.

'*You* stay the hell away from her!' Josie bolted to her feet, dragging the chair with her. Danni scooted aside with Franklin, her eyes wet ovals, her mouth wide in a silent squeal. The gunman lunged in and pressed a hand to Josie's chest, forcing her to halt. She pushed against it. 'I swear if you touch her I'll—'

'What? What will you do, bitch?' The creep's eyes flashed in challenge. 'Maybe I'll cut out your tongue instead of the fuckin' dog's. Should I? Want to see me cut out your mum's tongue, Danni?'

'That's enough, Callum,' the gunman snarled. 'Back off and leave this to me.'

'Well, thank you very much, *Toby*, you arsehole. You've just gone and told the bitch my name.' Callum the creep aimed his blade like a toreador, the point directed at Josie's face. 'You know what that means for you now, bitch?'

'Get out there. Now.' The gunman – Toby – stabbed a finger at the hallway. When Callum was slow to obey, he snatched up the pistol, reminding both Callum and Josie who was in charge. 'Sit down, Mrs Lockwood, and don't dare try anything. I'm going to speak with him. If any of you try to escape, I'll be back in here in a second. Do you understand?' He snapped his gun between Josie and Steph, and both women lowered their heads in acquiescence. He stared at them a moment longer, then strode out of the kitchen. He was out of sight, his voice lowered in a harsh whisper, but it was apparent he'd lost patience with his aggressive helper.

'Josie!' Steph's voice was lowered too, but strident. She bent her upper body over the table: her face was paler than death. 'These men mean business. If you know what they're looking for, just tell

them. Danni remembers more than she first let on; maybe she's
mentioned stuff to you before? Tell them before it's too late.'

'This is the first I've heard of anything from before the crash,'
whispered Josie. 'I don't know anything about any of these people
or what they're interested in.'

'Then encourage Danni to remember. She has to tell them, Josie!
We've learned their names now and they won't want us giving them
to the police.'

'We've also seen their faces,' Josie reminded her, a fact she'd
been aware of since the gunman forced his way inside her home.
She'd seen enough crime dramas on TV to know that hostages
who see the faces of the criminals usually ended up dead. 'It's
better if I make Danni stay silent. That way they need to keep us
alive!'

'You've seen the way that nutter with the knife acts. If Danni
doesn't give them something soon, he's going to hurt one of us!'

Josie shook her head. 'His friend won't let him.'

'How can you say that? He's just as crazy. He's only acting like
he cares because he thinks that will get him answers. But it won't
last. He didn't bring that gun for nothing.'

'I don't think he has it in him to shoot us.'

'How can you say that? We've no idea what these animals are
capable of. Josie, for God's sake, just get Danni to tell them what
they want to hear.'

'If I can make her keep quiet, I will,' answered Josie. 'The longer
we hold out . . . well, maybe help will come and—'

'There's no help coming! We're going to die . . . I'm going to
die. They'll kill me first to force you to get Danni to speak. Josie,
please! I don't want to die! I shouldn't even be here; I'm innocent
in all this!'

In the hallway, the men's voices rose in volume in line with
Steph's, and then their conversation ended abruptly with Toby
snapping, 'Just remember who's in charge, Callum. Do as I fucking
well say, and leave the rest to me. Now let's see what all the
racket's about in there.'

The duo filled the doorway, Toby pausing to check the tableau.
Steph was in the act of straightening up again, but it was apparent
there hadn't been an attempt made at escape. Josie watched him as
he eyed Steph in turn, and wondered what question just passed
behind his eyes. When she glanced at her friend, the woman's

expression was hidden because of the way her hair had fallen forward.

'Check she's still tied up,' Toby told Callum.

'My pleasure.' Callum strolled past and Josie caught a quick look at his hands. He'd put away the knife: Toby still held his gun, though.

As Callum bent around Steph, her head snapped up. 'Get away from me! This is unfair! I've nothing to do with this.'

Without a care for her discomfort, Callum palmed her face aside, and gave her wrists a shake. 'All good.'

'Good.' Toby considered for a few seconds then said, 'Drag her out here in front of the counter.'

'No! No! Let me go!' Steph threw her weight around, the chair legs hopping across the floor.

Callum grasped the back of her chair and yanked it around, dragging it across the floor tiles. Steph dug in with her heels, but there was unexpected strength in the skinny man's frame. He roughly jostled her until he was satisfied she faced Josie and Danni. He pulled out his flick knife and snicked it open. Steph howled in alarm, until he placed the sharp blade across her bottom lip. 'Keep yackin',' he warned, 'and I won't havta cut yer tongue out, you'll do it yersel'.'

Danni buried her face in Franklin's fur, but Josie stared. Adrenalin was bubbling, making her nauseous with fear . . . and also a feeling she couldn't quite pinpoint. Steph's thighs trembled, her head held stock still as the knifeman threatened her: Josie cast the knifeman a look of sheer revulsion.

'You don't have to hurt anyone,' Josie said, her words aimed at Toby rather than his bully boy.

'You're leaving me no option. Think I couldn't hear you when I was in the hall? You'll keep Danni silent, will you? Let's see how long that lasts while I have Callum slice the skin off her face.'

'No!' She'd underestimated them; in particular Toby, who she'd mistakenly believed she could appeal to. There was a reason he was the leader, and not because he was a soft touch.

'Then let's get back to where we were before,' said Toby.

Callum folded a palm over Steph's forehead, and inserted the tip of his knife in her right nostril. If she was rigid before, now Steph was petrified. He said, 'Just a little nick to get us started?'

'P . . . please, Josie,' Steph moaned through clenched teeth, 'just get Danni to tell them what they want to hear.'

'Please don't hurt Mrs Steph,' Danni cried. 'I'll try really hard to remember.'

Though her hands were bound, Josie desperately wanted to hug Danni. Danni stood up and moved away, cradling a squirming Franklin as she tried to intervene. Callum's intention to cut Steph looked very real, and Josie's heart almost burst with pride at her daughter's bravery. But she was also terrified that Callum's sadism would transfer to a new target.

'Danni, don't . . .'

Toby got between the girl and their hostage.

'We don't have to hurt her, but you must speak to me. You said you were in the car with Mel after she left Barker stranded. I don't care about you wetting yourself . . . that's unimportant. What I need you to do is tell me where Mel drove to, and how you ended up seventy miles away in that crash.'

Danni looked back at Josie for support.

Josie rasped, 'How do you expect a girl of five to know where the bloody hell somebody drove to? Did you have any idea at that age about directions or distances you were ever driven?'

Ignoring her outburst, Toby cajoled Danni. 'Why don't we go back to when you saw the flying saucer and pick it up from there?'

'Bloody flying saucer . . .' Josie was halted by a stern look from Toby.

'Danni recalls a flying saucer, and that's good enough for me. What happened after that, Danni?'

'Mam drove very fast.'

'North?'

Danni frowned.

Toby said, 'Did she continue the same direction the car was going before Barker got out?'

'They were on a fuckin' motorway, whaddaya think?' said Callum.

Toby scowled. He was obviously fully aware of the direction of travel; he was only attempting to prompt the girl's memory.

Danni finally dredged up something useful. 'We didn't stay on the big road for long.'

'Mel turned off the motorway? Good. Where did you go next?'

'I don't know. It was dark. Mam parked and she cried and then she tried to help me get cleaned up, but then she said we had to get going again and I'd have to stay wet.' Danni's bottom lip wobbled

again at the subject of peeing herself. 'She promised we were going
to be safe. We were going to go away together, and didn't have to
worry about *any* of the bad people again.'

Danni halted, struck by the realization that her mam's promise
had been an empty one, because here bad people were again threatening her.

Toby noted the change in her demeanour, and before she could
clam up again, he crouched down and ruffled Franklin's ears: a man
being kind to a dog couldn't be all bad, could he? 'Did she go back
on the motorway?'

'I . . . I can't remember.'

'Danni, try harder, please!' cried Steph. 'Otherwise this bad man
will cut me.'

And Josie finally got a grip on what had been bothering her.

JOSIE

'You can stop acting now,' Josie said.

The two men exchanged frowns, but Josie wasn't interested in their sham any longer. She jutted out her chin at Steph. 'I'm not a complete idiot. For a while there I bought your act, but you can quit now.'

'Wh-what are you talking about?' Steph asked.

Josie exhaled sharply. 'That stuff with the camera earlier was to make me think Callum was a journalist. To be fair, I believed it. But why pretend to be a journalist when all along Toby had already been inside my home, and already they'd planned their invasion? You must've been alerted by one of these two that I'd walked Danni to the shop. It's no coincidence you were seated on the village green when you were, and you ensured I'd notice you by having Franklin with you because you knew Danni couldn't resist petting him. You pretended to come to my rescue, chasing off Callum, because you knew I'd feel vulnerable and wouldn't refuse if you offered to walk back with us. You only wanted inside, so you were in position to let him in through the back door while I answered Toby at the front.'

Steph didn't answer. Callum lowered the knife enough for the woman's scarlet mouth to hang open in shock.

'I noticed the grass cuttings you tracked across the floor earlier,' Josie went on, now staring at Toby, 'and made sure I locked the back door. Steph, you had to have unlocked it to let Callum inside.'

'I . . . I thought it might be your partner at the door,' Steph began, 'and by the time I realized my mistake, it was too late to slam the door closed.'

Josie shook her head. Danni openly stared at Steph with fresh distrust. 'Lies,' Josie said. 'While I was at the front, you let Callum in because you expected him to be there. That was who you were texting earlier, wasn't it, while I was busy with the groceries? You gave your friends here the go-ahead because you had me exactly where you needed me.'

'No . . . I . . .'

Toby shrugged aside Josie's accusation. 'It's pointless arguing, Whizzer; you're not going to convince her.'

'I suppose you're right,' said Steph, and pulled out of Callum's grasp. She stood, unhindered, and it was obvious that she never was shackled to the chair as Josie was. The woman shook her wrists and two separate plastic hoops dropped to the floor. She also discarded her tinted glasses on the counter because they were all part of a disguise and no longer necessary. She wanted Josie to read the disdain in her eyes as she sneered at her. Josie returned the sneer.

'Smug bitch,' Steph called her. 'You probably think you're clever for working it out.'

'I didn't need to be clever . . . you tried too hard.'

Steph drew in her bottom lip, but then directed her ire at Callum who was still at her shoulder. 'Back off, will you, Grieves? The game's up; you don't have to pretend you're guarding me any more.'

'Who's pretending?' Callum offered a sickly grin, and Steph averted her face from his breath.

'Another thing,' Steph warned, 'kick my dog again and I'll have your balls. Do you get me?'

'Promises, promises,' Callum laughed, but moved aside. Now the game was up, he moved towards some of the treats Josie had purchased in anticipation of Grace and the boys' arrival. He tore open a packet of chocolate biscuits and fed one into his mouth, even as he reached for a second. At the same time, Steph held out her hands to Danni. She didn't speak; the command was clear.

Danni was reluctant to give Franklin back; the dog had settled in her embrace and didn't seem interested in returning to his mistress. Roughly, Steph grabbed the dog and yanked it away. Danni blubbered afresh, even as the little dog whimpered in distress. 'Be quiet!' It was unclear if Steph's harsh command was for the dog or for Danni, but Josie's hackles rose.

'You're worse than either of these two monsters combined, you horrible bitch!'

'Yes,' Steph agreed, 'and you'd do well to remember it.'

Now that the charade was over, Steph assumed her natural position; she was the actual one in charge of the trio. Toby was easy with their arrangement, but Josie sensed the tension between Steph and Callum Grieves – yes, she had pieced together the creep's entire name due to their slips of the tongue made in the last few minutes. Steph glared at him as he wolfed down another chocolate biscuit, a sound of disgust in her throat. He licked crumbs off his lips with a grub-like chocolate-coated tongue. Apparently, Callum's overenthusiasm in playing his part hadn't gone down well with the pale woman, not only through his mistreatment of her dog. Distractedly, she scrubbed at her ear and side of her neck where his horrid mouth had touched her. She ignored Josie, concentrating instead on Danni.

'Have you given things any more thought?'

Danni squeaked, 'I'm being quiet!'

'I don't want *you* to be quiet.' Franklin yelped as Steph squeezed the dog for emphasis. 'I want you to talk. Have you remembered where your mother drove to next?'

Danni's head shook.

'Think.' Steph bent at the waist to stare directly into Danni's eyes. 'Think, you little wretch. You said your mother stopped to cry. What happened then?'

'She said I'd have to stay wet.'

'Yes, we've already established *that*. What happened next?'

'She was five years old at the time!' Josie was repeating herself, but it was as if those awful people weren't getting the message.

Steph's mouth pinched as she transferred her gaze to Josie. 'She's had no problem recalling stopping at a service station and what happened immediately afterwards. If she thinks hard, she'll remember something else.'

'How can you take any of what she remembers seriously? Among other things, she's talked about UFOs, for Christ's sake!'

Toby spoke up, 'And she's right on the button with her description.'

Even Danni glanced back at Josie, disappointed that the only adult in the room who should trust her was the one to disbelieve. 'I . . . I did see . . . a UFO, Mum,' she hiccupped.

Josie attempted to impart her love and belief in her child through her features, but Danni lowered her head. Steph clutched her shoulder, roughly turning the girl towards her.

'Get your bloody hands off her!' Josie kicked out, grazing Steph's shin. The woman retreated with a pained snarl, even as Callum lurched in and grasped Josie's throat in one hand. His knife was back in the other. He jabbed the tip perilously close to her left eye, and Josie had no option but to surrender.

'Try anything stupid like that again and I swear to God I'll blind you,' he growled. 'D'you hear me, skank?'

Josie's throat constricted, unable to answer. Callum, however, looked confident his message had been clearly received. He shoved her back into the chair and backed away a few steps, jostling Danni as he passed. Deliberately, he grabbed a handful of the girl's sweatshirt and yanked her so that she was again at front and centre.

Josie fought the urge to react again. She had no illusion that Callum was lying; he'd willingly use his blade on her and was searching for the slightest reason. A harsh and terrifying realization shook her to the core. She croaked the words, 'Bobby Charters wasn't killed by a random mugger.'

'No,' Callum admitted, 'he wasn't.' Robert 'Bobby' Charters was Danni's saviour, the truck driver that'd plucked her from the conflagration to safety. His death wasn't the result of a street robbery after all, but down to the severe-faced creep. He grinned at Josie, and to further enlighten her, waggled his knife. 'It might not look that big, but stick it in the right place and it'll make anyone scream.'

His lewd double entendre wasn't lost on anyone – except Danni – eliciting a frown from Toby, and a sharp cluck of Steph's tongue. Callum was emboldened by their disgust.

'Ol' Bobby was a stocky little bugger, but I still got my knife into his liver, gave it a few twists and opened up an artery or two. Fucker was bleeding gallons inside, and before he died, I watched his belly blow up twice the size.'

Josie didn't wish to hear the horrible details, and neither should Danni. Sobbing, her daughter had hidden her face in her hands. Toby showed a spark of humanity that Josie thought she'd spotted in him before. He wrapped a protective arm around Danni as he said, 'All right, Callum, you've had your fun. Now give it a rest, you're only upsetting the kid.'

'As if I care about her,' said Callum.

'Stop frightening her. While she's blubbering, she's not giving us the answers we need.' Toby stabbed a finger at the open packet of biscuits, reminding Callum there was something else he did care for. For a change, Callum didn't need telling twice.

Steph moved close enough to Danni that Franklin's nose almost touched the girl's. The little dog craned, licking between her fingers. Comforted, Danni lowered her hands. Her face was blotchy and wet, and the dog licked at her salty tears. It raised the ghost of a smile on her lips. Steph asked, 'Come on, Danni. Let's try to remember, eh? You were telling us where your mam drove you next.'

For a few seconds more, Danni thought, then her head rose and she nodded. 'We went through some big mountains.'

Steph and Toby exchanged wondering glances.

'Were you on the big road?' Toby prompted.

'I don't think so,' said Danni. 'We stopped and there was a big train, like Hogwarts Express.'

Josie thought that Danni's imagination was getting the better of her again, with her talk of the train from a Harry Potter movie she'd watched a few days ago, and it equally confused her questioners. Surprisingly Callum added validity to Danni's claim this time. 'Wait a minute,' he said around a mouthful of chocolate biscuit. 'If she's talkin' about a steam locomotive, I think I know exactly where they were.'

'Really?' Steph looked unconvinced.

'Yep. Remember I was out at Barrow-in-Furness a few days ago? When I was on my way back to Lancaster, some roadworks held me up just after Ulverston, near this spot called Newby Bridge. Probably wouldn't've noticed otherwise, but I was stuck on a red light for ages outside this old railway heritage centre. I could see from the road that they had some ancient locomotives on display, like the one from Harry Potter. I think that's probably what she's talkin' about.'

'That's speculation at best,' said Steph.

'Nah, think about it,' said Callum, on a roll. 'Mel dumped Barker at the services just south of Lancaster. I think it's fair to say she drove at a fair clip but didn't travel far before she got off the M6. It's what, a fifteen-to-twenty-minute drive from the services to the turn off towards Barrow?'

'She can't have,' Steph argued. 'She crashed north of there on the M6.'

'So she turned round and came back,' Callum pointed out. 'Don't forget, between givin' Barker the slip and crashin' the car there's a gap of around three hours. Plenty time to have driven out west, hidden the stuff and then returned to the motorway and gone north again.'

Steph looked at Danni as if the girl could confirm the creep's theory. Danni only stared up at her. Her skinny legs quaked, one knee knocking the other.

'What happened after you saw the train?' Steph prompted.

'I . . . I don't know. Mam got out the car, but she locked me inside. It was foggy and I was scared. She was gone for ages.'

'Did she take anything with her? A bag or something?'

'I don't know.'

'Did she open the boot?'

Danni looked back at Josie and her eyes were huge wet pools. 'Mum . . . I can't remember.'

'You've done well, Danni,' Josie reassured her. 'It's OK if you can't think of anything else.'

'No, that's not good enough,' Steph snapped.

'Well, it's going to have to be. Leave her be. You're putting her under too much pressure. All this stuff about a train, don't you realize she could be mixing up her memories, her timeline could be all to pot? You're trying to get details from an eight-year-old about something that happened three years ago.'

'It's best I push for more while it's fresh to her,' Steph retorted. 'You said earlier that she had no memory of what went on before the accident. That plainly isn't true. She's remembering now, and from what I've heard has been able to string events together quite naturally.'

Josie exhaled. There was no arguing with these people.

Steph asked Callum, 'Where exactly was this train museum?'

'Like I said, some shithole between Ulverston and Newby Bridge.'

'How soon can we be there?'

'Hour or two.' Callum crumpled a biscuit wrapper and dumped it between his feet. He shifted, as if ready to set off immediately, then thought better of it and clutched a four-pack of cupcakes originally intended for Danni and Grace's boys; snacks for the journey.

'Put her in the car,' Steph ordered.

'My hands are full,' Callum replied.

Toby interjected. 'I'll take Danni.'

'Yeah,' agreed Callum, 'best you do that, Tobe, before Whizzer has you taking the dog out for a leak.'

While this had been going on, Josie struggled to escape her chair, fighting her plastic restraints, desperate to jump up and pull Danni to safety. 'You aren't taking my daughter!'

'Yes I am,' Steph stated. 'You, on the other hand, are staying here.'

Josie lunged, dragging the chair as she launched after Danni.

Callum was the one with the sadistic streak, but Steph showed she wasn't a stranger to doling out punishment either. She struck Josie with the heel of her right hand, a swift, solid jab that impacted Josie's chin, igniting an explosion in her skull. The initial white flash turned crimson, then black; next Josie was aware, she was lying on her side on her kitchen floor and the tableau had changed.

JOSIE

She had no idea how long she'd been unconscious, but it was more than a few seconds. Nobody was where Josie had last seen them. Franklin scampered around Danni and Toby's feet. Toby held the squirming girl tightly against his body, halting her from rushing to her mum. Steph had retreated towards the hall, and there was no sign of Callum. From the front of the house she heard a rumble of feet, a brief exclamation of outrage, then Pete Walsh's shout.

'Josie! Josie, where are you?'

'Shut it, you tosser,' Callum commanded sharply, and there followed a solid thud, and a squeal of agony from Pete. Despite her dazed state, Josie feared the worst: that Callum had finally used his knife. She cried out to him, and heard Pete yelp her name in reply. He had returned home early and unannounced from work – maybe not; that was probably him calling the house phone earlier before Toby yanked the socket off the wall – at quite possibly the worst time imaginable. Pete, for all he was a good guy, wasn't the heroic type. He wasn't a fighter who could save her and Danni from the awful invaders.

In the next second, Pete was shoved into the room. He held his bandaged hand over his left eye, and blood trickled from both nostrils. His dark hair was as lank as usual, but standing up wildly, as if he'd been dragged inside the house by it. Callum filled the doorway behind him, employing the sole of his right foot against Pete's backside to propel him further inside. Pete crashed down flat alongside Josie.

Josie wanted to reach for him but it was impossible. Her hands were still secured behind her, bound to the rungs of the chair. Pete was dismayed, terrified, and searched her face for answers. He pawed at her too, but was immediately dragged away by Callum. Pete was forced to lie on his side at the base of the kitchen counter. As he tried to sit, Callum kicked him solidly in the gut. Pete retched, almost vomiting, and curled his knees up around the point of agony. Josie and Danni both screamed at his abuser but their shrieks fell on deaf ears. For no other reason than he could, Callum kicked Pete again.

There was no way possible Josie could protect Pete. She couldn't right herself, not while tied to the toppled chair, not before being forced down again. 'Leave him be,' she squawked, only for Callum to cast an evil grin and then slam his foot into Pete's face. The creep was wearing deck shoes, and impacting hard bone, he too felt the contact. He gasped at the pain in his instep, and took a limping step to one side. He clutched at the counter with his empty hand, and for a second Josie was terrified he'd switch weapons to his knife. Steph shoved him roughly out of the way and peered down at Pete. Pete's face was crumpled up like the biscuit wrapper Callum had dumped on the counter. She snorted, unimpressed.

She ordered Callum to set Josie upright once more.

He winced as he took weight on his abused foot, but did as instructed. He jostled the chair so that he was well out of Josie's kicking range when he moved away. Without being asked, he grasped Pete's collar and yanked him up on to his backside. Fearing further punishment, Pete covered his head with his arms, and Callum zoned in on the bandaged digit. He grabbed it and twisted and Pete squealed again.

Josie hollered at him to let Pete be. It elicited another twist of Pete's injured finger, so Josie snapped her mouth closed on her next shout. She searched for Danni. The girl was still clutched against Toby's body and, despite knowing better, Josie could swear the man protected rather than imprisoned her. No, she couldn't believe any of those people had an iota of compassion in them.

Steph glared down at Pete once more, before aiming her words at Josie. 'This is most unfortunate. I thought your partner was supposed to be at work.'

Josie could only theorize, blurting out breathlessly. 'He hurt his finger yesterday and had to go to hospital. Maybe he's been sent home because of the pain he's in.' Her gaze was laser hot on Callum. 'That sadistic bastard is hurting him for nothing.'

'Not for nothin',' Callum corrected, 'but for my own fuckin' amusement.'

Steph held up a finger, silencing him.

She regarded Josie again.

'We hoped to have what we needed from Danni by now and to

have left. It's unfortunate that Pete's sore finger has caused us all
so much trouble.'

She instructed Toby. 'Put the girl in the car, we'll be out in a
moment.'

'No!' Josie screamed. 'You can't take her.'

Ignoring her, Toby jostled the girl, carrying her through the hall
while Danni kicked and shrieked. He clamped a palm over her
mouth. It was unlikely a neighbour would hear, but there could be
someone passing the house who might overhear Danni's screams
and get nosey. Franklin scampered after them, and Steph allowed
the dog to go. She picked up the pistol left for her on the counter
by Toby. She wagged it up and down in thought. 'Now, what to do
with you two?'

There was little hope of anything less than death, because Steph
wouldn't allow either of them to set the police on her tail. Josie
knew living witnesses couldn't be tolerated. Especially after
Callum had just confessed to the cold-blooded murder of Bobby
Charters.

'Please, Steph! Don't take my daughter.' Right then, Josie couldn't
care less what happened personally to her, but she couldn't bear
Danni being dragged kicking and screaming from her.

'I must. I can't chance any other unexpected visitors. This house
is getting far too crowded for my liking.'

'Why take her? What more do you hope she can tell you?'

'That's still to be ascertained.' Steph sniffed in disdain and turned
to appraise Callum. 'What do you suggest?'

The creep appeared surprised that his opinion had been sought.
He ran fingers through his spiky hair as he considered. 'Cut their
throats. Leave them the fuck here to die in their own blood.'

Pete moaned in horror.

'Jesus,' Callum aimed at Josie, 'what do you see in this cowardly
pussy?'

'Humanity,' Josie immediately replied. 'You though, you're just
plain evil.'

Callum laughed, amused by her summation. 'You've got that
right, girl.'

Steph collected her discarded sunglasses and her phone. She pushed
both in her coat pocket. She pulled her woollen hat on. She was still
considering her and Pete's fates, Josie realized, while preparing to
leave.

'Are you taking Danni to the train museum?' Josie asked. 'Are you taking her there to see if it prompts her memory?'

'You know that's why I'm taking her,' Steph said.

'Take us with you. We can help. If Danni's frightened, she'll clam up on you, she won't say anything more.'

'She will if she's motivated,' said Callum.

Josie ignored him. She appealed directly to the leader, not the attack dog. 'Please. You don't need to kill us, Steph. Once you've got what you're looking for, you can let us go. What can we tell anyone about any of you? We don't know your full names; we don't even know what you're looking for. Once you have it, you can leave us someplace remote, to buy yourself some time to get away. I mean, there's plenty places in Cumbria that are remote, aren't there?'

'We've neither the space nor the patience to take either of you with us.' There was a squawk from outside, Danni making her outrage heard as she was bundled into Toby's Range Rover. Steph considered things and changed her mind. 'Actually, you might prove helpful in keeping the little brat quiet. Callum, cut her loose and bring her with us.'

'What about *Peter the Pussy*?' Callum asked.

'I can't keep a close eye on the two of them. That means Pete must stay here.'

'We'll behave,' Josie promised. 'All that matters is Danni's safety. We aren't going to do anything stupid to jeopardize it.'

Steph's head shook. 'Pete stays. I'm making a concession in bringing you along. Don't make me regret my decision.'

'I won't. I promise. Just . . . please, Steph, don't hurt Pete. Tie him up, put him in a locked room, just don't hurt him.'

Steph and Callum exchanged glances and Steph shrugged. 'He needn't die, as long as he can't raise the alarm.'

'Suit yersel',' said Callum.

He warned Pete to stay put then Callum cut through the plastic garden ties securing Josie's wrists. Blood rushed to her fingertips. They burned. She rubbed her hands vigorously as she stood. Callum grasped her collar and shoved her towards Steph. The gun in the pale woman's hand was aimed at her gut. Josie raised her tingling fingers, displaying compliance. She looked back at Pete. His mouth hung open in utter dismay.

'Everything will be OK, Pete. Don't fight, just do as you're told, and don't give Callum a reason to hurt you any more.'

He hadn't given Callum a reason to hurt him before, but it hadn't stopped him. Callum rolled his tongue over his bottom teeth, poking out his lip.

'Well, watcha fuckin' waitin' for, pussy? Get the fuck up and sit yer arse in the chair.'

Pete scrambled to obey. Josie hoped to watch, to ensure Pete was treated reasonably well, but Steph jabbed her with the barrel of the gun.

'You wanted to accompany Danni. Move, before I change my mind.'

Josie looked pleadingly at Pete.

'Don't worry,' Steph said, 'I already told Callum there's no need for him to die. Callum *will* obey me.' Her latter words were expressly for the knifeman's ears.

'Yeah, yeah, I heard ya, Whizzer.' He pulled fresh zip-ties from his jacket pocket and began securing Pete in the chair. Josie was ushered out the front door. She couldn't hear what was going on back in the kitchen for the blood rushing through her inner ears. She stumbled down the steps, her attention now on the grey Range Rover parked at the bottom. Pete's blue Ford Focus had been parked alongside it, and near the exit gates was Callum's Audi. When he'd arrived home unexpectedly, she couldn't imagine what had gone through Pete's mind when spotting the strange vehicles in the drive – perhaps he'd thought Grace had brought one of them, but couldn't account for the other. He'd blundered directly into an ambush, as he'd let himself inside through the front door. If only the presence of the strange cars had alerted him to what was afoot and he'd retreated to call the police. If only . . .

Danni's face appeared at a window in the back of the Range Rover. Tears streaked her cheeks and twin strings of mucus ran from her nose. Josie hurried towards her but was intercepted by Toby. He looked questioningly at Steph.

'She's coming with us. She can babysit the kid, keep her quiet on the drive up.'

Toby shook his head at the change of plan, but didn't object further. He had to unlock the car to let her get inside. Josie scooped Danni into her arms and hugged her daughter as if she'd never let her go again. Franklin, she discovered, was also in the back with Danni, as the little dog clambered over the two of them. It yipped in bewilderment, aware of the strangeness of the situation and of their emotions. Josie gently moved the dog aside, but Danni reached for it and pulled it into the hug. Josie settled beside her, one arm around Danni's quaking shoulders, hushing her, promising everything would be all right, but without any belief in her own words.

Toby sat in the driver's seat. His gloved hands gripped the steering wheel. He watched his hostages in the rear-view mirror without comment. Steph was yet to get in the Range Rover; she stood watching the front door. Her vivid red lips were pursed in impatience.

They were waiting for Callum.

How long should it take to secure and silence her partner? The longer the better, Josie decided, because it would be too quick and easy for Callum to simply slit his throat. It was more than a minute before the creep appeared in the doorway, offering Steph a lopsided sneer as he pulled the door shut. He limped down the steps. They spoke briefly but Josie couldn't hear. Steph's face grew hard for an instant, and Josie felt her heart judder. Then the woman shrugged and jabbed at the Audi and Callum loped towards it, grinning as if he was the cock of the roost.

Steph got in the front of the Range Rover with barely a glance back at her hostages. To Toby she said, 'I've sent Callum on ahead. He'll meet us at the museum. Do you know where it is?'

'I'll find it.'

Callum was already driving away. Toby started up the large 4x4.

Josie asked, 'Please tell me that monster didn't hurt Pete.'

Steph twisted round and eyed her. Her pale irises were as cold as marble. They shifted to observe Danni, and it was obvious to Josie that Steph decided she'd get more cooperation from the little girl if she dropped the scary persona. 'Pete's going to be perfectly fine,' she said directly to Danni. 'Callum has tied him up and locked him in the utility room, where he'll be safely waiting for you when you get home. You needn't worry about him for now, just concentrate on remembering.'

Danni didn't answer, and Josie didn't push for further answers either. Steph had proven herself a liar, and a poor one at that. Josie only hoped that this time the deceitful bitch was stating fact. Josie needed Pete to be alive, and not only because she cared for him; he was their only hope of rescue. She'd primed him with the information he'd need, mentioning Cumbria and the railway museum while pleading with Steph. Pete was in pain and shock, but hopefully he'd absorbed her words and be able to repeat them if somehow he escaped confinement and alerted the police.

STEPH

'Do you see it, Danni?' Stephanie Wyszogrodzki gestured. 'Is that the UFO that you remember from when Mel drove you away?'

Toby had pulled off the M6 motorway a little over midway between Preston and Lancaster. He hadn't halted the Range Rover, only made a slow circuit at the far end of the service station's car park. Other northbound travellers had alighted their vehicles, heading to and from the services in search of sustenance or to relieve aching bladders. Toby took care not to drive too close where a witness might take note of the hostages huddled together in the back. He brought the car to a crawl so that the little girl could clearly see what she'd misinterpreted when she was a five-year-old child.

'It doesn't look like a UFO now,' Danni opined.

'It does to me,' Toby said.

Steph checked it out. Looming over the service area was an unusual hexagonal structure, designed to resemble an air traffic control tower, originally home to an upmarket restaurant and sundeck but long since shut down. It was a unique design, and a landmark to motorway users in the north. With its concrete base shrouded in mist the day that Danni was last here, Steph thought the derelict restaurant deck would have appeared to hover in the sky like a B-movie flying saucer.

She was doubtful of Danni's supposed childhood amnesia, having heard how much she had already recalled under duress. She was aware that children lost their earliest memories as they grew and the brain developed, but she was having the girl cast her mind back only three years. Even Steph, in her early forties, had memories of her early childhood; her first day at school; the first time she rode a bike without stabilizers; her first trip to a swimming pool – she could even recall the taste of the over-chlorinated water on her lips. As a coping mechanism, some children suffering a trauma would selectively block certain memories, but the memories were still there, only hidden. Usually they could be coaxed back to the surface with a little stimulation.

'This is the place,' Steph told Danni, 'and that was what you thought was a flying saucer. I've showed it to you to help you remember more.' She directed her next words at Toby. 'OK, she's seen enough, let's get going.'

Toby drove them on to the access road around the side of the petrol station and down the short ramp on to the motorway. He picked up speed but didn't exceed the limit. While they were on the motorway, Steph told Josie and Danni to keep their heads down, but they'd already complied without need for instruction. Soon they were past Lancaster and on to a quieter stretch of the motorway as they headed north for the Lakeland county of Cumbria. From what she'd heard from Toby and Callum, she was confident they were on the right track, so didn't demand further directions from the little girl. Shortly, Toby took the junction west and headed towards Barrow-in-Furness through the picturesque landscape of the Cartmel Peninsula. On their left was the muddy expanse of Morecambe Bay at low tide, on their right, cliffs of craggy stone crowned by gorse and trees budding with new life. Steph noted road signs for Kendal, Ulverston and Newby Bridge. They were places she'd heard of but never visited. It was doubtful that once things were over with there that she'd ever return. It would be madness to return.

She'd obviously lied when telling Josie she lived in her village. It was a trick to make the woman more comfortable around her, as if they had something in common, and after she'd picked up on Josie's urgency to sell her home, it'd given her an opportunity to visit the house. It had been almost unnecessary for Callum to play at being a pushy paparazzo because she was certain now that Josie would've invited her back for coffee – and a tour of the house – without his involvement. It was a grand house that Josie and her family lived in, the type of home Steph could've only dreamed of when she was younger, but one attainable if she successfully delivered on this job. She was on a 20 per cent finder's fee, from which she must pay Toby and Callum, but her take from the reward would be ample to put down a deposit on a house equally grand. Presently, home was a two-bedroom flat in Uxbridge, where passenger planes out of Heathrow to the south or fighter jets from RAF Northolt to the north disrupted her sleep patterns. On her doorstep she had Colne Valley Regional Park, but through it ran the clotted and noisy vein of the M25, so it had lost most of its tranquillity for her. She'd love to move home to somewhere as peaceful and eye-catching as the Cartmel Peninsula but knew this particular place could never be a home in her future. Once business concluded there, she must avoid the place as if it was plague-ridden.

Unless you were stupid, or you wished to be caught, you didn't abide where you planned to bury your victims.

Failure wasn't a word she'd entertain. She needed the money, but more so she intended staying alive. Michael Barker, a man too conceited and arrogant for his own good, had fucked up badly when he'd allowed Mel to give him the slip, and had paid for his mistake.

Toby had collected Barker from the service station and brought him back to face the music. Their employer, Leonard Freda, was generous in reward but demanded equally high payback for failure. Barker's mess-up had cost Freda to the tune of over two million pounds. Instead of showing remorse, apologizing and promising to work his arse off in reparation for the loss, Barker couldn't even guard his lip. Freda said nothing as Barker flew into a tirade. Everyone was to blame but him, and there was no fucking way he should be held responsible for the whore burning up the loot in the car. Barker had thrown his hands in the air, swearing and puffing up his chest. Seated immobile in his wheelchair, Freda was showered by Barker's spittle. He still said nothing, only raised a finger. His attendant, Jakub Holstein, handed the old man a tissue, and Freda dabbed at the droplets of spit on his cheek. Only then had the arrogant fool realized he'd gone too far, and Barker tried to apologize. It was too late for Barker.

Up until that point, Kolacz had stood as broad and silent as a clay golem and, when he'd lunged for Barker, it had been so sudden that even Steph had yelped and jumped aside. Kolacz had hands the size of boxing gloves, and fingers capable of putting dints in a bowling ball. They'd circled Barker's throat and squeezed down the apology before it had left Barker's tongue. Barker was a big guy himself, a tough guy, but he had been a straw doll in Kolacz's grasp. The giant hauled him on to his tiptoes, throttling him, and Steph winced at the crackling of pulverizing vertebrae and collapsing cartilage. Closing her eyes hadn't spared her the details of Barker's death because the sounds of it painted their own picture. She sure as hell didn't want to be the next person Kolacz throttled the life from, because her head wouldn't require severing afterwards, it'd probably pop off her shoulders like a champagne cork.

This was no vivid nightmarish fate she'd dreamed up. Barker's hands and head had been severed and his sundry remains dumped overboard, miles apart, to the bottom of the English Channel. Even if they were ever trawled up in the future, encased in concrete, it was unlikely they'd ever be identified as human remains.

They entered Newby Bridge, a pretty little town at the gateway to the southern lakes, and a tourist destination. It boasted some fine hotels nestled alongside a riverbank. Again, Steph warned her hostages to keep down as Toby slowed the Range Rover to negotiate a roundabout. They were stalled by traffic in front, and directly facing them was a police car. Toby timed it so they crossed the roundabout even as the police did the same, so the cop was concentrating on the manoeuvre rather than on them. Steph kept her gaze front and centre. The cop continued on without having even noticed them. As the police car receded in their mirrors, Steph said, 'Good. They can't be looking for us.'

Josie moaned.

'Don't worry,' Steph reminded her, 'it only means that Pete hasn't done something stupid like escaped and called the police.'

Josie said nothing. Steph knew the woman didn't believe a word she said any more. It didn't matter. Thinking that Pete was dead – despite Steph's promise he wouldn't be killed – might not be a bad thing. Fear that they could expect a similar fate if they caused problems was great motivation to obey. Josie wasn't stupid; it didn't escape Steph that the woman's main reason for being there was to protect Danni. She'd be plotting an escape and biding her time. Steph didn't believe the woman would shout and scream from the moving car, trying to attract a passer-by's attention, so there was little concern about a drama unfolding whilst travelling. Josie's escape attempt would probably happen once they'd arrived at their destination, except Steph wouldn't allow it.

A dual carriageway swept through some bends, and into a river valley, a steep crag on one side, and the forest-shrouded River Leven to their right. They crossed the river, and the abruptness of their arrival almost took Toby off guard. He slapped at the indicators and decelerated hard to cut into the turning lane. His reward was an angry blare of a horn from a truck driver that blasted past them, and the Range Rover was left rocking on its chassis. A break in the oncoming traffic allowed Toby to peel across and into the entrance to the heritage railway museum grounds. There were a few visitors' vehicles in the car park, but the people must have been inside the gift shop, tea room or inspecting the exhibits because – for all but one person – there were no pedestrians about. Toby drove over to where Callum Grieves sat on the bonnet of his Audi. He had parked at the far end of the car park to avoid close scrutiny, but it hadn't stopped him visiting one of the shops because he chewed down on a fried bacon roll. A blob of tomato ketchup clung to one hollow cheek. The man disgusted Steph in every possible way. Toby drew the Range Rover alongside the Audi and the sinuous man hopped down from his perch, gesticulating with his bread roll for Toby to wind open his window.

'Took yer bloody time gettin' here, didn'tcha?' he announced around a half-masticated pulpy mass of bacon and bread.

'We can't be that long behind you,' Toby responded, 'seeing as you aren't even halfway through your lunch. I bet you didn't hang around before feeding your damn face again.'

'I finished those cupcakes on the drive up. Whadd'ya expect me to do, sit here twiddling my thumbs till you decided to show up?' Callum aimed the remnants of his food at the teashop. 'Besides, I had to do a recce, and had to have a good reason for goin' inside without attracting attention.' He grinned around the pink mush. 'Perk of the job; this buttie is friggin' lovely.'

'Mel's unlikely to have hidden the bag in a teashop where it'll be easily found.'

Callum ignored him; instead he bent and peered in the back window at their hostages. When neither of them met his scarecrow grin, he said, 'The kid tell you anythin' helpful on the drive up?'

Toby shook his head.

Steph didn't answer either; instead she turned and craned between the seats. Franklin sniffed her, and she pushed the little dog aside. 'Danni. You're allowed to look up now. We're here. Where you saw the Hogwarts Express.'

Danni buried her head into Josie's chest. Josie said, 'What more can you expect her to tell you? She already explained that her mother left her in the car alone and it was misty. She knows nothing about where Mel went or what she did when she got here.'

Ignoring Josie, Steph said, 'Danni. Take a look around. Try to remember where it was your mam parked, and think about which way she went. You said you were scared when she left you, so I bet you watched her walk away, hoping she'd hurry back.'

Danni extricated her head from the circle of Josie's arms. She looked first at Steph then stretched a bit more to peer out the windows. After searching around, her attention fixed a moment on some nearby engine sheds. 'We were over there, at the front of that big shed. That's where I saw Harry Potter's train.' Her gaze tracked across the car park towards the teashop, but she decided it was the wrong direction and checked to the right again. The girl's eyebrows arched towards her hairline. Steph followed her gaze to a foot-bridge over the railway lines.

'Your mam went over the bridge?'

'I . . . I think so. She was gone for ages . . . hours.'

'Good,' said Steph, and offered a smile of encouragement that was lost on Danni. 'Now that you're remembering, can you picture your mam walking over there for me? Think back, how scared you felt, and you were hoping she'd turn round and come straight back. Was she carrying anything . . . a big bag?'

Danni scrunched her face in thought, and in frustration. She dipped her chin against her chest.

'Danni . . .'

'Let her be for a minute,' Josie snapped.

Mouth pinched, Steph held up a warning finger.

'Danni, just think about it,' she said, without taking her gaze off Josie. 'Was she carrying a big bag? A holdall.'

Wiping his mouth with the back of his wrist, Callum stated the obvious. 'Stands to reason doesn't it, Whizzer? She wasn't going to take a dump in those woods over there.'

As much as he annoyed her, Callum was right. There was only one reason why Mel would've left her daughter alone in the car and crossed the railway tracks. It was to hide the bag somewhere it wouldn't easily be discovered by any of the staff or visitors to the museum. The footbridge gave access to a raised platform, at the end of which a set of steps led to a fenced-off recreation area. Beyond it the hillside was densely wooded.

Steph retrieved a slim dog lead from her jacket pocket and reached for Franklin. 'Time for walkies,' she said to the dog, then shifted her attention to Josie. 'We're all getting out of the car together and going for a little stroll. Don't scream, or try to alert *anyone*, or I'll have Callum cut your throats.'

GRACE

The original plan was to bring her boys for a play-date with Danni, while she and Josie had a good natter and catch-up, but those plans hadn't fitted well with the boys' dad. David could be capricious at the best of times, so announcing he'd purchased tickets for him and the boys at a theme park – even if it wasn't his weekend for having them – came as no real surprise to Grace. She sometimes wondered if David's erratic ideas were his attempts at continuing to control her life, despite them being divorced for more than eighteen months now. But no, when they'd been a couple, he'd been equally unpredictable. It was one of the things that'd first attracted her to him. Back then his surprises had been welcomed: a romantic weekend in Paris; a trip to Venice; a fortnight's holiday to the Maldives. It was easy to believe that he was displaying his love for her through lavish gifts and trips, and it had taken Grace some years to realize the opposite: David was in control, and she was at his whims, never the other way around. If she'd announced organizing a surprise weekend break, he'd have gone out of his way to ensure it didn't happen – claiming he must work, or feigning sickness, and sometimes even refusing flatly in order to get his own way – before springing a different sudden plan of his own. After their kids had come along, with barely a year's gap between them, she'd taken an extended time off work to raise them, and this had pleased David. It didn't occur to her at first that it suited his ideal to isolate and control her, and it wasn't until the boys were of school age and she'd planned a return to work that he'd shown his true colours. Controlling their finances, her home, her body and even her social interactions, he had Grace exactly where he'd wanted her, in the palm of his hand. She'd still be stuck in the unhealthy relationship if not for the sudden death of Josie's husband, Gary. Out of her sister's tragedy, Grace's liberty had been won back.

Grace had wanted to attend Gary's funeral. David Dean had said no.

Josie was having nothing of her brother-in-law's selfishness, though, and had gone to fetch Grace and the boys. David was apoplectic, but how could he deny Josie her sister's company, or Danni the company of the boys, without being exposed as the controlling shithead that he was? Once she was free of his direct grasp, Grace had taken the opportunity to distance herself further. Announcing their separation, she and the boys had lived in Josie's rambling home for months while divorce proceedings were finalized. David had joint custody of their children now, but again, it was a fluid arrangement as far as he was concerned.

For a change, Grace wasn't annoyed at his off-the-cuff reorganization of her plans; if anything, David had done her a favour. She'd enjoy more quality time with Josie if she wasn't constantly wrangling her rambunctious boys. The person seemingly losing out this time could be Danni. Her original reason for visiting was so her cousins could help entertain Danni, but to be fair, Grace wasn't sure she would be overly upset, as the boys teased her remorselessly, and any game they played was at their discretion – sadly, there was no denying who their father was.

She'd brought a bottle of wine and some nibbles. She must drive home, but a small glass of vino with her lunch was permissible, right? Maybe a slightly larger glass if she ate plenty to absorb it.

She'd tried ringing Josie to tell her there'd only be one coming for lunch, to save her catering for the boys, but there had been no reply. Her subsequent text went without a reply too. Grace had gone old school and tried Josie's landline, but the phone was out of service. It was odd, and inconvenient, but not alarming. Josie had probably gone out to the village shop, or was playing with Danni in the garden, and unaware of the connectivity problems.

Grace drove through the village, passing the grocer's and the green, on the lookout for her sister and niece, and then along the quiet winding road to the house. She indicated, even though there were no other road users, and pulled on to the drive. Gravel was picked up in the tyre treads, some tinkling against the undercarriage. She barely noticed. Pete's Ford Focus was parked in a strange location, only midway up the drive, and its presence elicited a moment of disappointment – Grace had hoped to have her sister to herself for an hour or two. She was sure that Josie had mentioned Pete had to work today, but obviously their routine had changed. Never mind, Pete wasn't a bad guy to have around, and besides, if needed, the house was big enough that the women could find a room far enough from him to enjoy a private girly natter. There was no sign of the family out in the garden; perhaps they were out of sight around the back.

She grabbed her purchases off the back seat and strolled to the front door, peering up at blind windows that reflected the early afternoon sun. The gravel was all churned up, deep tyre tracks in it: it wasn't like Josie to leave the drive untended and unkempt. Grace had known her to be out here, raking the gravel as smooth as a Zen garden. When she wasn't raking, she'd be vacuuming the carpets, or cleaning up after Danni; it was a wonder she ever got any paid work done.

Grace rang the doorbell, and immediately tried the handle. The sisters didn't rest on formality: *mi casa es tu casa*, sis. The door didn't open because the latch was on. She knocked, thinking she heard a thump from inside. It was distant; somebody perhaps was in the kitchen. Grace pressed the bell again, waited. When the door didn't open, she lugged her purchases around the house, looking in windows as she went. Nobody was in sight. She passed the bins, and turned up the short path for the back door. It stood open a few inches, so Grace let herself in, passing the utility room to the kitchen door. About to call out to announce her arrival, the shout caught in her throat. The kitchen was in disarray; something was decidedly *wrong*.

The table where Josie had been working had been shoved away from the wall. The scattered pages of a manuscript littered the table and floor. Josie's laptop and phone were bundled in a heap on the corner of the kitchen counter, the cables wrapped around them, a crumpled pile of empty biscuit wrappers on top. One of the dining chairs was abandoned in the gap between the table and sink. Severed plastic ties lay on the floor. Then there was the blood. There weren't gallons of the stuff. Only a small spatter of it on the floor, a few more droplets a few feet distant, then larger drips and smears of it tracked into the hall.

What has happened here?

Had somebody been cut so badly they'd been rushed to hospital?

It could explain why the house was deserted. Maybe an ambulance had to be summoned and the entire family had accompanied the injured party to A&E. Was that why Pete's car was left parked so haphazardly outside? Perhaps Danni was injured somehow, and Josie had alerted Pete and he'd sped home to find his way blocked by an ambulance, into which he'd then piled with his family. Was that why the gravel was so badly churned up too: the ambulance hadn't hung around. All those thoughts tumbled through Grace's mind in as many seconds as it took her to lurch inside and shout in alarm for Josie. Maybe they weren't at hospital, but upstairs in one of the bathrooms, attempting to staunch the blood.

She dumped her carrier bag beside the sink, the wine bottle clunking so hard it was close to smashing. She didn't care. She straddled the largest splash of blood, staring a few seconds in dismay, trying to comprehend. Her head snapped up. 'Josie?'

She rushed for the hall but halted at the foot of the stairs. 'Josie, are you up there? Is everyone OK?'

A drumming sounded, something hammering on wood. It grew louder, more desperate. A stuttering moan accompanied it.

'Josie? Danni? Where are you?'

Unable to pinpoint the source of the noises, she could tell only that they were from somewhere behind her. She spun around, lurched back into the kitchen. She tracked through blood. The sounds were louder, calling her to the utility room. She hadn't noticed them before, but there were drops of blood in there too. A century or more ago, another room at the far end was part of the original kitchen, a cold store where meat and perishables were kept. These days Josie used it as a place to hide her clutter. The door vibrated in time with the frantic hammering, but Grace was caught in a mild panic, dreading what she might find behind the door. The moans rang out again, a mixture of fear and frustration. It wasn't a sound she could imagine coming from Josie or Danni.

'Pete? Is that you?'

'Uuuuhhhh . . . huhh . . . huuurrrppp!'

'Pete!'

She lunged for the door, about to yank it open. Her fingers fell short by a few inches.

What had happened here? Some kind of struggle had occurred in the kitchen. Had Pete come home and got into a fight with Josie? Would he be a threat to her sister and niece if she let him out?

'Pete,' she said tremulously, 'what's going on? What happened here?'

Pete gurgled something unintelligible. He scuffed feebly at the door. Whether or not he'd instigated the fight, he was in no fit shape to chase anyone now. She grasped the handle and tugged. The door resisted her. She checked for a lock. There was an ancient keyhole, painted over. Pete hadn't been locked in with a key. A wooden doorstop had been kicked into the gap between the door and floor.

'Pete, I'm going to open the door now,' Grace announced. She used her heel to loosen then kick aside the triangular wedge. She pulled the door open, but stepped backwards too, ready in case Pete darted for her throat. He barely moved. His head lolled back and his eyes rolled up with no recognition in them.

'It's me, Pete, it's Grace.'

'Huuurrrrppp muuuhhh . . .'

Surrounded by junk, he was seated in one of the kitchen chairs, hands behind him, ankles fastened to the legs by plastic ties. His face was messed up, bruised and bloody. A cloth gag had been applied so tightly that it stretched his lips agonizingly. Hanging from the sodden rag, twin rivulets of stringy saliva, thick with blood clots, stuck to his chin.

Josie hadn't tied up Pete like that!

Hyperventilating, she reached for Pete. She again drew back. If not Josie, then who had done this to him? Were they still in the house and . . . *where are Josie and Danni!*

There were no other sounds than Pete's moans and the pulse beating a tympani inside her skull.

She again reached for Pete, trying to ease the gag from between his teeth. It wouldn't budge. He shook his head, kicking slightly with his feet: it was his toes hitting the door that had made the drumming sound before. Grace could barely find room to reach around him, and the knotted rag defeated her attempts to untie it. She grabbed Pete around his middle and dragged him and the chair clear of the cupboard. Seeing how he'd been tied up, she didn't think her fingers would loosen the plastic ties. She rushed to the kitchen, found the wooden knife block and picked the sharpest one in it. On her return, Pete flinched in horror at the bared steel and Grace understood how much he'd been terrorized and by what.

'It's OK, I'm only going to cut you free.'

He groaned but in relief.

She attacked the ties around his wrists first, taking care not to cut him because the plastic was so tightly embedded in his flesh. Pete moaned and winced as she snicked through each plastic tie. As the last one snapped open, he slumped forward. Grace grasped him, holding him up so he didn't spill into the utility room altogether. While he was nestled against her chest, she worked the tip of the knife under the knotted gag and began sawing. It felt like forever before the rag parted, and she could help him spit out the bloody rag. He reared back in agony as she tugged it free, and she realized the source of the blood was from his tongue.

'Oh my god!'

As he opened his mouth to speak, she saw the tip of his tongue had been split neatly down the centre. The two sides moved independently of each other. He slumped forward, cupping his mouth with his hands. His fingers must've been numb through the lack of circulation. One finger was bandaged, but it looked as if it was done prior to his latest injuries. More blood dripped between his cupped fingers. She placed a comforting hand on his shoulder while stooping to cut his ankles free of the chair legs. Reaching was awkward, so she took his weight against her shoulder as she dipped lower and sawed through the garden ties.

Finally he was free and Grace tried coaxing him up, to follow her to the kitchen. He was in shock or something, because he didn't move.

'Pete,' she urged, 'you have to let me help you. You need to get to hospital—'

His head snapped up, eyes feverish, skin marbled where the circulation was returning. 'No hoshpi'al!'

His mouth sounded full of marbles, and it must've been difficult to speak. He spat, worked his tongue and tried again, 'No hoshpi'al! No poleesh!'

'What? What are you talking about? You have to get help.'

'No, no, we can't, Grashe.' He shook his head wildly. 'We can't, for Jothie an' Danni'th thake.'

He clawed at her to help him stand, and she supported him as he stumbled through to the kitchen. Bracing his arms over the sink, he regurgitated a mass of congealed blood that plopped into the sink in a livery mass. It was surprising he hadn't choked to death on his own blood before now. Was causing him to choke what his abuser had intended by slitting open his tongue then gagging him with no way of expelling the blood? Whatever had been in the monster's mind, it was an act of sheer barbarity.

Pete spluttered, while Grace patted his back in a feeble attempt at helping him. She couldn't think clearly. She asked, 'What did you mean, we can't get help for Josie and Danni's sake?'

He turned to squint at her dumbly. No, as if she was the dumb one. The answer should've been obvious to her.

'Somebody has taken them?' she asked tremulously.

He nodded. 'They did thish to me.'

He still slurred, but having expunged most of the clotted blood he could form words more clearly.

'Who Pete? Who did this?'

He threw his hands in the air.

'You have to help me to understand—' she said.

'I don't know, Grashe! There were three of them. I don't know who they were.'

Grace stood in silence, her thoughts a maelstrom of confusion.

'Two men. A woman. They took Jothie an' Danni,' Pete slurred, then had to spit again. 'They warned me they'd kill them if I called the copth. We can't call the police, Grace. The bastard that did thith to me . . . he will do ath he warned.'

Grace shivered head to foot. 'We have to call the police, Pete! We have to.'

He grasped her arms with bloody fingers. His fingertips dug in painfully. 'No, or Jothie and Danni will be murdered. Don't you get it?'

'But we have to help them—'

'We help by *not* calling the copth . . . uh, cops.'

'How? How is that helping? Pete, for god's sake, they've been kidnapped and—'

'They'll be released unharmed if we follow instructions. The one that did *this* . . .' he indicated his mouth, and it was apparent he was more comfortable with forming words without lisping as hard, 'he promised they'd be freed. But he also promised what would happen if he even got a whiff of the cops.'

More blood trickled from the corners of his mouth. Grace searched for something to staunch the flow. She'd no idea where Josie kept her first-aid box, so delved in drawers and came out with a laundered tea towel. She handed it to Pete, who wadded it to his mouth. Questions were forming in her mind at a million miles per hour.

'Why did these people take them?' she demanded. 'Who are they? What do they want?'

Pete shook his head. He checked the towel, finding it already scarlet. He adjusted it, pressing a thick wad inside his mouth.

'Pete,' Grace said, 'you have to speak to me. I need to understand or I'm calling the police right now!'

'Hurts to talk,' he whined.

'I know, but you must try.'

He tossed the dirty towel in the sink, went to the drawer and found a fresh one. He hacked more congealed blood into the bowl. He said, 'I came home from work and they were already here. They grabbed me, they beat me up. I . . . I . . .' He shook his head again, as if it would help reorder his mind. 'They were most interested in Danni.'

'Why, why would anyone—'

'Not Danni; they wanted something and they think she knows where they can find it.'

'I don't understand. *What?*'

He rolled back his head, groaning in misery, with the towel concealing his lower face.

'Pete? For crying out loud! Speak to me.'

He nodded, but the towel was again soaked with blood. If he didn't stop the bleeding, he'd likely faint, and then there would be no answers.

Grace picked another cloth and ran it under the cold tap. She squeezed out the excess water and handed the damp towel over. Pete wiped around his mouth, wincing. While she steadied him, he shuffled over and sat on the nearest chair. Grace allowed him a few seconds to get composed. All colours had bleached from his features.

'You need to go to hospital,' she opined.

'I told you—'

'*You could die from blood loss!*'

'It's not as bad as it looks.'

'Are you fucking kidding me?'

Grace was certain that if she caught sight of her reflection, it would be as pale and dismayed as Pete's face was. She was jittery with anxiety, but a hot ball of anger had also formed in the centre of her chest. Violent strangers had invaded Josie's home and taken her and Danni hostage. There was once a time when Grace had been the prisoner of a control freak, and her sister had stood up for her, because that's what family was supposed to do. It had been a life lesson for Grace, who'd sworn she'd be stronger, and that she'd never allow anyone to control her again, and god pity anyone that tried to hurt her or her loved ones.

'Pete, if you don't tell me something I can work with, I'm phoning an ambulance, and then I'm phoning the police.'

'Please don't. You weren't here. You don't know what that evil bastard is capable of. Grace, he wasn't bluffing. He laughed when he cut my tongue. *Laughed*. He was under orders not to kill me, but he still hurt me anyway. He swore he's going to do worse to Josie and Danni if we call the cops, and I know he wasn't bluffing.'

'OK, OK, I hear you and believe you. But think, Pete, you must have heard something important.'

'I told you. I arrived home late, so I don't know what they were looking for. After they took Danni, they were going to kill us, I'm sure of that. But Josie bought us some time. She went with them so she could protect Danni. She said . . . wait! She said something about a train museum.' Pete was suddenly agitated. He thrust up from the chair, his eyes bulging from their sockets. 'Josie was dropping me clues. She said about the train museum. She begged the woman to let them go, somewhere remote in Cumbria.'

Grace and Josie had grown up in Carlisle; their parents still lived there now. She knew Cumbria. It was mostly remote, a county of hills and lakes and woodlands. 'It doesn't really narrow it down . . .'

'There can't be that many railway museums in one county, can there?'

It wasn't a subject Grace knew about, so she went for her mobile phone.

'Whoa! Wait!' Pete clawed for her phone.

She turned aside. 'I'm not calling the police. I'm searching the Web.'

She frowned. Ordinarily when she visited Josie, her phone automatically picked up her Wi-Fi signal. There wasn't a signal, and the best she could get was 3G coverage, not good enough for an Internet connection. She looked over at Josie's computer bundled on the counter, and concluded what must have happened. The Internet signal, as well as the phones there, had been disabled. Hopefully she could re-establish them if she plugged in Josie's router once more. She was unsure which room the router was in and didn't care to waste time searching only to find the wires ripped out, the way the phone lines had been. More concerning was bringing her sister and niece home safely. She opened her contacts list and hit one number in particular.

The phone rang twice and was picked up.

'Kyle,' she said without preamble, 'it's Grace. I desperately need your help.'

KYLE

'Come again?' said Kyle Perlman. Music kept a steady beat, and the thudding of fists against leather surrounded him. He juggled his phone, trying it against his other ear. Asking her to repeat her words wasn't because he'd missed what she'd said, only that her name meant nothing to him.

'It's me, Grace Dean, you know from school?'

Kyle took a quick check of his surroundings, as if a phantom image of the woman might present herself, boxing in the ring or maybe even grappling in the padded cage. 'You one of my MMA students?'

'No. I'm Jake and Lucas's mum. You know, from junior school? We got talking at the gate when you came to pick up your kids that time.'

'Oh, aye, right.' Kyle frowned, her identity still unclear to him. Over the last couple of years, he'd spoken with many of the young mothers at school pick-up time, and if he were to be honest, few of their names had stuck in his memory. He was certain he hadn't randomly handed out his mobile number to any of them. 'How'd you get my number again?'

'You gave it to me.'

'I don't know about that . . .'

'You were selling your Mercedes,' she reminded him, 'and I was in the market for a new car. You gave me your number, and I called and arranged to look at it.'

Her face came back to him then. Smart-looking young woman with an elfin cut of black hair and a dark beauty spot on her chin. He thought she'd the look of one of those chic Parisian girls, but she'd spoken with a definite northern English accent – he couldn't decide if she was a Geordie or a Jock, or maybe from somewhere in between. Her accent certainly didn't originate in Cheshire. As he recalled now, he'd found her attractive and tried picking her up.

'Dean? I'm positive that wasn't the name you gave to me.'

'I was rebelling at the time and might have used my maiden

name then. I'm divorced now, but still use my ex's name for the kids' sake.'

'Didn't we go out on a date?' he asked.

'You took me out twice for lunchtime drinks.'

'That's right. I remember now,' he grunted in humour. 'You turned me down the third time.'

'Yeah, isn't it what they say, the third time's the charm?' she said. 'I was worried things were getting too serious and about who I could be getting involved with. From what I'd been told by some of the other mums, I got the impression you were a bit of a bad boy.'

'Yeah,' he laughed, 'well, I've been told some women like bad boys.'

'Maybe so, but at the time I was only interested in your car.'

'Is that right? So much for my roguish charm and my sales skills, eh? You dumped me and didn't even buy the Merc in the end.'

'It was out of my price range,' she admitted.

'If you're after another motor now I can—'

'No wait! That isn't it.' She paused, and in the background Kyle thought he could hear somebody else making pained groans. Grace came back on the line. A groan of agony was a sound he was familiar with in his line of business. 'Look, were you serious when you said you were connected?'

He grunted, wondering what the bloody hell he'd told her. Grace had been good-looking, and he wouldn't have put it past himself to try impressing her with some outlandish claim or other, never about his military career or his current business dealings, though. 'What do you mean by "connected"? I'm not in line for the throne nor nothin'.'

'I mean *connected*, as in you know *certain types* of people. Not all of them law-abiding.'

'Depends what you're after. If it's drugs or that kind of shit, I don't go near it.'

'You told me that you ran a dojo, and that you had some tasty fighters in your camp. You said some of the lads you managed worked the doors for you, but the impression I got was that, well, maybe there was more they'd do for the right price.'

'Nah. You got the wrong end of the stick there. Yeah, I supply doormen to the pubs and clubs, but that's as far as it goes. Everything I do is above board.'

'You know I'm not a copper,' she said. 'I'm not trying to catch you out, or to get you to say something incriminating. Jesus Christ, Kyle. I called you because I'd nowhere else, *no one* else, to turn to. I'm neck-deep in trouble, and I need some tough guys to back me up.'

'I can hear moaning in the background. Somebody's been hurt, yeah? Are you next? Is that what this is about? Somebody's threatening you with a hiding?'

'Trust me, if this was only about me getting a beating, I wouldn't be calling you. I wouldn't be begging for you to put me in touch with someone I can trust not to run when the going gets really tough.'

He looked around his gym. This time in the day, his paying customers were fewer than in an evening. He wasn't taking an active part in the day's coaching, and could leave it to some of his more advanced students. 'I'm at a loose end. My trust can be bought at the right price.'

'I don't have much,' she said, 'but maybe we can, I dunno, come to some sort of arrangement.'

'How'd you know I'm not a happily married man?'

'Happily married men don't flirt and go on dates with mothers they meet at the school gates. Besides, that isn't the type of arrangement I meant. Perhaps I can pay so much now, and so much after completion?'

'My terms are a grand a day and you pick up any expenses. Way I recall, you were short on the cash when you were after my motor. How can I trust you to pay me. when you've already admitted to being skint?'

'I never said I was skint, only I wasn't in a position to pay what you asked for a second-hand car. It's different when it comes to helping my sister and niece. I love them so much that I'll pay whatever you ask. Kyle, please don't turn me down. This really is a matter of life or death.'

'So call the cops.'

'I can't. You know I can't. I wouldn't have reached out to you if I'd anywhere else to turn.'

'I must admit, you're beginning to intrigue me.' He wasn't lying. She'd been a touch ambiguous about what exactly she wanted from him, other than she needed somebody tough, fearless, and that things could get very heavy: A matter of life and death. Maybe she was being overly dramatic, but he had to admit his interest had been piqued. For months now, his life had been way too cosy and domesticated for his liking, and it sounded as if Grace was offering a distraction. Shit, if she'd pleaded harder to begin with, he might even have taken the job *free gratis*. 'When do you want me to start?'

'The second I hang up. Do you still have your Merc?'

'Nah, I let it go. But I've got other wheels.'

'How soon could you meet me at . . .?' She named a service station on the M6 he was unfamiliar with. He asked for clarity, and she told him it was just over the Lancashire county boundary in Cumbria.

'Oh, yeah, I know where you mean now. It's just before you hit the fells. I could be there in . . .' He made a quick calculation in his head. 'Say, three hours?'

'Let's say two hours or you won't be of any use to me.'

'Two hours will be cutting things fine.'

'Kyle, it will already be two hours more than I can spare. Get there in under two hours and I promise I'll pay you another grand's bonus on top of your daily fee.'

'And agree to joining me on a third date?'

'OK, and I'll also go out for drinks with you again.'

'On those terms I'll risk a speeding ticket.'

'No,' she said, 'whatever you do, you mustn't draw the attention of the police.'

'What am I getting into here, Grace? You planning on doing a heist or something?'

'You could say I'm planning a snatch of sorts, but nothing illegal. At least I don't think it's wrong to try rescuing a pair of hostages, whatever I have to do to their kidnappers to get them back safely. The police might have a different outlook, so I'd prefer they don't get in our way.'

'The way you're talking, things might get heavier than a fistfight. Say nothing, I'll pack for any eventuality.'

He waited, his words having given Grace a reality check. For Christ's sake, what did she expect? From what she'd intimated, her sister and niece had been kidnapped, and she wanted to take them back from the bad guys. What? She might think a few harsh words would do the trick, but Kyle would deserve having his arse handed to him on a plate if he went in with less than all-out war in mind. He was going to tool up, or she could forget about him. 'You got a problem with that?' he finally prompted.

'No. Just wondering if you could fetch me a weapon too.'

GRACE

'Are you barking mad?' Pete had regained enough strength to stand at the kitchen sink, bracing his hips to the counter to avoid falling. His mouth was a mess, but the more she'd seen of him speaking, Grace had realized the slit to his tongue wasn't as horrific as she'd first thought. It had been parted at the tip, but not so he looked snake-like. The blood had mostly stopped flowing, so he didn't have to constantly spit and drool into the bowl as before. However, when he'd exclaimed in shock at her plan, she was showered in tiny crimson droplets. She averted her face, the smell of his breath so coppery it was sickening.

'What do you expect me to do, Pete? Stand here and do nothing?'

Still lisping, but not as obviously as he had before, Pete cried, 'You're planning on running off and meeting a total stranger, who, reading between the lines, is some kind of lunatic, to do what? Try to save Josie and Danni from *armed criminals*? Are you a complete nutter?'

'He's not a total stranger. I've dated him, and well, he seemed like a good guy.'

'You know nothing about him.'

'I know he can handle himself.'

'He can talk the talk, but what if he's full of hot air? He sounded to me like he's watched too many Guy Ritchie movies. I mean, who does he think he is, bloody Jason Statham?'

'This is about helping Josie and Danni. You're in no fit state to fight for them, so I have to do *something,* and by asking for Kyle's help I hope to even up the odds.'

'You could get yourself killed.'

'I have to try!'

'Worse, you could get *them* killed. Is that what you want, Grace?'

'Of course not!'

'What about your boys if anything happens to you? Do you want them living with David the entire time and turning out just like him? We should just wait, and once they're done we'll get Josie and Danni back home again."

'*You* don't get it, Pete! Once they have whatever the hell it is they're looking for, Josie and Danni will be worthless to those bastards. In fact, they'll be fucking liabilities. Do you genuinely think they'll be allowed to live when they can identify their abductors?'

'So we have to call the police.'

'I know. We should. But we need to try my way first. Until they've found what they're looking for, the bastards will keep them alive: if they think the cops are on to them they might just cut their losses and murder Josie and Danni before making a run for it.' Grace stared at Pete, hoping he'd register hope in her words. There was none though, nor the slightest sign of courage. 'I can't stand around here debating with you. Every second counts, Pete, and I have to go.'

'No, wait. Where do you think you're going to find them? Cumbria is a big county.'

'I know that,' she snapped. 'That's why you're going to make yourself useful. Come on, Pete. Give yourself a shake, will you? You've been messed up, but you're not finished: I've bitten my tongue worse than you've been cut. I always thought you were a good man for Josie; well, why not bloody prove it? Get your phone and Wi-Fi up and running again, and search for railway museums in Cumbria. You can call me on my mobile and let me know. Once I meet Kyle, I'll—'

'You'll what? Charge in like the bloody Seventh Cavalry to save them? I think it's a really bad idea, Grace.'

'If I must, I will. Wouldn't you, Pete, if you thought you might be able to save them?'

He held up his bandaged finger. Whatever he meant, it was lost on Grace. She saw only a pathetic attempt at concealing a cowardly streak as thick and yellow as spilled custard. He couldn't hold her gaze for more than a couple of seconds, before turning aside. He bent over the sink and a dollop of clotted blood slipped from between his teeth into the bowl. He might be looking for sympathy, but in that moment Grace despised his weakness. 'I was going to ask you to come with me, to help. But you're more useful here. Do what I asked, Pete. Find where I need to go.'

'It's a wild-goose chase,' he spluttered.

'Not if you think about it. Search your memory. You heard more than you first realized, and there will be other clues in there. Do what

I asked, Pete. *Do it.*' She backed away as she spoke, gaining speed with each step, and then she spun around and headed through the hall towards the front door. Yanking open the door, she cleared the front steps, and then charged across the churned-up gravel to her car. Without thinking about it, she had pulled out her keys and inserted them in the ignition: the engine caught first time. She pulled out her mobile and threw it down, screen up, on the passenger seat. Hopefully Pete would do as she'd instructed and have a location for her before she made it up the motorway to her rendezvous with Kyle Perlman. If he let her down, well, she could always run a web search of her own once she'd reached the service station.

From previous trips she'd made to visit her parents, she knew it was about a ninety-minute drive from Chester to the Cumbrian county line. She always looked out for the service station and the scoured fell opposite, as they were landmarks of sorts, signs welcoming her back to her ancestral lands, and well beyond the mid-point in her journey. She'd pushed Kyle to meet her within two hours, with the proviso he didn't drive in a manner that'd alert the police. Wasting more time on convincing Pete of her plan than she'd have liked, she had to get a move on if she was going to beat her own schedule. Her car roared through the village, past the green, and took the tight right turn that'd take her back towards the M56. She almost struck a cyclist, but swerved at the last second. Her driving was affected more by the fear of being too late to help Josie and Danni than by the stinging mist the tears caused in her vision.

Josie might not have literally saved Grace's life, because it was doubtful her overbearing husband cared passionately enough about her to do her actual bodily harm, but she'd saved her nonetheless. Josie had come and collected her and her boys, given them a place to stay until they found a rental more suitable to them in the city, and had done so without fear of personal reprisal or inconvenience. It was the way the sisters had behaved all of their lives. Ask Josie and she'd swear that Grace was the tough one who looked out for her, but it wasn't entirely true; Josie sometimes required more motivation to fight, but not when her little sister was in trouble. Back then, anyone who threatened her had her big sister to contend with too. She knew for a fact that Josie would fight tooth and nail if Grace ever needed her, no questions asked. It would be wrong for Grace to do anything less.

JOSIE

Josie and Danni crossed the footbridge, with Steph leading the way. Oblivious to the dilemma of his new-found friends, Franklin was joyful, enjoying stretching his legs after being confined in the car for too long. He sniffed at everything, slowing their progress, but Steph allowed him, so they didn't attract attention from the few people they'd spotted in the railway yard. Josie and Danni came next, and they were hemmed in closely by Toby. He kept his gun out of sight, but he was an ever-present reminder of what could happen if the hostages tried to force past Steph and run for it. Callum, looking unlike the others, stayed back until they had crossed, then followed, walking idly, as if bored and searching somewhere fresh to assuage his inquisitiveness. His knife was out of sight, but Steph's threat to have him cut their throats kept Josie and Danni obedient.

Josie clutched her daughter's hand. Danni's fingers felt slim, fragile, and her skin was cold and paper-thin. Her limbs were spindly, and she walked with a tripping gait. Yet she was proving to be stronger than her physical appearance belied. Her earlier tears had dried, and she no longer displayed any outward fear of their abductors. She even managed to smile and emit a giggle or two when Franklin stretched to the end of his lead so he could stand on his back legs and yap at her. Josie wished she too could forget they were in mortal danger, but she couldn't and shouldn't. She had thought about trying to attract the attention of somebody in the yard, to somehow impart the peril they were in through facial expressions alone, but the opportunity hadn't arisen. Callum had got between her and any potential saviour, and eyed her over the last mouthfuls of his bacon roll; his eyes had twinkled in humour, the creepy bastard enjoying her discomfort as much as he had the food.

The footbridge quaked underfoot. It was highly likely theirs was the largest party to cross it at any one time in months. Josie hoped that the entire thing would collapse and bring the emergency services flocking to the site: of course, the caveat was that she, Danni and Franklin survived without a scratch, while the others got crushed under the steel girders. Within seconds she'd discarded the notion. No miraculous bridge collapse was going to save them. She must look for another escape route, one where there was a slim possibility of survival. Once beyond the opposite platform and small picnic area, the terrain was dominated by a densely forested crag. She thought the landscape shouldn't trouble her or Danni too much – Danni could be agile when necessary, and wasn't always gangly and awkward – but the same could be said of their abductors, too. Steph had first presented as somebody used to finery and an easy life without toil or drudgery, but it had all been an act. She was a hard-hearted criminal, and as hardened – Josie assumed – as either of the men under her command. Once she'd dropped the 'Steph-sham' and reverted to Whizzer, her entire demeanour had changed. Josie wouldn't like to meet a sour-tempered Whizzer in a dark alley. Toby looked fit enough to run most athletes into the ground, let alone a frightened mother and child, while Callum was a serpent able to squirm his way through the undergrowth to find them in whatever nook or cranny in which they tried to hide.

Steph paused on the platform. There was no hint of a train arriving, but who knew? She glanced sharply at Josie, and nodded for her to take Danni into the adjacent picnic area. A couple of mossy tables sat unloved at the end of the green space. The grass had been left to grow unattended for several seasons. Litter dropped by careless visitors had caught at the foot of a wooden fence. Josie took in her surroundings without concentrating on any single facet: she sought an escape route. Other than clambering over the wooden fence and on to the railway tracks, she could see no other way out, except for a beaten path into the woods. Over the past century or more since the railway station was built, people had found reason to go poking around at the foot of the crag. It was unlikely that Danni's birth mother had tried concealing a bag of loot in the picnic grounds where it would easily be uncovered; rather, she might have taken it into the woods nearby.

Steph was apparently of the same opinion.

'You were watching Mel from the car, Danni. Think. After she crossed the bridge, where did she go?'

Danni shrugged expansively.

'Not good enough. Think, Danni. Did she go that direction, into the woods?' Steph aimed a nod at the crag.

To Josie, the bulwark of stone rising out of the ground looked sheer and unscalable. However, there were fissures, and perhaps nooks and hollows where a holdall bag could have been secreted.

'I couldn't see her from the car,' Danni said. Her tone had gone from despairing to defiant. 'It was misty, *remember*?'

Toby approached close enough for Josie to pull Danni into the protection of an embrace. He barely noticed. He peered up at the crag and then allowed his gaze to track west and then east. 'When Mel stopped here, she was probably thinking only of hiding the bag until she could return for it. She was unfamiliar with the place, and didn't have a shovel or anything to dig with. It's likely that she found somewhere she could stuff the bag and then cover it. I doubt she'd have gone a mile before hiding it, so my bet is that she only went a short distance into the woods. See there, a path. She probably followed that in and then moved off the path to hide the bag. We should do the same. Look for anything that she would have used as a landmark to lead her back to its hiding place.'

'I like your way of thinking,' Steph acknowledged.

Without announcing his arrival, Callum had also sidled close behind them. Josie could smell his breath: an unpleasant mixture of frying oil and something sickly sweet, like old-fashioned boiled sweets. She tried making space but had nowhere to move. His breath hot on her neck, he said, 'For all we know, she could'a crawled up the cliff like a bloody spider and stuffed the bag in one of those crevices up there.'

'You want to climb up and check, go ahead, Callum,' said Toby. 'Me? I'm going to try the easiest route first.'

'The kid said she was gone for a long time. She wouldn't have needed hours if she just went off the trail into the woods,' said Callum.

'The passage of time isn't the same for a scared five-year-old as it is an adult,' Toby said. 'A few minutes can feel like ages to them.'

'Yeah, I know that, genius,' said Callum. 'But Mel still could'a gone up the cliff. I could climb it.'

Ignoring his boast, Steph said, 'Mel can't have taken hours to hide the bag, because in *only* a few hours she'd made it back to the motorway, and driven far enough north in time to die in that wreck. I'm in agreement with Toby: she went into the woods. She hid the bag somewhere she would be able to find it again. She probably intended returning in a few days, so we have to consider that the hiding place wasn't that secure from the elements.'

'Could be a bag of rottin' paper by now,' Callum grunted. 'I still expect to be paid, but not with soggy notes that're fallin' to pieces.'

'Truth is it could be long gone,' Steph admitted, 'but we aren't leaving here until we've checked every nook and cranny, or the darkness beats us. But we must search intelligently, and methodically. We begin down here, then only if we must, you can show us your climbing skills.'

'What we gonna do about these two?' Callum asked, placing his palm on Josie's backside.

She jerked away with a yelp, feeling violated by his touch.

Toby stared at him.

'Whassup, Tobe?' Callum sneered.

'Keep your filthy hands off her and the kid, do you hear me?' Toby snapped.

'A quick grope never hurt anyone,' Callum said in complete defiance. He rolled his tongue in his bottom lip.

'I swear to God, if you ever try touching Danni like that, I'll kill you.' Josie meant every word of her threat.

'Chill out, I'm not a fuckin' nonce,' Callum growled.

Steph finally took a side, saying, 'Then stop acting like a pervert, and get moving. I've changed my mind; go and clamber up that rock and see if you get lucky. Toby, you bring these two, and keep an eye out for anything Mel could've used as a landmark.'

'Expecting a big-arsed "X-marks the spot" is out of the question?' Callum quipped, but again nobody was laughing. He turned his back, and walked off muttering under his breath.

The path into the woods hadn't been used for a while. It was not so much beaten as a slick strip of mud winding between tufts of coarse grass and fragments of the same rocks that formed the crag. Josie's trainers could handle the dirt, as could Danni's, but it gave Josie a tiny bit of smug satisfaction to hear Callum's discomfort: his deck shoes let in muddy water that squelched up around his ankles. Neither Steph nor Toby's footwear was appropriate for the terrain, but they didn't complain. They were possibly so close to finding their loot they were overcome with excitement, not that it showed in their demeanour. Toby remained expressionless, while Steph's visage held a similar cold aloofness from which Danni must've first identified her as a vampire. Was her expression due to dread? What would happen to those sent to seek the lost money if they failed to return it to their boss? Josie had heard and determined enough from what they'd said to know that the man in the wheelchair – Freda – was somebody to fear. Could she use Steph's anxiety against her, or would it end her and Danni's usefulness to the criminals? While there was the suggestion that Danni might still be useful to them, then it meant they would stay alive. Josie wasn't naïve, and knew that – whereas they might spare Danni – Josie wouldn't be allowed to live once they had their hands on their dirty money. Sparing Danni's life should be all she would hope for, except they'd possibly take the girl back with them and into the clutches of terrible people that'd make her life a living hell. It was one thing the man Danni named Coal Axe gifting her with sweeties when she was a little girl; another that, approaching puberty, she'd be constantly around sick perverts like Callum Grieves.

Josie clutched Danni's hand tighter.

Her daughter looked up at her. Her eyes were haunted.

'Don't worry. I won't let anything bad happen to you,' Josie whispered.

'Mum,' Danni replied, 'bad stuff is already happening.'

'I won't let them hurt you,' Josie promised.

Danni wormed her fingers, showing discomfort, and Josie relaxed the pressure. Danni responded by tightening her own grasp. She said, 'I'm more afraid they'll hurt you, the same way they hurt Pete.'

'Pete's going to be fine, you don't have to worry about him.'

'What if Pete tries to rescue us, Mum?'

Josie had no reply. She didn't expect him to come riding to their rescue on a white steed. He might call the police, and she hoped that he would, but not if it meant jeopardizing Danni's safety. Callum, she fully believed, would make it his mission to cut them if he caught the slightest sniff of a cop.

'Let's just behave and do nothing to make anyone angry, eh?'

'Good advice,' Toby intoned, barely loud enough for her to hear.

Josie exchanged a glance with him, but the man's face gave nothing away. She was frightened enough of Callum, a self-confessed murderer, perhaps she should be more so of Toby.

The path petered out as they approached a wooded slope. The crag continued within the woods, but not as exposed as at the cliff face that Callum had headed towards. Steph stood, with Franklin sniffing around her feet. Her pale gaze scanned the wooded slope, seeking where Mel could have scrambled upwards several years ago, to hide the bag of money somewhere out of sight but easily enough recovered from on her planned return. Josie had no idea what Steph hoped to see: there were a few barely detectable game trails and also loads of rabbit holes on the slope, but nothing that hinted that a woman hefting a heavy bag had clambered up it years ago. Who knew, perhaps Steph was a seasoned tracker who could read the slightest anomaly in the terrain?

'Anything?' Toby asked, possibly wondering the same thing.

'I thought she might have blazed a tree or something,' Steph replied, 'to show where she went up. There's a mark on that tree over there, but it looks too recent to me. What do you think, Tobe?'

Toby approached the tree indicated by Steph and raised two fingertips to a scar in the bark. He dabbed at the exposed flesh, and tested the resulting stickiness against the pad of his thumb. 'Could've been done months ago,' he surmised, 'but I doubt Mel was responsible. I'd've thought it would've discoloured more than this over three years. Then again, I'm no expert.'

Toby distractedly wiped his sticky fingertips on his trousers while he checked around. 'The branches of that tree there have been broken off, and the damage doesn't look recent.'

It was dumbfounding listening to their warped logic. They were less than half a minute's walk from the pedestrian bridge and adjoining picnic area: Josie would bet that any number of kids and teenagers had ventured into the woods after visiting the railway museum. The broken branches could have been caused by any of them, or even by one of the storms that'd hammered the county during previous winters. She kept her opinion to herself: while their abductors followed unlikely clues, she and Danni had gained some time. Plus, with their attentions fully on finding the loot, they were less attentive about watching their hostages.

When Steph took a couple of steps after Toby, Josie held Danni's hand, gently pushing back on her palm, signalling her to wait. Surreptitiously she checked for Callum; the living scarecrow was nowhere in sight. Could they possibly make a run for it, and make it back to the bridge before Toby caught up? Surely he wouldn't shoot in earshot of witnesses, and try instead to catch them and force them into obedience again.

Josie checked with her daughter. Danni had proven more resilient and mature than anyone would've previously given her credit for. She was mentally stronger than some adults Josie had met, but there was no way she'd force the girl to run if Danni wasn't ready.

Danni surprised her, almost as if she'd read her mother's intention in that fleeting perusal. 'I'm stronger than I look, Mum,' she whispered, and offered a gap-toothed smile. Her smile flickered and then dissolved. 'I can run faster than any of them, but what about you?'

'I'm not over the hill yet, kid,' said Josie, going for light-hearted.

Danni took her literally. 'We shouldn't go that way. We should go back to the tracks.'

'We will. But wait.'

Even as she uttered the warning, she caught a searching look from Toby. He saw that they hadn't moved, and possibly believed they were cowed into total obedience by now. He turned back to inspecting a barely visible trail up the slope.

'What about Franklin, Mum?'

'Franklin will be fine. Steph will look after him. She's a horrible person, but she still cares for her dog.'

'Callum doesn't. He will kill Franklin, quicker than he'd even kill us if he gets his way.'

Josie pulled Danni under her arm, squeezing her gently. 'I won't let Callum hurt you, I swear.'

Danni's noncommittal shrug sent a spear of regret through her heart. Danni didn't believe in her mum to save her, but – to be fair – Josie hadn't done much to sway her. 'Till now,' she whispered, 'I've been playing along with them. I'm waiting for them to think I'm weak, and useless, and their guard lowers. Then we'll show them they picked on the wrong people when they messed with us Lockwood girls.'

'Mum,' Danni whispered conspiratorially, 'I've been playing along with them too.'

GRACE

The sun was a bloated orange disc descending over the fells to the west when Kyle Perlman arrived at the designated service station. As motorway services went, this was not the largest and did not have a corresponding twin serving the southbound carriageway. The slip road accessed almost directly into the car park, so Grace watched the car approach – as she had dozens of others in the past half-hour – with a sense of trepidation. She had placed a lot of faith in a man she'd barely met, and if the rumours were true about his lawlessness was not the most trustworthy of souls. Perhaps she was doing his reputation a disservice: what she actually meant was that his rep was solid, only that he was known for unsavoury behaviour of the violent type. The important point was that his aggressive nature could be put to third-party use, if purchased.

Since Grace had arrived, she'd split her attention between her phone and watching the slip road. She'd checked the news updates, dreading to learn of some terrible fate befalling her sister and niece, and was relieved when there was no hint of them. She tried searching for possible locations to check, but her phone's search engine spat out so many useless links that she'd given up. She'd hoped that Pete would've got back to her by now, so she was ready for action the minute Kyle appeared. But Pete was still yet to call. She had contemplated ringing him, but knew she'd only hinder him in his search: best she didn't distract him.

After crawling it into the car park, Kyle parked his new Nissan Qashqai adjacent to her car. She had lowered her window, and hung out a hand at his approach, flagging him. He powered down his passenger window.

'Did you bring my fee?' he asked.

'Straight to the point.'

'Is there a better way?'

'I suppose not. I'll be straight with you too. I'll pay you when you prove you're not going to take my money and drive off,' she said.

'You contacted me, Grace, not the other way around. If you don't think you can trust me, then let's go our separate ways and no hard feelings. You can reimburse my fuel bill next time you see me picking up my lads.'

'I'll pay you. I'm good for some of your fee upfront, but you might have to wait till we get my sister back before I can give you the rest.'

'My advice: keep your money and phone the cops.'

'My response: I already told you I couldn't. I still can't.'

'The cops are better equipped to handle things. You should call them, tell them about the threat to your family and they'll take things extra cautious, like.'

Grace shook her head. 'Kyle, if it was your kids those bastards had taken, and you were warned not to call the police or they'd be killed, would you call?'

He rocked his head on his shoulders. 'I wouldn't have let anyone take my kids from me, tooled up or otherwise. They'd be dead, or I'd be dead, so there'd be no calling the police by me.'

Jesus, Grace thought, *Pete's right. He does sound like a gangster out of one of those Guy Ritchie movies*, and she couldn't decide if he was deadly serious or just full of bullshit. His stone-hard glare looked sincere enough.

'You want to get in?' he asked.

'Maybe it's best if we travel separately,' she said. 'We might need both cars at some point.'

He shook his head. 'I'm not going into anything blind, Grace. Don't think I'm a mug you can use, then leave to the wolves when the going gets too tough. I've agreed to work for you, but there's only so far I'll go. I'm a dad, with an ex-wife that expects regular maintenance payments: she'll get nothing to help raise my lads if I'm in prison . . . or worse.'

'I have no intention of leaving you to take the heat,' she said.

'Maybe not right now, but who knows how you'll react if the shit hits the fan. If we're doing this, we're doing it together. Now get in or the deal's off.'

She thought about his instruction for no less than a few seconds. She still thought it was best to have the manoeuvrability of two separate vehicles, but she couldn't risk him backing out and leaving her alone. Where was the advantage in that scenario?

'OK, hold on.'

Before she got in his car, he stepped out. He kneaded his lower back, while arching his spine, head thrown back. He exhaled loudly at the heavens. His breath was visible, indicating a drop in temperature. Evening was coming. Grace clutched her phone and her handbag, but brought nothing else from her car. Earlier, when prepping to visit Josie at home, it had never occurred to her to fetch a coat, and who would need a hat and gloves while indoors? She shivered, but wondered how much of the chill was psychosomatic. Kyle was dressed as if he'd come directly from the gym, which indeed he had. He wore a black jacket over a branded MMA T-shirt, and tracksuit bottoms and trainers. He sported a thick gold chain around his equally thick neck, and several conspicuous gold rings on each hand. For all intents and purposes, Grace believed the rings were not only status symbols but also knuckledusters hidden in plain sight.

Kyle's face couldn't be described as handsome. His nose had been broken and reset on more than one occasion, and one ear had been permanently disfigured: Grace could see a chunk had been bitten off, and she'd bet the biter hadn't been a dog. He had several scars on his cheeks and forehead, and even beneath his short-cropped greying hair. If he was the winner of all his battles, as she'd heard, she felt sorry for the losers.

Rather than get directly in his car, she moved around to his side and held out the two hundred pounds she'd withdrawn from an ATM in the service station. He studied the notes with a frown, then snapped his gaze up to hers. 'You promised me a grand, plus a grand's bonus if I made it here inside two hours. What's with the measly two hundred quid?'

'It's all I could draw out of the cash machine in one go . . . what, you think I normally go around with thousands of pounds in my purse?' She returned his stare, challenging him to see her logic. 'Sorry if I didn't leave home expecting to have to hire a mercenary today.'

'I'm not a mercenary.'

'You're ex-forces, though,' she said, demanding confirmation of what she'd heard. 'You told me you were in the SAS or something.'

'I was flirting with you, hoping to impress you by talking bollocks.'

'But you do have military experience, don't you?' she pressed.

'If I admit it I'll have to kill you,' he quipped, but it was the confirmation she was looking for. He was taking great pains to deny his background. Not that she thought he was ashamed of it, no way, but by admitting it he possibly tended to attract the wrong kind of attention. She'd heard that – up until ten years ago – he had been a soldier, one of the most elite.

She held out the notes. 'I'm good for the rest. I promise.'

He took the small bundle of twenties and shoved them in a pocket, and zipped it closed. She took a less than discreet check of his waistband, perhaps expecting to find a pistol tucked into it. He coughed out a laugh at her naivety. Then he nodded sharply at her car. 'You should lock up your motor. We don't know when we'll return to collect it.'

Taking his instruction as meaning they were about to leave, she checked her phone. 'I was waiting for some info coming through before we could leave.'

'What, you don't know where your sister's being held? Why'd you have me meet you here?'

'The kidnappers were overheard talking with my niece about a train museum in Cumbria. This seemed like a good place for a rendezvous.'

'You intend checking all the railway stations in the county? For fuck's sake . . .'

'Not all of them; only those that double as museums. It's OK – Pete, that's my sister's partner, has messaged back. He's pulled a list together for me. There's a miniature railway attraction about a mile away from here, but I don't think that's what we're looking for. The nearest heritage museum is at Haverthwaite and sounds more promising.'

'I know it,' said Kyle, surprising her. 'I took my kids there once. We'd been to the wildlife park near Barrow and called in on the way back. They had a replica of Thomas the Tank Engine on show and my kids were well into it at the time.'

Bemused, Grace shook her head.

'What's up?' Kyle demanded.

'Just trying to reconcile your tough exterior with your softer side.'

'I can be a good dad and still be a hard bastard when the situation needs it.'

'I believe you. The same can be said for me as a mother or, in this case, an aunt.'

They each held the other's gaze for a moment. Then Kyle smiled and jerked his head. 'Get in the car.'

It was high time they got moving, but Grace couldn't help experiencing a slight reservation about getting into a virtual stranger's car. He could very well be as dangerous as some of his detractors whispered, and maybe hid darker crimes than anyone knew of. She held up her mobile. 'Pete knows I'm with you,' she said, but left a clearer warning unspoken. If Kyle was astute enough, he'd understand her message.

'Good,' he said. 'Keep him on speed dial in case we do end up needing back-up.'

DANNI

B eing tall for her age came with pros and cons for Danni. There was the fact that some adults believed her to be older, and therefore that she shouldn't act as childishly as she sometimes did. However, those who got that she was younger than she looked could make the mistake of treating her as naïve. They'd have conversations within earshot of her that they believed she couldn't possibly understand, thinking she was lost in blessed innocence, or ignorance.

She was young enough to see the magic in nature, but understood the difference between fantasy and reality. She still wanted to believe in Santa, even if deep in her heart she knew that it was her mum, Pete and Aunt Grace who bought and wrapped her Christmas presents. She was happy in her own wonderment to love the idea of unicorns and dragons, but she believed in them no more than she'd genuinely believed that Steph was a vampire queen. She understood that the goblins and ogres and witches of this world were only people – Callum and Toby and Steph-Whizzer – but they were all the more dangerous because they could hide in plain sight.

Danni thought it fair that she too could hide without trying too hard.

Toby first, and Callum, and then once she'd revealed her true nature, Steph had all questioned her, pushing and prodding to ignite memories of the day her mum, Mel, was killed. Danni had purposefully buried the awful images of that day. Who wanted to recall the fear and anxiety when they'd first fled from Barker, or the sense of abandonment Danni felt while Mel went to do whatever it was she needed to do in the woods? She certainly didn't want to bring to mind the horrible impact, or the flames that engulfed her mum, and forced her to scramble out of a broken window and stagger, blind and choking, through noxious smoke and into the arms of a stranger. But once one memory surfaced, others had too, like circling sharks emerging from the depths to chew and bite free of the self-imposed fog. Once those memories broke through, Danni had found it necessary to redirect the worst, and to manipulate others into visions she could contend with. Some, she'd even managed to twist to her favour.

She'd played things straight at first. Mel had driven the car here, and made Danni wait inside while she did whatever was necessary. Now, with a more mature outlook on events, Danni thought Mel might have contemplated abandoning her there for the authorities to find, and had gone off alone to think things through. She hadn't taken any bag from the car boot then, and hadn't gone any further than the midway point of the bridge over the railway tracks. Danni hadn't exactly lied; she'd given enough detail to allow Steph to build a picture, a version of what could have happened, and think that Mel must have buried their loot below the crags. She knew that she had placed her and her mum in a scary position, because the criminals could do away with them in those woods. But with that risk came the advantage that she had guaranteed them some extra time, because it was doubtful that they'd be killed before the criminals found their treasure, and they sure as heck weren't going to find it there.

Danni was comforted by her mum's presence, but on the other hand, could have done without her being there. If Danni had been alone, she'd just bet that the bad guys would've forgotten enough about her that they wouldn't keep a regular watch on her: thinking her a scaredy-cat little girl, they'd assume she was afraid of the woods and would stick close, when really she hoped to put more and more distance between them. Till now she'd kept her secret even from her mum as, once Josie knew that she was playing along, then she might act differently than before and give the game away. Mum would make it her duty to control any escape attempt, and that could jeopardize their freedom. Danni was prone to tripping over her own feet in adult company, but she wasn't as gawky as she sometimes pretended. She could run like a cheetah when the situation demanded, and could beat her cousins in a straight foot-race. She thought she could beat any of the three baddies there too, but was doubtful that her mum could keep up. No doubt her mum would try something heroic like sacrificing herself so Danni could escape, but that would be plain stupid.

She gave her mum's hand a gentle squeeze. 'Try not to let my secret show,' she whispered.

Her mum's eyes seemed to protrude from their sockets for a second, her mouth making a tight slash, signalling that she was thinking only worst-case scenarios.

'The treasure isn't here,' Danni continued *sotto voce*. The gap at the front made her lisp, so she switched to aiming her words out the corner of her mouth.

Her mum's eyes grew even larger.

'I told them that so they'd waste time searching,' she whispered. 'When their backs are turned, we must run away, Mum.'

'No,' her mum whispered, squeaky with fear. 'We have to wait for another opportunity. We can't outrun a gun.'

'Course we can. We just need to get the trees between us and Toby, and he can't hit us then.'

Her mum looked up the slope. Steph was scuffing aside fallen twigs that'd been brought down during the winter storms. Checking in the depths beneath a fallen tree bole, Toby momentarily had his back to them, arched over as he rooted among dirt and spidery roots. As if aware of her perusal, Toby straightened up, and turned to eye them over one shoulder. He could be emotionless, but right then Danni recognized pure, unadulterated hatred in his gaze. She was unsure if his ire was directed at them, or at the fool's errand he was engaged in. He turned away, continuing to search. He touched marks on another tree trunk, but discarded the idea they pointed to the loot. He gestured to Steph and she moved closer to him. Franklin strained at the end of his lead, interested in a woodland smell rather than finding a bagful of money. Steph yanked him unceremoniously after her.

'See,' Danni said, 'Steph doesn't care for Franklin at all.'

However, she knew that her mum was right. Steph did care for her dog; she was only acting a little rough with him, the way a harassed parent sometimes resorted to physical control of their kids. As it happened, Danni was prepared to get rough with her mum and drag her too if it would help speed her along.

They'd come a fair way into the woods, but not in a straight line. The crags had blocked them and made them turn parallel to the railway track. It was probably less than a hundred metres through the trees to the railway museum. If they went in that direction, Danni felt that they could give Toby the slip and get help from the staff at the railway station. She tugged on her mum's hand, and when she had her attention, she discreetly nodded at the downslope to their left. 'We can reach the tracks that way,' she said, barely above the volume of a breath.

'We could slip and fall,' her mum said, equally quietly, 'and that would be it. No, we have to use the same path we came in on.'

'It's a lot further that way. Can you run that far, Mum?'

'I told you already; I'm not over the hill. I can easily make it that far. It's running fast enough that worries me.'

Danni added gentle pressure to the hold on her mum's hand. 'I'll help you.'

Her mum strained out a smile, but her eyes were shiny, pinched by the sting of tears.

Danni said, 'It'll be OK. I promise.'

Her mum returned the squeeze of her hand, but said, 'Wait.'

They needn't wait. The time for escaping was while Steph and Toby were fully engaged in the hunt. For the moment their attention was wholly on the search and not watching their hostages. But her mum had a point: where was Callum? They'd best check that he was still halfway up the crag and not close enough to cut them off.

'I don't see him,' she whispered.

'He can't be far away,' her mother warned.

'He's in the wrong direction if we go the way I said.' Again Danni gestured down the slope to their left, but her mum was resistant to the idea. Danni wished that her mother would trust her plan, but she was the adult and therefore the one expected to make all the important decisions.

'Get behind me,' her mother said, with a pull on Danni's hand.

Danni understood what was happening. This was the set-up for the sacrifice. Her mother would deliberately get between Danni and a bullet, and would probably deliberately retreat slowly to ensure she acted as a shield. Danni didn't want her to get shot, especially when there was no need. She pulled out of her mum's grasp and immediately danced to the left, digging in with her heels so that she could crab safely down the slope. Her mother made a futile grab for her, but already Danni was out of reach. She urged her mum to follow with a roll of her eyes, and took another sidestep. Her mum darted looks around, checking they were unobserved. She followed Danni.

The slope was gentle enough, but was uncultivated. The turf was filled with ridges and hollows, and hidden tree roots and fallen branches added to the trip hazards. The latter also made stealth difficult. Twigs crackled underfoot, soft enough that the sound shouldn't carry too far, but it was to ears that were on the alert to possible danger. Probably the sounds were too low for either Steph or Toby to take note of, but not the alert little canine. Franklin spun and trained his gaze on them as they traversed the slope at an angle. He grinned, button eyes lighting up. He yipped. Danni was torn about leaving him behind, and to her his high-pitched bark sounded like the loneliest sound on the planet. Franklin barked again, a trio of yips. This time the sounds were of betrayal, and she wished he'd just shut up.

'Hey!' Steph said.

'Where the bloody hell do you think you're going?' Toby was already on the move, each word punctuated by a step. He covered more ground than Danni and her mother had in less than a second and a half.

'Run!' her mum urged.

Danni didn't need telling twice, but again she feared that her mother would place her body in the way of a gunshot. Danni grabbed her clothing and clung on, pulling her mother along with her. They went across a dip in the earth and up a shallow embankment, and then on to a steeper down-slope. With momentum, and fear, pushing them downward, they kicked through twigs and wild grass, panting and gasping at the sudden effort. Toby raced after them.

He could cut them off before they reached the tracks.

'This way,' said Danni, and yanked at her mum's clothes. They cut away from Toby, heading down the slope still, but putting distance and a thicker stand of trees between them; he'd soon make up the difference by cutting across the slope at the same angle. Once they had the trees as a shield, Danni urged her mum to run in a direct line along the embankment. If she was right, then they'd meet the path they had followed in no time.

She glanced up the slope. A pale blur caught her eye. At first she thought it was the white of Franklin's fur as he joined in the race. But that wasn't it. Steph's hat had come off, disclosing her white hair, and it framed her equally stark face. She reminded Danni now of a living statue, her features were set so hard. Steph suddenly terrified her more than even Creepy Callum did.

'Down, down, down,' she bleated, and cut in front to direct her mum down the slope at a sharp angle. Her mother tripped. She tumbled, barrel-rolling almost until checked by a hummock of coarse grass. Danni hauled on her, trying to help her rise. She struggled up, but with an arm clutched tightly across her midriff: the fall had winded her.

'Go on,' her mother croaked, and pushed Danni.

Danni shook her head. 'I'm not leaving you.'

'You must. Run, Danni. Get help.'

'No, they'll hurt you. I'm not leaving you, Mum. Come on, we can still escape.'

Danni snagged her fingers in her mum's waistband. She tugged and, with each step, her mother moved with a little more ease. She began unfurling, but the redness in her cheeks extended into her eyes, showing she was in pain. She limped badly on her right leg, where a dark splotch marked where something hard had dug into her thigh. Danni couldn't tell if her mum's jeans were bloody or if it was just mud.

Toby appeared to their right. Several trees still separated them, but he was agile and moving surefootedly where Danni and her mum both lumbered. Thankfully he had not drawn his gun, but he wouldn't need it in a few more seconds. Once he had a hold of Danni, her mother would give up to try protecting her instead. Danni grabbed a branch off the floor and brandished it.

'Get away from us!' she screeched.

Her weapon didn't faze Toby. More likely, he held no fear of skinny, gangly girls.

He lurched in, hands outstretched, and Danni took a swipe at him. She missed completely, and the swinging branch almost twisted her into a knot. Her mother, injured as she was, was at her most primal. She snarled, and she battered at Toby's head with both hands. She hit him in a flurry, and then her fists unfurled into claws, and she raked at his eyes and lips with her nails. Danni struck at his legs with her stick, only for it to break into rotted splinters. Toby grabbed her by her throat, and held her at arm's length. Her mum screeched in fury, and again tried to tear his face off. He struck her, his other palm ramming up under her jaw. Danni heard the clack of her mum's teeth, and the audible groan as she sat down hard on her backside, feet splayed apart. Toby pushed in, forcing her mother on to her back with his foot on her abdomen. He trod down, forcing out the little air left in her mum's lungs. Danni twisted and squealed and hollered, battering futilely at him with the disintegrating stick. He gave her throat a simple pinch, and red-tinged darkness overwhelmed Danni's vision.

JOSIE

J osie blinked the crimson fog from her vision. Her jaw ached, but there was a sharper pain at the base of her neck. By the feel of things, Toby's palm-strike had come close to dislocating her skull from her spine. She didn't care about her discomfort. All she cared for was Danni. Her child was standing, but looked out of it. She'd fainted, but the swoon had lasted only a moment and she'd regain her full senses in no time. Josie wanted to hold her, to comfort her, but Toby had one hand on her collar, while he dabbed at the raw scratches on his face with his other fingers.

Twigs crackled behind Josie, followed by the thud of feet coming to a distinctive halt. She didn't look, because she knew who it was. She could smell his sickly sweet breath.

'I leave you alone for a few minutes . . .' Callum mocked his friends.

'Shut up,' Toby growled. 'I'm not in the mood for any of your crap.'

'Typical, though, innit?' Callum went on. 'Trust me to miss all the fun.'

'Callum, make yourself useful,' Steph ordered as she adjusted her retrieved hat over her pale hair. 'Take hold of Josie, and make sure she doesn't move.'

'By the look of what she did to Toby's mush, that's good advice.'

Callum strode in and, without any preamble, he grabbed Josie under an armpit and dragged her up. He was stronger than his emaciated frame might suggest. He dug in with his fingernails, ensuring she felt their nip even through her clothing. 'Try scratching me like that and I'll rip you a new arsehole.'

His threat sounded as disgusting as ever, but Josie believed it.

She gave no cause for him to hold her tighter, but his sadism required satisfaction. He continued digging in with his fingernails, causing her to squirm, her knees turning to liquid.

'Stand up,' he sneered, then forced her to wilt with another painful squeeze of her armpit. Finally, he lessened the pressure, and Josie stood. She checked if Danni had recovered. Her daughter appeared

starry-eyed, still a little confused by Toby's painless form of stran-
gulation. Franklin pulled at the end of his lead, snuffling inches
from Danni's trainers, but she was oblivious to the dog.

'Danni . . .' Josie called.

'Shut it, slag,' Callum growled, at the same time that Steph held
up a warning finger.

'You risked your daughter's life trying to run away from us and
you can see where that got you,' Steph said. 'Don't think that
screaming for help will do any good either.'

'Wh-what are you going to do with us?' Josie croaked.

'Obey me, and don't try anything stupid, and you'll both be
released once we've found what we're looking for.'

'You're lying,' Josie said, and she could no longer hold back the
tears stinging her eyes. They rolled down her cheeks, hot, viscous
drops. She dashed them with her free wrist.

'Lying how?'

'You have no intention of freeing us. I don't care what happens
to me. But, please, Danni's only a little girl. You must let her go.'

Callum's hot breath scalded her neck. 'You don't get it, do ya?
Her mother, Mel, was Freda's property. By default, that makes Danni
his property too. The bag of money Mel stole isn't all Freda wants
back.'

'Callum, that's enough!' snapped Steph.

'Just telling the slag her future, Whizzer.' He spoke out the side
of his mouth, so that his next words were specifically aimed at
Josie. 'See, you're probably a bit too old to be of much use to
Freda, but Danni's another story altogether.'

Josie thrummed like a plucked bowstring.

'You'd really love to scratch my eyes out, wouldn't ya?' Callum
laughed.

'You've said enough,' Toby stated. 'Now keep your bloody mouth
shut, and do as Whizzer said.'

Josie was under no illusion. Toby, again, wasn't coming to her
rescue, only reminding Callum that he was a hired hand, and his
services could be dispensed with if he wasn't careful.

Steph said, 'I take it that searching the crag was a bust?'

Callum only looked at her. Then he turned to Toby. 'So am I to
keep my mouth shut or answer?'

'Don't be arsey,' said Toby.

'Does it look as if I found where Mel stashed the loot?'

'We had no luck either.' Steph looked up through the treetops, seeking the sun. 'The light isn't going to last much longer, and I've a feeling there's more ground to cover than we have daylight. Fact is, I think we're going to need a few more eyes and hands to help us search.'

'Whaddaya mean?' Callum demanded. 'If you're gonna bring in others, it'd better not mean my cut gets less.'

'You'll be paid what you're owed,' Toby told him.

'Yeah, so you've promised before. Same as you said you'd cover my expenses. You seen the state of my feet? I'm adding the cost of a new pair of shoes to my bill.'

Toby ignored Callum. He peered directly into Josie's face. 'We are going to return to the car. Play up, I'll have Callum hurt you.' He touched the fresh gouges marring his Hollywood good looks. 'Don't think I won't.'

Steph pulled Franklin in close at her side, folding the lead into a shorter loop to fully control the dog. She nodded at Toby, and he nodded back. The agreement was clear: she'd lead the way, while each of her male companions physically controlled their hostages. Josie felt Callum's arm slip around her ribs. She gave no cause for his squeeze to tighten as they fell in at the rear.

Danni plodded, her soles slapping the ground with each step. Her shoulders swayed and her arms were bent sharply at the elbows: Josie thought her daughter hadn't fully regained her senses yet. Toby's grip on her was more a guiding hand than restraint.

Within minutes Josie spotted the bridge over the railway track. Steph paused. A couple of teenaged boys were on the bridge, but they took no notice of the small group emerging from the woods. Within seconds they moved away, returning to the railway platform on the far side. Steph dragged Franklin forward and the others followed. Before climbing the bridge, they all bunched together at the foot of the stairs.

'Where are you taking us, Steph?' asked Josie.

'It's not as if we can take you to a hotel room or anything,' Steph said, airing her thoughts aloud, more for the benefit of her companions. 'But that's OK. I know a place. I'll make arrangements for the others to meet us there.'

Josie opened her mouth to speak, but Callum nudged her forward. She trod up the steps, again giving no resistance. Toby came next with Danni, and this time Steph brought up the rear. She allowed the group of four to move toward their cars before she also alighted from the bridge, and angled across the grounds towards Toby's Range Rover. Josie could hear her speaking into her phone, but it was unclear what she said; Josie was just thankful to have made it back to the car alive. While she had a breath in her, she could hold on to hope that she could free Danni. Their next escape attempt had to be planned better than the last, and have a chance of success that Danni's had lacked. Actually, that was unfair. If it had been solely down to Danni, then her daughter would probably have evaded her pursuers and made it back to the railway tracks. But what then, if she had? Involving witnesses at the railway museum might have caused Toby or Callum to grow more violent, and who knew then who might have died?

Josie slid on to the back seat of the Range Rover. She pulled Danni into a hug and placed her lips alongside her daughter's ear. 'We're OK for now,' she whispered, 'and will get another chance to escape.'

'Yeah,' Danni breathed. It was the only confirmation Josie required: being strangled unconscious had failed to dim Danni's spirit.

GRACE

'Is something the matter?' asked Kyle, without taking his eyes off the road.

Caught without a ready answer, Grace didn't make a discernible reply. She grunted, shifted awkwardly in the passenger seat.

'It's just you keep on staring at me as if I'm some sort of alien with two heads.' Kyle flicked a hand at his nostrils. 'Or do I have a bogey hanging out of my nose or something?'

'I'm wondering if I have any right asking you to risk your life when you also have kids at home.'

'You're paying for my services,' he reminded her. 'I'm not going to lie, Grace. I don't want anything bad happening to any kid, but I wouldn't've come for free.'

'I don't think that's the entire truth.'

'This better not be you trying to wangle your way out of paying me the rest of my fee. By playing on my soft side.'

He had taken his eyes off the traffic ahead for all of about two seconds, ensuring she caught the smile that ghosted across his lips. Reassuring her he was joking was unnecessary, as was her counter-reassurance. 'When this is over, the money will be there for you, I promise.'

Besides that, the last thing she wanted was for Kyle's soft side to dominate his decisions. She had reached out to him because she required somebody tough as nails and unafraid of the consequences of going up against a bunch of desperate criminals. She'd been sneaking him glances, wondering if indeed he was the man for the job. Being a father, his responsibility was to protect his own children, rather than Danni, and she feared that when the worst finally happened, if he'd decide his skills would be better used elsewhere, and abandon the rescue attempt.

Or was she simply superimposing her own fears over Kyle? She too had children, and they should always be her priority, and of course they were. However, Josie was her sister, and Danni her niece – whether related by blood or not – and she loved them to their bones. Grace would fight to the death for them.

'Did you bring those weapons you mentioned?' she asked.

'Locked in the boot.'

'Guns?'

He glanced again at her with a frown. 'Hopefully we won't need them, but you know the old saying about not bringing a knife to a gunfight . . .'

'One of them uses a knife. He sliced the tip of Pete's tongue, to warn him from talking.'

'Yeah, so you said. He sounds like a right piece of work.'

'A piece of shit,' she corrected.

'The other has a gun?'

'Yes. Pete said he was armed with a pistol. He was unsure about the woman. She seemed to be in charge, so she probably leaves the rough stuff to her thugs.'

'We should hope for the best but plan for the worst. I've met some vicious women in the past, and some of them wouldn't think twice about sticking you with a knife.' He thought a moment, then said, 'You should call Pete, see if he has remembered anything else useful about them.'

'Yeah, good idea.'

Before she reached for her phone, she checked their location. Their conversation had taken them along several miles of dual carriageway and up a steep hill and around a roundabout. There were directional signs for Lindale and Grange-over-Sands, and another sign warning of an upcoming end to the dual carriageway ahead. It was several years since Grace had been along that unfamiliar section of the A590. 'How far to Haverthwaite?' she wondered.

'About ten minutes, maybe less.'

'Is that all?' Grace left her phone tucked in her pocket. Adrenalin shivered through her body. Her tongue darted over instantly dry lips.

'Having second thoughts?' Kyle asked.

'Second, third, fourth . . . pick a number,' she admitted.

'You're bound to be nervous. I'd guess that it isn't every day you get involved in a hostage rescue situation.'

'Only once before, and on that occasion me and my boys were the ones being saved.'

'Oh, aye?'

'It wasn't as dramatic as this. In fact, my big sis just came and collected us when my arsehole of an ex was out. There weren't any guns or knives involved then.'

'Is your ex out of the picture now?'

She didn't answer immediately. There was a hot sensation at the back of her neck. Finally she said, 'Why do you ask?'

'I'm divorced. But my ex-missus is still in my life. She's the mother of my kids, so I suppose it's inevitable. But she's OK, and we've stayed friends for the sake of our little ones.'

'And you guessed that the same can't be said of my ex-husband and me? Well, you're partly right. I have as little to do with him as possible, but he still tries to find ways of controlling me.'

'Was that why you escaped him, he was too controlling?'

'He was manipulative and selfish. It hadn't gone as far as violence, but there was the potential for it. Like I said, my rescue wasn't as dramatic as what we're about to attempt, but I still needed to get away from him.'

'He sounds like a bit of a dick. Blokes like that tend to be cowards, as well as bullies. After we're done here, d'you want me to have a word in his ear and get him to back off?'

She looked across at him, again feeling heat at the base of her skull. Any second and she expected the flush to spread to her cheeks.

'You know my daily charge,' he added, 'it'll be a grand well spent when I put the fear of God into him.'

'Jeez, altruism isn't dead,' she sighed.

'Never claimed to be an altruist, no more than I claimed to be a mercenary. I'm just a bloke trying to make a living.'

The dual carriageway was coming to an end. It had only been a short stretch, more of a passing place for car drivers to get ahead of slower trucks and agricultural vehicles that used the road. Kyle hadn't taken the advantage of speeding past slower-moving traffic, having remained at a steady sixty miles per hour since the round-about. It was lucky he hadn't sped on, so that when they were adjacent to another vehicle on the opposite carriageway, Grace caught a fleeting look at a girl's face before she ducked down below the window. A strip of grass no more than three metres wide separated the opposing carriageways. Each lane was about three metres wide too. That placed the passing car close enough for Grace to make out detail, even though most of it was absorbed unconsciously. She saw the blonde braided hair, wide pale eyes and gap-toothed mouth of her niece, Danni.

Doubt assailed her though.

What if the girl was a complete stranger, and Grace had

superimposed Danni's features over her, the way she'd earlier super-imposed her fear of failure over Kyle? She'd got no more than a one- to two-seconds look at the girl before she bobbed down once more. Had Grace also spotted the hand of an adult reach up to cup the girl's head, and urge her down, or was this a fantasy of her own making?

She must have squawked or made some other form of outcry, because Kyle's head had snapped around, and his mouth hung open in question. 'There, back there in that grey Range Rover,' she cried, 'I swear to God I just saw our Danni.'

'What?' His response was less than erudite but, to be fair, he had little to go on. He searched his mirrors, looking for the Range Rover. Grace twisted in her seat, trying to keep the car in sight, hoping that she might again spot Danni, or even Josie, showing their face above the seats. Already the two vehicles had put too much space between them for her to be sure, but she thought there had been at least a couple of figures in the front.

'It was her,' Grace said, her voice strident. It was as important that she convinced herself, as it was convincing Kyle. 'I'd bet my life on it.'

Without another word, Kyle decelerated sharply. They'd already left the dual carriageway, and only a pink strip of painted tarmac and white chevrons separated them from oncoming traffic. The chevrons ended in no distance. Kyle's sharp braking almost caused a pile-up. He bumped his car up on to the grass verge, and then spun it partly in the opening to a farm track. Directly opposite them, there was a footpath, and a hardstand area marked POLICE ONLY. Drivers leaned on their horns as they picked up speed again. One driver passed, mouthing curses and jabbing at the side of his head, indicating that Kyle was insane. Kyle gave no response: after all, his manoeuvre had been a reckless one. It was nowhere near as dangerous as the stunt he pulled next. He hit the throttle and swerved out of the farm track, and directly across the road. Grace, in the passenger seat, cringed in dread at the delivery van speeding towards them. The driver must have stood on the brake with both feet, because the van juddered to a halt, its back end almost jumping skyward for a second. Kyle didn't hang around; he spun his car in the POLICE ONLY stand, and then accelerated with two wheels on the footpath until he could bump back down on to the carriageway. More horns blared and Grace was certain she could smell overheated tyres. Kyle sped in pursuit of the now obscured Range Rover. Grace looked back, and saw the van had avoided an accident, and was slowly picking up speed again. She hoped the driver wasn't furious enough at Kyle's driving to make a complaint to the police.

Kyle had other ideas about police involvement. 'Get on the blower and tell the police we're following them.'

'Not yet,' said Grace.

'What? Why not? We can have them pulled over and—'

'What if they use Josie and Danni as human shields? After what they did to Pete, I think the last thing they'll do is give up without a fight.'

'We don't know that for certain,' said Kyle, but his words helped convince him that Grace was possibly right. 'We don't know how they'll react if the coppers come in heavy-handed, but if we can set up a trap, have them stopped before they can harm their hostages—'

'I can't imagine any scenario where my sister and niece get out unharmed.'

'I don't think they'll harm them once armed coppers are surrounding them. Unless they have death wishes, they'll give up.'

'I asked you once before and know what you replied, but this scenario's different: if it were your kids in that car, would you risk it? I'd rather we follow, wait for a better chance at freeing them.'

Kyle didn't slow down; he kept his face forward and his eyes were like flint shards. 'You're the boss,' he said. 'Actually, that's not right. You're only the one paying me. If at some point you start making the wrong decisions, I'll bloody well tell you.'

'For now that means I'm still right then?' It sounded sarcastic, and she fully meant it to, but she elicited a grunt of mirth from him. His flat eyes sparkled anew.

'Where are they going?' she wondered. 'I thought they'd have been at the railway museum longer than this.'

'Maybe they found what they were looking for already.'

'I had this horrible feeling they'd do away with Josie and Danni the second they had their hands on their loot.'

He glanced across, and bit down on his lip. 'Maybe they did. Are you absolutely certain you saw the right girl?'

'It was definitely Danni. Someone pulled her back down in the seat, and I hope to God that it was Josie. The bad guys must've found what they were looking for and have decided to keep Josie and Danni as security till they're safely away.'

'That's pure speculation,' he warned her.

'I know, but it's also why I'm afraid to call the police yet. They'll be on a high, and probably determined not to get caught.'

Kyle had driven well over the speed limit on the return leg. Already Grace spotted signs warning of the roundabout ahead. The grey Range Rover was nowhere in sight. There were only two directions it could have gone. Either the kidnappers had continued on the main road, back towards the motorway, or they'd circled around and taken the road towards Grange-over-Sands. There was no reason to assume they'd headed anywhere but along the main road. Kyle took the turn off without consulting with her. He floored the throttle, picking up the speed they'd lost in negotiating the turn. In less than a minute they were forced to decelerate and tag on the back of the queue of traffic in the passing lane, all of them trying to overtake a convoy of slower-moving HGVs. Several cars and a pick-up truck was all that separated them and the Range Rover.

'We should keep back a few cars so they don't spot the tail,' said Kyle.

Grace concurred with a nod. Until they knew where the kidnappers were taking their hostages, they couldn't do a thing other than follow, and – crucially – to follow without being spotted. As long as they kept a few vehicles between them, the driver of the Range Rover shouldn't grow aware of them. She wondered if he was as savvy as to expect a tail, and therefore to check for it. He was a criminal not a spy: she'd bet that he was on the lookout for marked police cars, but would miss Kyle's Nissan Qashqai if they stayed back far enough.

It was a pity that Grace hadn't shown similar street smarts. Both she and Kyle were unaware of the black Audi A4 that'd stuck closely to them since Kyle's dangerous driving stunt.

CALLUM

Sometimes Callum Grieves felt that those he worked alongside underappreciated him. If he cared what people thought about him personally, then he might get upset but, frankly, Callum didn't give a fuck what anyone thought. They could hate the ground he walked on; however, he was mildly pissed off that Whizzer and Tobe both looked down on his skills and experiences, mostly overruling any ideas he had. He thought that dragging the gap-toothed kid and her bitchy mother with them was a complete and utter waste of time and energy, their presence more inclined to attract the wrong kind of attention. If it had been left to him, Callum would have left their hostages locked in the pantry with the cowardly stepdad, all three of them with their throats opened so there'd be no chance of them talking. Case in point, back there at the woods, there'd been no need for the kid or her mother to be present; it only hampered the search, and everything almost came to a screeching end when 'God's Gift Tobe' took his eye off the ball and allowed them to almost escape. Danni had already told them enough to identify the railway museum as a possible location for the hidden cash – and they shouldn't forget that it was he, Callum Grieves, who'd pinpointed the location from the girl's description – so taking her there served no other purpose than he felt Stephanie Wyszogrodzki was reluctant to make the most severe decisions.

Steph worked directly with Leonard Freda, and Toby worked with her. Callum worked *for* them. It was the difference that made them undervalue him. If he were a member of their inner circle, he'd bet they'd show him more respect, and pay attention when he spoke.

Just look at them, oblivious to the danger they'd got into by failing to listen to his advice. They'd picked up a tail, and they remained blissfully unaware. Good job then that he was there, the undervalued one, to watch their scrawny arses.

Minutes ago, back where the road met the dual carriageway, he had almost rear-ended a van when the driver had slammed on the brakes. Callum had been too engaged in avoiding smashing into the van to give much notice to the other car that had straddled the road in a mad attempt at a U-turn on to the dual carriageway. By the time the van driver had regained his composure and got the lumbering vehicle moving again, several cars had zoomed past and pulled between Callum and the rapidly diminishing SUV. He had rolled his tongue in his bottom lip, and floored the Audi's accelerator, and swept around the slowly moving van. He gave the van no further consideration as he worked up the gears and was moving at almost ninety miles per hour in less than ten seconds. He soon slipped the car into a gap between slower-moving traffic, and decelerated to match them. The Nissan Qashqai was four positions ahead when they reached the roundabout. Callum followed, and watched the Nissan zoom off, trying to close a gap. Without knowing for certain who its driver was trying to catch up to, he had a very strong inkling. It was no coincidence that the driver had performed a reckless manoeuvre, risking involvement in a pile-up, seconds after passing Toby and Steph on the opposite carriageway. Sure, it could be a random driver who'd suddenly realized they were going the wrong direction and was trying to make up time and distance, but Callum didn't buy the explanation. He didn't believe in coincidences, no more than he did in the divine intervention that'd supposedly whisked Danni out of the midst of the flames and toxic smoke and placed her in the arms of her saviour, Bobby Charters. If some god or other had saved the kid, then it was a fickle bastard, because it subsequently neglected to save the lard-arsed truck driver from Callum.

The Nissan decelerated once Toby's Range Rover was in view. It added credence to Callum's notion that those in the SUV were tailing his employers, and it could be for only one reason. He doubted they were coppers, but they were there on some mission or other, probably a rescue attempt. Earlier, it had amused him to convince Josie that Leonard Freda wanted the girl back as much as he did his money, but it was simply a tale he'd come up with to terrorize the woman. Steph and Toby had shut him down sharply, and again, he didn't believe in coincidence. Maybe Freda did want the kid back, the reason why Steph had them brought along; maybe somebody else was also after the kid. It had become known by several interested parties that Freda was missing a huge wedge of cash and that the amnesic girl could possibly lead them to it. Had one of those other parties got wind that Callum had identified where the loot could be hidden and dispatched searchers? Were they rival criminals now tailing Steph and Toby with the idea of snatching the girl from them, or more likely stealing the loot if it had been recovered?

He used the hands-free system in his Audi to contact Toby. 'Wotcha, Tobe,' he said the instant his call was answered.

'What is it, *Cal*?'

'You owe me, mate.'

'How's that then?'

'Take a look in your mirror and tell me what you see.'

'What exactly am I looking for?'

'If you were as good as you make out, you'd have spotted the tail yersel', mate.'

'You're talking about the SUV?' Toby asked for clarity. 'Yeah, I've been keeping an eye on it for a few minutes now.'

'Yeah,' Callum sneered, 'of course you have.'

Steph butted in. 'We have been aware of it, but have been trying to determine if it's a threat or not.'

'If it had you worried, why not let me know?' Callum countered.

'Because we haven't made up our minds about the threat level yet,' Toby said, enunciating each word slowly and clearly.

'They haven't made any move to close distance on us,' said Steph. 'At first we worried that it was an unmarked police car, but that doesn't appear to be the case.'

'Earlier, did you let Freda know where we were going?' Callum asked.

'You think he sent others without informing me?' Steph replied.

'Wouldn't he?'

Steph didn't immediately answer, meaning Callum's suggestion that she wasn't entirely trusted by Freda to complete the job must have been in her thoughts. Finally she said, 'I'm heading this op; it'd be disingenuous of him to send other hunters without alerting me. Besides, I've only recently spoken with him and asked for more hands to meet us. If he'd already sent someone—'

'He'd have owned up, would he?'

'I believe he would've, yes. I'm confident that whoever's in the Nissan they have nothing to do with Freda. In fact, I'm not even convinced we are the ones they're following.'

'We should find out,' Callum suggested. 'Make a move, see if they follow.'

'Yeah,' Toby cut in, 'we were planning on doing that.'

'Course you were, Tobe. Course you were.'

'There's another roundabout coming up. I'll take it, but go all the way around, and see how the driver in the Nissan reacts. You can get close enough to watch what he does, yeah?'

'It's too unnatural a move, Tobe. If you try that kind of bollocks, he's gonna realize you're on to him. We want him oblivious, so we can lead him into a trap.'

'So what do you suggest, genius?'

'Take the first turn, it goes towards Kendal. If he follows, it's good. Not far after, you'll come to another spot, where you can turn and head back in this direction again. There's a petrol station you can pull into. That way he'll believe that you took a short detour to get petrol, rather than an obvious ploy. If he follows you, it's gonna become kind of obvious, eh?'

'Unless he's also short on fuel,' Toby said, without conviction. Yeah, he knew as well as Callum that coincidences didn't happen.

'I'll follow but sit back from him, watch how he reacts to your turn, and see how he wants to play after.'

'Yes,' Steph said, 'do that, Callum. But don't engage with them. Not yet.'

'Wasn't planning on it. I want somewhere less public than a dual carriageway to run the fuckers off the road.'

JOSIE

For what felt like the hundredth time, Josie drew Danni down so that her head remained below the edge of the window. And for what felt like the hundredth time, Danni resisted and within seconds tried taking another sneaky peek outside.

Josie was desperate to take a look too, to see who it was that Steph and Toby had grown concerned about, especially after Creepy Callum had called them and confirmed that they were being followed. Actually, there was still some debate about whether they were under surveillance, and the thugs were planning to trick their pursuer into confirming it. The general consensus was that whoever was in the Nissan Qashqai, they weren't police. Josie was thankful, because who knew how her captors might react if they thought they were about to be arrested? Josie, for definite, would be cannon fodder, while Danni would prove extremely valuable as a human shield. Not for the first time, Josie had considered begging Steph to release them unharmed, with a solemn promise they wouldn't tell a soul what had happened. It was time wasted on such thoughts because it might never happen, not least until after Leonard Freda's stolen cash had been recovered. The best-case scenario would be to go along with instructions, not offer any problems or rebellion, and the attention of their captors might slip again: Josie wouldn't try an escape through a muddy woodland again, though; she hoped for a better opportunity to arise that would allow her to get Danni safely out of the way of an armed stand-off with the police.

'Danni, what are you doing?' Her whisper was low enough not to carry to those in the front seats.

'Trying to see.'

'See what?'

'Just this place,' she said, enigmatically.

Josie cupped a palm over Danni's head and gently pulled her down out of sight.

'There's nothing to see,' she said.

Danni shook her head. She craned so that she could meet her mum's gaze, to convey something important, and it was instantly apparent: she was watching for the location where she'd now remembered that Mel had hidden the cash. In hindsight it must have been left somewhere between the railway museum and the motorway north, because once on the M6, there'd have been no safe opportunity to stop and conceal the holdall.

'There was a baldy hill,' said Danni, her words no louder than a tickle in her ear.

'Like a bald head—' Josie pointed at the side of her own head, and Danni's mouth opened in agreement. The tip of her tongue protruded through the gap in her teeth.

Josie couldn't imagine what the girl referred to, or what she might have conjured in her memory from something as mundane as the odd architecture of a motorway service station that had become a flying saucer. She darted gazes around, but she was seated too low in the seat to see anything except the trees at roadside and clouds licked by the sunset. It would soon be fully dark.

The thought that the world would soon be veiled in darkness sent a quiver through Josie. The sun was setting on one of the worst days of her life. Would she or her child live to see the sun rise again, to feel its warmth on their faces?

Another thought balanced her dismay.

Could the darkness become their ally?

Given the opportunity to run, it would be best if the night helped conceal them. The problem back there in the woods was that they were constantly in view of one or other of the bad guys, but that might not be a problem once it was fully dark.

Danni bobbed up again.

'Keep her out of sight,' Steph warned, 'and stop her from yattering.'

It hadn't occurred that Steph's attention had been drawn, but thankfully she hadn't made any sense out of what she might have overheard. She obviously hadn't gathered that Danni was on the lookout for the true location of the hidden treasure she sought.

'She needs to pee,' Josie said, the lie coming easily enough to her lips – she too needed to urinate.

'You both should have gone back there in the woods,' said Steph.

'Yeah,' Josie agreed drily. 'The opportunities were endless.'

'You should've thought about relieving yourselves instead of your pathetic escape attempt.'

Josie ignored the woman. Instead she drew Danni around, and

helped her bend her knees high enough to check her trainers. One lace had come partially undone. Josie tied the lace in a double knot, then again for good measure.

'No, no, no,' said Steph. The woman reached through the gap between the car seats towards Danni's feet. Having taken off her gloves, her slim fingers were translucent in the dimness; she wore several silver and gold rings. Josie was tempted to clench the slim fingers in her fist and bend them until they broke. Instead, she only pushed against Steph's hand, guiding her away from her daughter.

'Don't touch her,' Josie warned.

'Take off her shoes.'

'Why?'

'I said take off her shoes.'

'Where's the sense in *that*?' Josie demanded. But she knew exactly what Steph meant: if Danni were barefooted, there'd be less chance of her running if she tried again to escape.

'Do as you're bloody well told!' Toby exploded. He even reached back, as if he would yank off Danni's trainers if he could get his fingers on them.

Josie drew Danni away, and they both shuffled on their backsides to one side. 'OK, OK, I hear you. I'll take them off.'

'Take off your shoes too,' Steph ordered.

Josie held up a soothing palm. 'OK, I will.'

To argue would only convince their captors that Josie was planning another escape attempt. Agreeing to go barefoot could only distract her true intention.

'My trainers smell,' Danni informed them.

Nobody answered.

'It's because they have manure in them,' she went on, 'it's why I'm so tall for my age. I grew really quick, like a stick of rhubarb.'

Her jokes were infantile at best, disarming, and were a reminder of how naïve Danni could be: it was a clever act; the girl was giving them reason to underestimate her.

She stood on the back seat in order to push her heels out of her trainers. Whilst standing, Josie noted, her daughter did a brief perusal of the front and sides of the car, then turned and leaned on the back seat while pushing one shoe off with the other. Her attention was rapt on the road behind.

'Get out of sight this instant,' Steph hissed.

'Come on, Danni,' said Josie, cajoling her to sit, 'do as Steph says.'

Under her fingertips, she felt tremors of excitement flooding through her daughter. Josie stayed silent, only helped Danni to snuggle closer. The gap between them was alive with Danni's excitement. The sensation was catching, and Josie too felt a buzz go through her entirety. She slipped off her shoes before being reminded, but it didn't matter for now, not while they were driving at speed.

Within a minute the Range Rover was on the steep approach to a major roundabout. Josie placed them on a mental map of south Cumbria. They were on the western approach towards the motorway, but also only a few miles away from Kendal. From what she'd overheard, Callum had advised turning to the left, which would take them towards the town. It had been years since Josie had travelled out that way, but she could almost picture where they planned to launch their trap on their pursuer.

As advised, Toby took the first turn off the roundabout and immediately accelerated to pick up the loss of momentum. Behind them, Josie imagined the Nissan driver taking the same turn, and revving to match their speed. Callum, in his Audi, couldn't be too far behind: the creep still gave instructions over the car's hands-free system. Judging from his voice, he was enjoying this sudden elevation in his importance to their team – to Josie it sounded like self-importance. It didn't matter – what did was that the three criminals were again fully engaged in detailing their plan. Josie brushed Danni's ear with her lips, she whispered so closely. 'What is it, Danni? What did you see?'

GRACE

'Look at her. It's definitely Danni!'

Kyle didn't know Danni from any other kid, but Grace knew her well enough for the two of them to be certain.

'What is she doing, standing like that? Get a little closer, Kyle. I need to see—'

'It's risky getting too close,' Kyle counselled.

'I know. But just for a moment. I need to see, Kyle.'

'Is it or isn't it her?'

'Yes. Definitely.'

'Then why get closer?'

'Please, just a little closer.'

Without being over-dramatic, Grace hoped to get her eyes on her sister too. Except for the hand that had briefly appeared to urge Danni down into the seat earlier, she'd seen nothing to indicate that Josie was in the car. For all she knew, it was one of the abductors who was controlling – or struggling to control – Danni, and not her big sis. Josie might already be dead, and all Grace wanted was the faintest glimmer of hope that Josie had survived until now. Her mind's eye pictured Josie bloodied and beaten, her tongue split as Pete's had been slit, but still alive. Even in that awful state was better than the alternative: Josie could already have been murdered and buried back at that railway museum.

Kyle exhaled, his knuckles almost creaking as he gripped the steering wheel. He sped up marginally, closing the gap between them and the Range Rover.

Through its back windscreen she spotted Danni again, but only for a second or two. The setting sun caused orange and grey patterns to shift on the glass, reflecting the sky. But then the road took a sweeping turn to the left, and the reflections changed and then disappeared entirely. Again Grace spotted her niece; this time the girl was leaning over the back of the chair, and it appeared she was messing with her shoes. A head moved alongside her. There was a hint of dark, wavy hair and a slightly upturned nose, and then the head dipped down. It was the briefest of glimpses, but Grace would know her sister anywhere. She'd no way of telling if Josie was hurt, or to what extent if she was, but she was alive, and that was what mattered most to Grace.

The breath caught in Grace's chest. Confirmation that Josie and Danni were in the car made everything real, and served as a reminder about what she hoped to do, and how dangerous to them all it might prove. She was very tempted to ignore her previous fears about informing the police: they were the professionals and knew how to deal with abduction cases while she didn't. However, she'd seen too many movies, TV shows and news segments where the shit had hit the fan and the hostages didn't survive. For the time being she'd keep the police out of it, and only call them when there was no other option available.

'They're going towards Kendal,' Kyle announced.

Grace had also spotted the Range Rover's indicators begin flashing left.

Kyle hit his indicators, while decelerating sharply. The decline down to the roundabout was steep, and had probably taken several drivers by surprise over the years. The Range Rover was out of sight the instant it took the slip road. Kyle swung them around the short curve of roundabout and fell in behind. He had to change gear and hit the accelerator to match speeds going back uphill. They travelled for only a handful of minutes before they approached another slip road, and Kyle could be forgiven for believing the Range Rover was going to head on into Kendal on the A6: he followed closely enough that his feet stuttered on the pedals when the Range Rover swung around a secondary roundabout and headed back on to the same road they'd followed, now on the opposite carriageway. Kyle's Nissan had been positioned to go into town; he had to pull it over sharply, eliciting a squeal of brakes and the blast of a horn from a pick-up truck they cut in front of. He missed an instruction to give way at the next junction, and again was honked at by the alarmed truck driver. Kyle swore under his breath.

'What the hell are they up to?' Grace voiced aloud for him.

'Don't know. Maybe they took the wrong turn back towards the motorway . . .'

There was little conviction in Grace's answer. 'Yeah. Maybe.'

'Oh, look,' said Kyle.

On the way uphill they'd passed a petrol station and motel. It had a sister petrol station on the opposite side. The Range Rover's indicator lights flashed amber, and it slowed on its approach to the petrol station.

'They need to refuel?' Kyle wondered.

'Why not use the station on the other side?' Grace asked. 'Why wait till they reached this one?'

'Maybe they collect loyalty points or something,' Kyle suggested with a curl of his top lip. He slowed the car and pulled into the service area, but aimed the Nissan to an adjoining car park that also served visitors to a porcelain tiles showroom. He parked the Nissan so that they could see the Range Rover on the station forecourt. It sat next to the fuel pumps, but nobody got out to refuel the car. Across the carriageway, a black Audi had pulled into the sister service station. There, a severe-faced man with spiky hair lounged alongside its bonnet. He eyed them, but they were oblivious to his scrutiny. After a moment he took out his mobile phone and used it to snap a series of zoomed photographs: at that distance the images might not be clear of their faces, but anyone who knew them would recognize Grace or Kyle.

Still unaware they were being observed, they didn't see the man get back in the Audi and pull slowly off the forecourt. It rejoined the carriageway north, and those at the fuel pumps on this side gave him enough time to negotiate the turn and return south again. The Range Rover pulled away, catching Kyle unready. He scrambled to follow, but there was no need for panic. The Range Rover crawled its way back to the dual carriageway, and then drove on to it at a leisurely pace.

Kyle's Nissan followed.

Grace checked with him. He wore a frown so deeply lined it looked painful.

'What was all that about?' she asked.

'Absolutely no clue,' he replied truthfully and without the sarcasm this time.

Behind them, sitting at a casual speed behind a supermarket delivery truck, the Audi was once more on their tail.

JOSIE

She made several ooh-ooh-ooh-type noises, sounding like a baby chimpanzee, before Danni composed herself. Josie assisted, laying a forearm across the girl's thighs to deter her from bouncing up and down with each excitable hoot. Josie used her other hand to smother Danni's mouth, then immediately withdrew and touched a single finger to her own lips. Danni got the message. In the moment she'd forgotten that she was keeping the secret from those in the front seats, so her mum's reminder was timely and welcomed. She sank down, but jabbed her fingers, directing Josie to look out the side window.

After their detour to the service station, Callum had called on the phone again. This time Toby's hands-free system had not picked it up; the call had been made directly to Steph's phone instead. Apparently Callum didn't want the hostages to overhear what he had to say, but Josie feared that she already knew what the creep thought was best kept from her. Danni had earlier whispered back to her that Aunt Grace was following them. Josie couldn't imagine how it had come about, but she knew how deeply her little sister loved her, and if anyone would try to fight to free them from the bad guys, it would be Grace. It had always surprised her that Grace had allowed her husband to dominate and control her: Grace was never one to shrink from trouble, and when they were younger it would've been Grace that squared up to their bullies first rather than the other way around. OK, it was one thing scratching and slapping and yanking the hair of another schoolgirl, quite different from defending oneself against the manipulations of a narcissistic control freak. And it was a universe away in difference to taking on a gang of armed criminals. The conversation between Steph and Callum lasted until they were once more approaching the motorway. Toby must have gathered enough from the one-sided conversation that he didn't require directions. He took the slip road south, and that was when Danni began hooting like a chimp.

'What is it now?' Steph demanded as she dropped her phone into a pocket.

'Nothing,' said Josie, barely able to contain the lie. Beyond Steph, a local landmark dominated, filling the window and blotting out the darkening sky.

'There's something. Out with it,' Steph snapped.

'I told you already that Danni needs the toilet. She's growing desperate. I am too.'

'You're both going to have to hold it in. We can't stop here.'

Toby accelerated sharply, matching and then exceeding the speed of vehicles on the motorway. He slipped the Range Rover into a gap in the traffic. He was watching his mirrors, and grunted in satisfaction. Josie guessed that the Nissan Qashqai – with Grace onboard – was still taking the bait and following, the driver oblivious that they'd been spotted. Steph faced forward once more. Danni sneaked up her head like a tortoise coming out of its shell, and showed Josie a gaping grin. She nodded several times at the outcropping that for Josie always marked the approach to the higher Cumbrian fells. The motorway was barely above sea level at that point where the land met Morecambe Bay, so the hill was possibly the tallest point in the immediate area. It was distinct in that for years it had been denuded of trees and bushes, the craggy limestone rocks showing through and giving it a scoured appearance. Its actual name was Farleton Knott, but during previous journeys Grace and Josie had jokingly nicknamed the hill 'Bareback Mountain' – after the movie of a similar title featuring two cowboys falling in love in a tent – so it was no surprise now that Danni had thought of it as a 'baldy hill'.

Danni hadn't said it, but it was obvious that she'd recalled important details about the day her birth mother fled her abusers, and hid the loot she'd stolen with which she probably hoped to finance a new life for them. Where on Farleton Knott had Mel concealed the bag that was the source of Josie's current woes? A small part of her decided to come clean with their abductors and help press Danni into remembering exactly where Mel had stashed the bag. If she'd believed they'd be released unharmed afterwards, she would certainly have done that, but she knew their corpses would be exchanged for the bag. Better then to help Danni conceal the secret, and buy them time. If Danni was correct and Grace was following them, then perhaps her sister was already helping coordinate a hostage rescue team.

'Where are we going?' she asked.

'Be quiet,' said Steph.

'How far?' she persisted.

Steph twisted towards her, her mouth a tight line of annoyance.

Josie said, 'I ask only because there's going to be a couple of accidents soon.' She aimed her next words at Toby. 'Are you happy for us to pee on your lovely leather seats?'

'Don't even think about it,' he warned.

'You're going to have to come up with some other idea then,' Josie pointed out. 'You can't expect us to hang on for ever. Jesus, you're going to have to let Franklin relieve himself soon as well, or there'll be more than two puddles to contend with!'

Steph exhaled sharply. She had cradled Franklin in her lap. The little dog had dozed for the last few miles, but sensing it was the object of discussion, it lifted its head and batted its dark eyes at its owner. It squirmed under Steph's hand. 'Don't you dare go wee-wee,' she mock-scolded it. Hearing her speak in such a twee, babyish manner sent a dagger of annoyance through Josie's stomach.

Steph exchanged mumbles with Toby, and Josie saw the driver's shoulder rise and fall.

Steph looked back at her. 'If you hold on, we'll stop at the next service station.'

From experience, Josie knew that the next one they'd reach was the southbound site, across the motorway from where Mel had originally given Barker the slip. Hopefully there was some beneficial meaning to again visiting the service station where all of this had begun three years earlier. Could they escape their abductors in a similar manner – or escape the car and run to Grace, then speed off? She wondered if she should prepare, discreetly slip her feet into her shoes, and perhaps sneak on Danni's too, but to do so was tempting fate. If Steph noticed they'd put on their footwear, she would probably suspect they were planning to run: she'd ordered them to take off their shoes to deter another mad dash for freedom. Josie felt she could endure a short barefoot run across perished tarmac, but Danni's feet were soft and easily damaged. Suffering sore feet was, of course, preferable to the alternative.

The service station was situated a few miles south of Lancaster. They approached it within twenty minutes of leaving Cumbria. Across the way, a rising mist hid the tower and faux flying saucer on top. Toby hit his blinkers, giving plenty of notice they were turning in. Again he nodded silently when seeing that their tail followed suit.

It was approaching evening, and much of the traffic on the motorway was composed of commuters. Most didn't visit the service station, choosing instead to push on for home, so there weren't too many vehicles in the car park. Thankfully there were enough people to witness them if Steph or Toby chose to lead them to the toilets at gunpoint. Josie shivered with anticipation, feeling that freedom was in reach.

As Toby pulled the car to a halt, well back from the buildings, she reached to retrieve her shoes off the floor.

'No, no, they stay off,' Steph told her.

'What? We can't walk barefoot to—'

'You aren't walking anywhere. When I say, you can just open the door and pee alongside the car.'

'You're joking, aren't you?'

Steph exhaled sharply at the suggestion.

'People will see!' Danni squawked.

'They won't,' Steph reassured her, 'because I'll be blocking their view.'

'Mum, tell her,' Danni whined.

'It'll be OK,' Josie calmed her. 'I'll block you too, so nobody will see.'

Toby stopped the engine and got out of the car. He dug his knuckles into his lower back, arching his spine. He shut his door and moved around to the passenger side. Steph got out, and Franklin bounded out of her hands on to the tarmac. She'd already clipped him back on to his lead, so the little dog didn't get to range far. He urinated against a raised kerb. While their captors manoeuvred about, Josie whispered to Danni. 'Can you see where Aunt Grace is?'

'They're parked on the other side of the car park,' she whispered in return. 'We can't run to them, Mum.'

'Why not?' Josie avoided looking for where the Nissan was located, for fear she'd give the game away.

'Creepy Callum's parked near us. He's still in his car, but he can stop us getting to Aunt Grace.'

'Shit,' said Josie, and for once didn't receive a look of mock reproof from Danni.

The child safety locks had been activated. Toby opened the door, and stood with one hand on the window frame. He jerked his head to indicate that Danni should get out first. Josie moved to get out too, but Toby bumped the door against her, forcing her to stay inside. Once she got the message, he opened the door again. Steph blocked any escape for Danni, who stood open-mouthed alongside the gap.

'Crouch down there,' Steph said, and indicated the floor in the 'V' between the door and body of the car. Horrified, Danni blinked at Toby. 'Don't worry,' he told her, and averted his gaze. 'I won't look at you.'

'Mum?'

'It's OK, Danni. Just pee there.'

'I don't think I can now.'

'Yeah,' Josie assured her. 'You can.'

'You'd better,' Steph warned, 'because we won't be stopping again, not for at least an hour.'

Mortified, Danni pulled at the waistband of her jeans. She squatted, again checking that Toby wasn't looking. She made tiny huffing noises, and Josie was unsure whether or not her daughter was weeping in shame. It seemed an age before Josie heard the trickle of liquid. Danni finally stood, and even in the evening gloom her face glowed and her eyes shone.

'Climb back inside now,' Steph instructed, 'and crawl to the far side. Josie, don't get out until I tell you.'

She waited until Danni had clambered across and seated herself once more, before beckoning out Josie. Josie bit her lip in frustration: she'd hoped that they both might have been allowed out of the vehicle at one time; now the prospect of running for it was snatched from her because she had no intention of abandoning Danni.

'I've lost the urge,' she said.

'Your choice,' said Steph, and Toby shut the door.

'Now's not a good time for either of us to go,' said Toby. Somehow, Josie thought, he wasn't suggesting that they squat in the dirty gutter like animals, but that they might put off visiting the toilets inside the service station. He couldn't resist a turn of his head, checking out where the Nissan was located, but he made the glance look casual, continuing his scan to include the other vehicles in the car park too. 'They're just sitting there, watching us,' he explained for Steph's sake. 'That might not be the case if either of us leaves the other alone.'

They wouldn't be alone, not while Callum lurked nearby, but for now Grace and her friend were unaware of his presence. Seeing Steph in particular left to guard her hostages, it might provoke an attempt at a rush-and-grab rescue attempt.

Inside the car, Josie craned to spot her sister. She hoped to warn her about Callum, but circumstance conspired against her. A delivery van parked between them, blocking any view Josie might have had of the Nissan. Standing, and a metre or so forward of Josie's position now, Toby could see something of the car. He said, 'There's a bloke getting out.'

'Let's go,' Steph instructed, 'we can't afford a confrontation where there are witnesses.'

Toby ignored whatever the man from the Nissan was doing. He strode quickly around to the driver's side and got in, starting the engine. Steph hurried Franklin back inside, then slid on to the passenger seat as sinuously as a snake. Toby reversed back to get clear of a high kerb, then pulled away. As he negotiated a tight exit designed as a speed-calming measure, it gave Josie an opportunity to quickly bob up and search for her sister. She spotted the Nissan, and a burly bloke she didn't recognize standing at its raised boot hatch. A pale blur in the front passenger seat had to be Grace's face, turned to seek hers. Spotting it made her heart leap, and unbidden her hands shot up and she gesticulated wildly, stabbing fingers towards the black Audi and its dangerous owner. Both Toby and Steph's attention was on watching the reaction of the Nissan driver, who immediately lowered the boot hatch and rushed to get back in the driver's seat.

'He's about as subtle as a brick in the face,' Toby sneered as he swept the Range Rover around the site towards the motorway.

'Who was that?' Steph asked, and it took a second or more for the question to register with Josie.

'Are you asking me?'

'Who else?'

'Well, how should I know? I never even saw who you were concerned about.'

'Don't lie,' said Steph, sounding frustrated by the continuous dance they each played. She held up her mobile, showing Josie a photo on the screen. It must have been taken back where they'd pulled the stunt at the petrol stations, because the photo had been sent from Callum to her and showed a couple seated in the front of the Nissan. 'Here. Look closely. Who are those people?'

Josie tried to give nothing away, but seeing Grace's face more clearly than she had a moment ago set her pulse pounding behind her ears. She shook her head, dismissing the people in the photo, but took a longer look at the driver. He'd a broad face, misaligned nose and small, lumpy ears. His hair was shorn so short she suspected he was naturally growing bald. She honestly had no idea who he was, only that he looked more thuggish than any of her abductors. Was he a competitor chasing the same loot as Steph and her friends, who'd somehow forced or even coerced Grace into assisting him? Maybe Grace wasn't trying some insane rescue but was in as much danger as either Josie or Danni. Her gorge rose at the thought, and she had to slap a hand over her mouth to avoid drooling acidic saliva. The reaction wasn't lost on Steph.

'Who is he?'

'I swear, I've no idea,' Josie said, 'but his presence is frightening.'

'I don't think we've much to be concerned with,' said Toby, more for Steph's sake. 'His actions have shown he's an amateur. We'll easily deal with him once the time's right.'

Steph nodded.

For a moment, Josie didn't know how to feel about Toby's poorly veiled boast. If the Nissan driver proved a threat to Grace, she'd be happy to have him 'dealt with', but what if the opposite was true, and the man was the essence of never judging a book by its battered cover?

GRACE

'Hurry! Get back in the car, they're leaving already!' Grace needn't have raised her voice so sharply, because with the rear hatch open, her words had clear passage to Kyle.

'Just give me a second,' he said, more to himself, as he dug in the compartment holding the spare tyre and tools. He brought out a zippered bag, which appeared heavier than if it only contained his overnight toiletries. He quickly pulled down on the hatch, and returned at a trot to the driver's seat. He tossed the bag across into Grace's lap.

She held the bag tentatively, resisting unzipping it. She watched as the grey Range Rover performed a rapid reverse manoeuvre, then took off towards the far end of the car park. If Kyle didn't hurry, he'd lose them and have to drive like a lunatic to catch up. As the Range Rover slowed to exit between twin high kerbs, she caught a glance of Josie in the back. It was undeniably Josie in her mind now, having positively identified Danni climbing out and back inside the car, to apparently relieve herself. They had expected Josie to get out too, and Kyle had announced it time they arm up, rather than miss another opportunity to free the hostages. He'd barely exited the car when a van had pulled in, partly blocking her view, but Grace had seen enough to spot the change in the demeanour of the abductors. Trying to look inconspicuous, there was a definite change in their body language, especially in the manner in which the woman almost yanked the little dog off its feet and scooped it into the car. The big car was driven with a touch more urgency than had been shown before. Before Kyle could get the Nissan moving, the Range Rover was already on the exit road that encircled the site, and led back to the motorway. Kyle cut directly across the car park, ignoring directional signs and marked parking bays, and made up several seconds. He had to slow to negotiate the choke point, and frustratingly had to wait until a truck had gone past, before they could give chase. The truck diverted to the lorry park, and Kyle swung around its back end as it made the turn. He clipped the high kerb protecting the grass verge, and the car swerved when he momentarily over-steered. The bag almost slipped from Grace's lap. She clenched her knees around it, hands reaching for the dashboard to brace for a crash. Kyle corrected the car, glancing across to squeeze her a less than confident smile.

He didn't slow; in fact if anything he was driving too fast when he hit the slip road back on to the motorway. He gained more speed and then swept out into the first lane, forcing the following traffic to pull over sharply to avoid hitting them. Horns honked, but it appeared Kyle had the capacity to turn a deaf ear to them. Gritting his teeth, he accelerated, until once again the Range Rover was less than half a dozen vehicles ahead. Then he slowed to match its speed.

Grace buzzed with adrenalin. She fancied she could feel an electrical charge dancing among the shorter hairs on the back of her head. Her stomach felt as if it flipped, and for a second or two she fought against her rising gorge, holding down stinging bile.

'You OK?' Kyle asked.

'I am now. For a bit back there I thought you were going to kill us both.'

'Nah, I know how to handle a car,' he said, and grinned feverishly.

Did he though? Grace was beginning to suspect that a few sycophantic hangers-on might very well have exaggerated some of the rumours about Kyle Perlman. She didn't doubt that he was handy with his fists, or that he had maybe driven round town like a lunatic as a younger boy, but she was yet to see evidence that he was ex-Special Forces, or that he might know a thing or two about extracting hostages. She felt the weight of the zippered bag on her lap. It was heavy, but not as heavy as she'd expect it to be if it held two guns and ammunition. Without asking permission she drew the zip open, and peered in.

'What's this?'

'It's all I could access given the urgency,' he answered.

'Is it even real?' she croaked.

She took out what were obviously the butt, trigger and hammer of a revolver. To her it looked antique, like something her great-grandfather might have held on to after returning from the Great War.

'I can put it together in a few seconds,' he assured her as she took out more parts of the disassembled gun. There was also a half-moon feeder clip of bullets. To her eye, they appeared to have been wrapped in cellophane a decade or so ago, judging by the staining and fragility of the plastic wrap.

'Jesus,' she moaned, 'I'd be scared to fire it in case it blew up in my hand.'

'It's a Webley Mark Four,' he replied, as if that should allay any of her fears. 'They were the service weapon of choice for the British armed forces.'

'Were? Until when, the bloody Battle of Hastings?'

He clucked his tongue. 'Up until the nineteen sixties.'

'So it's older than our combined ages?' she said.

'I don't know about that, I'm—'

'I'm only being sarcastic.'

'Yeah, I noticed. Hey, you needn't worry about it. I've fired it before and it works as well as it did when it was first used. Anyhow, if all goes well, there won't be any need for shooting. I brought it more as a deterrent than anything.'

'I thought you were going to tool us up accordingly?'

'What more do we need?'

'You said you'd bring me a weapon.'

'Dig deeper in the bag.'

She slid in her hand and, under a fold in the cloth lining, found another hunk of metal. She pulled it out and blinked at it in dismay. 'You expect *me* to use a bloody knuckleduster?'

'Nah, that's for me. You get to carry the gun.'

'I've never fired a gun in my life.'

'I'll show you how. But, like I said, we hopefully won't need to. Just the threat of being shot should be enough for most people to give up.'

'From what Pete told me, one of them has a pistol: what's the chance he only waves it around for show?'

'You'd be surprised. Most wannabe gangsters haven't a clue about using firearms.'

'Unlike you ex-Special Forces chaps, eh?'

He again glanced over at her, his frown deeper than ever. 'Are you taking the piss?'

'It was meant as a compliment,' she said, rather than admitting that she was entertaining serious misgivings about his supposed background. But who was she to doubt him? He had never claimed to be former Special Forces; the closest he'd come to an admission was with a joke he'd have to kill her to protect his secret. They continued in silence, eyes on the steady, unblinking red lights of the Range Rover ahead. Finally Grace asked the question troubling her. 'Have you ever killed somebody, Kyle?'

'Would it make you feel better if I said no?'

'I hired you because I needed somebody with skills, but it never occurred to me what I really expected from you. If it comes to it, and it's a choice between defending my life, I suppose I could shoot somebody, but I don't think I could otherwise. What about you, Kyle?'

'Like I said, hopefully it won't come to that. See those brass knuckles . . . I've never used them before. But trust me, when it comes time, I won't flinch from knocking the shit out of any of those bastards.'

JOSIE

I t occurred to Josie well before arriving at their destination where it was that Steph planned on holing up for the night and to rendezvous with the reinforcements she'd requested.

At first, the realization had stunned her, then given her a trickle of hope, and then finally an intense feeling of dread.

The woman had lied about owning a small house in Josie's village. It wasn't her own front door she'd be throwing open to welcome the arrival of more hard-eyed thugs. Steph planned on using Josie's home, and Josie feared that it was with the intention of making it a mausoleum once her hostages lost their value.

Confirming matters for Josie, Steph had called Callum on his mobile. With her voice lowered she asked, 'I hope you followed my instructions when dealing with Josie's partner?'

'Told you already,' Callum replied. 'I didn't harm him. Well, not much. Just made sure he couldn't squeal to the coppers about us.'

'And you definitely secured him?'

'Aye. There was no way he could get free. I was in the Sea Cadets, y'know, so I know a thing or two about tyin' knots.'

It was an unlikely boast, even to Josie, who recalled that when he'd secured her it was by use of plastic ties. Steph was unimpressed by his announcement, and Toby made a sound of disgust in the back of his throat. Perhaps he'd heard similar unsubstantiated boasts concerning Callum's skills before.

'You're confident he's still tied up where you left him?' Steph went on.

'If he'd got free, wouldn't the rozzers have been on our arses by now?'

'Maybe he didn't call the police. But how else did those two in the Nissan know to follow us? I think that, maybe, Pete had a hand in it.'

'How'd he know where to send 'em?'

'I don't know,' Steph admitted. 'If I didn't believe otherwise, I might've thought they were journalists . . . Josie was worried that you were a reporter chasing a story. Maybe she wasn't far off the mark when it comes to these two.'

'Listen,' said Callum. 'I haven't been idle while following. I got on the blower to a contact and had them look up the Nissan. It's registered to an owner in Chester, bloke by the name of Kyle Perlman.'

'Oh,' said Steph.

Josie ran the name through the vault of her mind, but it meant no more to her than his battered face had in the photo.

'What do we know about him?' Steph prompted after a few seconds.

'Frig all,' Callum admitted. 'I've put out some feelers, though, and will let you know if anythin' comes back. Meantime, I wouldn't worry about him. There's nothin' to say he's any less of an amateur than he's already shown.' Callum ended the call.

Josie sensed Steph's turn before it came. She ducked her head, and snuggled against Danni. After her burst of excitement at the sight of Farleton Knott, Danni had fallen into an exhausted slumber: Josie feigned sleep.

'The name Perlman mean anything to you?' Steph asked aloud. Josie said nothing.

'Obviously it does, otherwise you wouldn't pretend to be asleep.'

'I'm not sleeping,' said Josie, without raising her head, 'I just have nothing to tell you.'

'You claim not to know Perlman. What about the woman?'

'Haven't a clue who she is either,' said Josie, and she felt Danni stiffen. Apparently Danni wasn't sleeping as deeply as she'd made out either. Josie had no fear of Danni blurting out that it was her Aunt Grace; her daughter had proven cannier than previously believed.

'If they were reporters, they'd have made a move before now. We have to assume they're competitors also after the money that Mel stole.' Steph's words were for Toby. 'I think it's safe to go back to the house. You?'

With her head down, Josie couldn't determine if he'd nodded, shook his head, shrugged or anything else. It didn't matter, because he didn't slow down and didn't make any alternative suggestion. She waited long enough for their attention to leave her, then Josie stretched up a few inches, so that she could peer over the rim of the window. It was too dark to make out the landscape beyond the motorway embankments, only the proliferation of lights that marked towns and villages. Under the circumstances, what should have been familiar terrain had an unnerving alien quality.

Toby negotiated the junction with the M56 so smoothly that it didn't impinge on Josie that they'd left the M6 and were once again back in north Cheshire. Despite her resolve to fight tooth and nail to protect her daughter, she snoozed. In her mind she felt she only micro-napped, but her periods of sleep must have been longer. It was perhaps half an hour's journey from where the motorways met to her home, but Josie was oblivious to perhaps twenty-five minutes of that. She only realized how close they'd got when Toby slowed enough for her to spot a directional sign to Chester Zoo. Spotting the sign, she rose up sharply, clearing her throat of tacky mucus. Her actions roused Danni, and also Franklin, whose head appeared between the front seats, eyes twinkling blackly in the subdued light from the dashboard. Danni, as ever, reached fingers to the little dog and fussed him. Steph grunted in annoyance, but didn't draw the dog away.

'Have you anything to drink?' Josie asked.

Neither of their captors answered.

'I'm thirsty, Mum,' Danni also said.

'You'll be wanting fed next,' Steph growled.

'We've gone all day with nothing to eat or drink,' said Josie. 'Giving my daughter a drink should be the least you do.'

'We've had nothing either. You'll eat and drink when we do,' said Toby. 'That's if you behave and give us no reason to punish you again.'

Toby took the expressway around the eastern side of Chester, then a connecting road that took them across the River Dee, and then towards the England/Wales border. They were on a country lane little wider than a single carriageway, bare miles from home: the last place on earth where Grace should follow them. Josie gently extricated her arms from around Danni, and had the girl sit down fully on the back seat. Josie reached across and clipped the lap belt over Danni's thighs. Once Danni was secure, she gave no warning of her intention. She leaped forward, one elbow slamming the side of Toby's skull. He reacted instinctively to the pain, rearing away. It cleared space for Josie to throw her upper body through the gap and she yanked at the steering wheel. Toby, and then Steph, fought for control of the car. The big 4x4 swerved erratically. Fingernails clawed for Josie's face, and she squeezed tight her eyelids to avoid being blinded. Inside the car was a cacophony of screams, terrified yelps and loud curses. Danni screeched, but this time didn't attempt to assist her mum. She cowered in the seat, a terrifying memory assailing her as the car swerved from one side to the other.

Until now the Range Rover had been driven too fast for Josie to risk forcing them off the road. Here though, on the winding lane, Toby had dropped to thirty miles per hour. Sending them through a hedge into a field could still cause them some injury, but not outright death, as would've been the case if she'd tried something as desperate on the motorway. As it was, no sooner had she lunged for control of the steering wheel than Josie regretted it. Steph tore at her face, then at her hands and wrists, shredding her flesh, but Toby recoiled quickly from her buffet to his head, and returned the honours with an elbow to her chin. His strike was pointed and on target, and snapped her head backwards so sharply that her thoughts were left several seconds in its wake. A tidal wave of crimson-tinged darkness engulfed her, even as she slumped on the bench seat. Josie moaned, but was totally unaware of the despair in her voice.

Toby fought for control but the Range Rover hit the grass verge. The car tilted, and for a few seconds came close to losing its battle with gravity, but Toby was no slouch behind a wheel. The big 4x4 dropped off the verge on to tarmac, and a quick adjustment had it travelling in a direct line again. However, it was directly at a tight bend in the road, where the scarred trunk of a tree showed where other careless drivers had misjudged their skill. Toby braked, steering the car away from a certain collision, but couldn't avoid clipping the verge once more. A pothole grabbed and held a tyre for a split-second, and then the Range Rover kicked free, and swerved across to the opposite side of the corner. The driver's side took the impact with the hedge on that side, and the screeching of abused metal overwhelmed the previous noises inside the car.

Toby brought the car to a shuddering halt.

Josie surfaced from near unconsciousness.

She was hurt, but not yet finished.

This time she avoided a direct confrontation with Toby, and went at Steph instead. She grabbed the woman's head, a hand each side of the headrest, and yanked up and backwards. Steph's hat came off, and Josie's fingernails dug into her fine white hair and the pale skin beneath. Josie raked and scored the woman's scalp, then reached to dig her nails into her eye sockets and the corners of her mouth.

'Let us out or I'll blind her,' she screamed at Toby.

'Like hell I will,' he snapped.

She wanted him to get out, to rush around the car and throw open the door, in order to control her. With the door open, she'd urge Danni to jump out and run to her aunt while she made it difficult for Toby to pursue her. He didn't get out. He spun on his seat, kicking for room and then leaned over to clasp her throat in one fist. She recalled from earlier how he'd the knack for choking the life out of her, so she reared away, and unfortunately lost her grip on Steph. Steph wrenched forward, her face going into her palms as she cried out in dismay. Josie batted at Toby's hand. He swatted her aside, and then darted in with his other fist. His knuckles raked her forehead, but without the force to knock her out. It hurt like crazy though, and crimson again flashed in her vision. She ducked his next punch, falling over Danni. Toby swatted at her a third time, but then decided he was getting nowhere.

Then again, neither was she.

'How many warnings will it take before I march you out into that fucking field and put a bullet through your brains?' he snarled.

Knowing she was done for now, Josie ignored him, and instead tried to calm Danni, who had degenerated from a screaming child to one hyperventilating in panic. 'It's OK, it's OK, it's OK,' Josie repeated, mantra-like, trying to soothe the girl's terror, and simultaneously hoping that she'd done enough to warn her sister of the danger they were in.

'It isn't OK, you bitch,' Steph yowled at her, 'look at what you've done to my face!' Her skin was a patchwork of weeping scratches.

'Yeah,' said Toby, the recipient of Josie's claws in the woods earlier, 'welcome to the club, Whizzer.'

GRACE

To avoid discovery, Kyle had dropped back from the Range Rover. Grace was confident she knew where the car was headed, back to Josie's house, so felt it was unnecessary to stick closely on their tail. Along those narrow, winding roads their headlights would obviously pinpoint them if they shadowed too closely, so he turned them off and drove by what little light remained in the heavens.

The last either of them expected was to approach a bend in the road and receive only a few seconds' warning that the route was partially blocked. Kyle braked and the Nissan halted mere feet from colliding with the big 4x4.

The Range Rover was canted up on two wheels on the right-hand side of the lane. Its headlights were on, and the backwash from them silhouetted the car's occupants. They jostled, and Grace let out a cry when she spotted the driver beating her sister. She looked to Kyle for some positive action, but he sat, open-mouthed in momentary indecision. The gun was still in several component parts and useless to him, and what good would a pair of brass knuckle-dusters serve under the circumstances: the least he might do was go and pound a fist through a window and help extricate Grace's kin from the back seat. Instead, Kyle hit reverse gear, and took the Nissan back around the corner, and out of sight.

'What are you doing?' Grace groped blindly at her seatbelt, trying to pop it loose. If Kyle had no intention of rushing to Josie's aid, then Grace definitely would. She unclipped and wrenched the belt aside, and was halfway out of the car in a second, before Kyle could even bring it to a stop. Her left foot bounced and scraped along the road, and the door banged back against her shins several times, before she could throw it fully open. Kyle grabbed her, grasping the waistband of her jeans. She fought for a few seconds, trying to twist loose, shouting wordlessly. For that moment, he was an enemy.

'Grace! For god's sake, what are you going to do?'

'I have to help them!'

'How? By getting yourself killed? Get back in here and think about it.' He gave her no space for argument, physically yanking her inside the car, and holding her while she again struggled. 'Listen. They're pulling off again. D'you want to try chasing them down on foot or what?'

She made a final half-hearted attempt at pulling free, but Kyle was correct. The Range Rover was moving again, its headlights bouncing off the trees that lined the road. Already it had picked up more speed than she could ever muster on foot. She prised at Kyle's fingers. 'OK, I hear you and you're right,' she told him, her eyes hot and stinging. She pulled her door shut, tried to regain some dignity as she settled once more into the chair. The bag and the weapons it contained had slid off her lap on to the floor. She bent and groped for them. To be doing something constructive was far preferable to sitting in silence, while her guts coiled inside from embarrassment. Her actions had been reckless and, let's face it, she decided, the height of stupidity. How had she ever expected to free Josie and Danni from their armed abductors with her bare hands alone?

'Stop the car, Kyle.'

'Why? You going to run across the fields to cut them off, or try something else as barmy?'

'I'm one hundred per cent confident they're going to Josie's place. We don't need to stick so closely to them. We were lucky they were too busy scuffling with Josie that they didn't spot us just now. We shouldn't chance blowing things again when it's unnecessary, yeah?'

He concurred with a shrug.

'I need to phone Pete and warn him they're coming. He has to hide, or play along – or whatever the hell he can do – to help us free them all safely. Or as safely as things can be where guns are concerned.' Grace hefted the bag and its heavy contents. 'I need you to show me how to put this together. I must be ready next time.'

CALLUM

'I dunno who this Perlman thinks he is,' said Callum, 'but he's actin' like he's ten men.'

'What do you mean?' Steph demanded over the phone.

'He's actin' as if he's afraid of piss all, like his bollocks are the size of ten men's. Fucker's lookin' for a ruck, y'ask me. He's still on your jacksie, and looks set for followin' you all the way to hell and back.'

'Sometimes I barely understand you, Callum. Are you even speaking English?'

'Says the fuckin' illegal immigrant,' Callum replied. 'Your jacksie is another name for your sweet arse, Whizzer.'

'Yes, that much I grasped.'

'Dunno what your problem is then. Wouldn't mind grasping your jacksie mesel', eh?'

Steph steadfastly refused to reply.

In the background, he heard Toby grunt and mutter something about showing some bloody respect. His command though was wasted on Callum, and he knew it. Instead, he said more clearly, 'It'll be best drawing him all the way to the house. That way we can contain the situation without any potential witnesses driving up on us. Stick with him, Callum, but let us know if he changes tack.'

'Will do, Tobe.'

'Toby,' Toby corrected him.

Callum grinned, amused that a single dig could still get a rise out of uptight Toby Davis.

'You said you'd put out some feelers, to see if you could learn anything more about him?' Steph prompted.

'Yeah. I came up with a load of blanks. He's not known to anyone I reached out to, but that could mean one or two things. It could mean he's squeaky clean, or that he's good at what he does and hasn't been caught. My opinion, he isn't the fuckin' latter.'

'So he isn't a competitor?'

'Doesn't strike me as one, but we can't rule it out. Could be somebody the jocks have hired and sent after the *wee lassie*, I suppose.'

'Doubtful,' said Toby, 'when the Scots have plenty of their own they could send.'

'Who else could have a stake in this except the jocks?' Callum asked. 'I mean, seein' as they're the ones that Barker was supposed to deliver it to, they knew what to expect and how much Mel stole?'

'It's not them,' Steph said, ending the guesswork. It was apparent that she knew more about the business relationship between Leonard Freda and his Scottish opposites, but wasn't willing to expound.

'Hang fire.' Callum, as had the driver of the Nissan, had been proceeding without the use of his headlights. To avoid suspicion, though, he'd switched on the sidelights, should he meet a copper coming the other direction: he could claim he'd simply forgotten to flick up the beam as it grew darker. Ahead, though, he'd just caught the flare of red that signified the Nissan braking again. Callum slowed, and knocked off his own lights in order to creep forward.

'What's wrong?' Steph asked.

'They've stopped,' he said.

'To do what?'

'How would I know?'

'What's your best guess?'

'Girl's giving him a blowjob.'

'Callum, for god's sake!'

'Ha! Well, how'd you expect me to know when they've just this instant pulled over? I'm doing the same.' He tucked the Audi into a wide spot in the road, next to a gated entrance to a pasture.

Inside the Nissan, somebody reached and switched on the overhead light. The two occupants turned to face each other, and Callum watched some animated nodding of heads and hand gestures. Without creeping up and spying inside, it was almost impossible deciding what they were doing. They messed about for a minute or more without offering any clues.

'Callum?'

He had forgotten for a moment that he had a phone call open.

'I'm still here, Steph, but I'm none the wiser. I can't tell what it is they're doing, but they've got their minds fully on it and wouldn't see me coming. Now would be a good time for me to sneak up and stick 'em both.'

'No, not yet.' From behind Steph's voice came another; a ragged squawk of alarm followed by frantic pleas.

'Sounds like I hit a nerve there. I don't think that Josie has been totally honest with you, Whizzer.'

'For once, we're in agreement,' she said.

'Wonders will never cease,' he said. 'Uh-oh, here we go. They're on the move again. I'll let you know if there's any more funny business.'

He ended the call, started his engine and gave them enough time to build some distance between them before turning on his sidelights and following. He had, earlier in the day, punched the location of the Lockwood house into his satnav, so despite making a different approach this time, he was in no danger of getting lost, even if they shot away and left him in their dust. From the digital map he concluded that they were mere minutes away and wouldn't even have to pass via the village green where he'd posed as a pushy journalist that morning.

The road took him towards the village church. Its spire dominated the sky. It looked out of place in a village as small as this, but Toby had mentioned at some point that there used to be a massive estate thereabouts, with a mansion in the grounds, and that the huge Lockwood home had served as its gatehouse. It stood to reason the gentry would splash out on an equally extravagant church. He made a silent bet that the modern congregation was so few they could tuck into one tiny corner, so its days were probably numbered as a place of worship and it would likely be demolished. To be honest, he didn't care a jot about the church, or any other religious building, be it temple, mosque or cathedral: he was a godless man, whatever you called Him.

As he recalled, a road ran adjacent to the Lockwood house's grounds, and then gave access to the other end of the village via a lane: it was where Steph had walked her little shit machine, Franklin, in order to survey the place and then make first contact with Danni. Logically thinking, in historical times villagers walking to Sunday worship would have used the lane as a shortcut. Callum had never used the lane, but he was confident that he could find it and access the house before even the Range Rover arrived with its hostages, let alone Perlman and his chick.

He slowed and crawled the Audi past the front of the church. It was early evening still, and there could be a few stragglers out and about, but there was nothing about his actions that should draw suspicion. He had his lights low, but streetlamps cast their own glows, so it didn't look odd for him to drive with his headlights down. He checked, and saw that the doors to the church appeared completely shut, and no lights burned within. An old burial ground wrapped around the church, much wider to the left where it had been allowed to expand into the open fields, whereas it was constrained by a cinder path pinched between walls to the other side. Beyond the path, there was a mixture of architectural styles, where homes hundreds of years old neighboured post-war houses and several modern bungalows. People were home in some of the dwellings, but none that took any notice of him. Callum parked the Audi at the roadside, a few metres shy of the entrance to the path. Anybody giving his car's location more than a second's notice would probably think it belonged to a dog walker: there was a handy poo bin tacked to a lamppost at the entrance to the path.

He took his phone off the dashboard mount and, after turning off the ringer, he secreted it in an inside pocket. His wallet, keys and knife nestled in his trouser pockets. His suit had grown rumpled over the past few days, and since scrambling about in the woods at Haverthwaite, it had become dotted with mud, with a splotch of ketchup finding its way on to the sleeve. His deck shoes were more discoloured than ever, clogged with dirt in the treads. He'd bet even his spiky hair didn't stand as jagged as before. He was hungry, his stomach roiling, but other than perhaps an indigestion tablet or two that he could scratch from the glove compartment, there was nothing to eat. Never mind, soon he'd be inside and there were still Josie's other treats he hadn't got to before leaving the kitchen.

The thought of chocolate bars and biscuits spurred him forward with almost as much alacrity as the thought of ending what he'd also started earlier with his blade. His patience with Josie and Danni was wearing thin, but he'd resisted the urge to stick them on several occasions, knowing that the longer the act was deferred, the sweeter it would be when it happened. The little torture he'd subjected the bloke, Pete, to had satisfied him for a few minutes at most, and since then he'd been itching to get back and finish him off, to a point where his skin was beginning to crawl like he was an addict jonesing for a fix.

If anyone noted him flitting down the lane, they could be forgiven for believing that the severe-faced man was a revenant arisen from its grave. He went slightly hunched over, his head jutting forward, knees lifting high so that the sharper cobbles in the path didn't pierce his thin-soled shoes. To his left the gravestones stood shoulder-to-shoulder, silent observers. If he believed in ghosts, he might have been freaked out, but he gave the subject of lingering spirits as much credence as an all-seeing, all-knowing deity, which amounted to *zilch*. If ghosts were the result of traumatic death, as some people hypothesized, then Callum thought he'd be trailing quite a retinue by now. He chuckled at the idea.

The path ended at an archaic turnstile. For ease of passage, though, an iron gate had been added within the past century: it had survived being culled for metal to go towards the war effort, but was rusted and the hinges had seized in the open position. Callum slipped through without giving those details much attention, and was on the dead-end road that passed the Lockwood house. Huge sycamore and yew trees threw their boughs overhead, adding to the darkness. The nearest streetlamp was a good distance away, probably almost adjacent to the driveway to the house. Callum appreciated the dark, it concealed him as he progressed, while seeking a way in to the grounds. A thick hedge surrounded the garden, and unless he scurried under on his belly, there was no obvious way to get in. But then he came across another old cast-iron gate, this one thickly layered by many decades' worth of paint. He tested it, but it was seized as resolutely as the first he'd passed through, but this one was shut. It didn't deter him for a second. He grabbed the top, dug a toe into the frame and powered up. He jumped down from the gate into a lawn spongy with moss and dotted with grass cuttings from a recent half-hearted mowing.

As he dashed towards the house, he left imprints in the soft grass, but they didn't concern him, as the lawn was already trampled in places, no doubt by the kid using it as her playground. As he approached the house, it struck him that there were more lights burning inside than there should've been. He paused in his tracks, concerned that he could be walking directly into a trap, and any second a squad of coppers might swarm him. But then, he couldn't swear that the lights hadn't been on last time he was there, he just hadn't noticed in daylight. His first instinct encouraged him to check that Pete was still secure in the closet, but he didn't have time before the impending arrival of the others. He preferred to be in place outside, and ready to move. Besides, if the shit hit the fan, and there were cops lying in wait, they could have Steph and Toby while he made himself scarce.

He took care approaching nearer, then moved alongside the house towards the front, peeking into windows of empty rooms. He stepped out on to the deep gravel turning circle at the front of the house, scanning the ground for signs that there'd been recent activity. It was churned up in places, but he couldn't tell which tracks were those of their own cars earlier, or if any other car had been there since. Only Pete's Ford Focus sat abandoned on the drive. If that coward had escaped his bindings, Callum was confident he'd have fled in it until he knew it was safe to return.

A car approached. Its headlights lit up the treetop canopy. It would be Toby's Range Rover, Callum decided, but all the same, it was better he got out of sight. He scurried away, cutting obliquely across a second lawn to a continuation of the boundary line: he settled into a gap between some rhododendron bushes. He inserted his hand in his pocket, and touched the handle of his flick knife. Its feel was more familiar – and more welcomed by him – than a lover's caress.

The Range Rover pulled into the grounds, tyres crunching on gravel. Toby had no inkling that Callum was there already, watching from the dappled shadows, but was on the alert for anyone else in the grounds. His head was on a swivel while he brought the car to the front of the house, then manoeuvred so that the bonnet faced the exit once more. Toby switched off the car's lights, but nobody moved to get out: as Callum had done a minute before, Toby and Steph were probably debating why there were more lights on within than there should've been. Callum's phone vibrated.

He took it out, cupping his hand over the screen to block the glow. Steph was calling, but he declined to answer. Instead, he swiftly typed a message to her: IN POSITION. UR CLEAR TO GO.

His phone vibrated once again, Steph preferring to speak directly, but he wasn't prepared to reveal his position by yapping. He cancelled the call, typed: WATCHING UR BACK. SHHH.

He put away his phone, and again felt it buzzing against his chest. He ignored it and finally Steph gave up. He watched her get out of the car, her little shit-machine dancing about her feet as she made a brief reconnoitre of the front of the house. She climbed the steps and tried the door handle. The door had locked behind them when they left. She turned about and lifted both palms and, as dark as it was, Callum saw a searching look on her face. Toby exited the car and Callum expected him to take out his lock-picking set. He didn't approach the house, but just stood, peering out across the grounds, checking the deepest shadows. At one point he looked directly at Callum, but the rhododendrons concealed him. Callum raised a middle finger at him, grinning in childish delight.

Toby moved to the back of the 4x4 and opened a door. He reached in, and came out clutching Danni by the collar of her sweatshirt. He commanded her to stand still, then jerked his head, ordering Josie out. The woman was cowed, her spirit diminished. She shut the car door, and then preceded Toby and Danni as they approached the house. Toby controlled Danni, keeping her very close, and Callum wasn't fully sure if he'd drawn his pistol again, but their body language suggested it. Josie mounted the steps. Steph indicated the locked door. Josie didn't give any resistance this time, she went to the edge of the steps, and dug among some plant pots: she picked up one of those stupid fake rocks and there must've been a spare key inside. Steph took it from her, and then unlocked the door. She was tentative as she pushed the door inward, and the relief was visible when a bunch of armed coppers didn't spring from conceal-ment. She snapped the lead a couple of times, and Franklin took the hint, leading Steph in. Toby told Josie to follow, and she did: she paused for a beat at the threshold, her head turning back towards the driveway, but Toby was in no mood for any further rebellion. His words were loud enough that Callum heard: 'Get your skinny arse inside before I break it with a kick.' Ha! Toby was finally showing his true colours.

Josie gave one last searching look towards the entrance, and unless he was seriously mistaken, Callum believed she was hoping for rescuers to come racing in. No, if the dread on her face was anything to go by, then she feared somebody else appearing there. Callum turned his attention on the entrance too. When next he checked, the others were inside, and the door was shut.

It was more than a minute before he heard the sound of an approaching vehicle. The driver had switched off its lights to crawl past the entrance. Callum couldn't see, but thought that the car continued on and must almost have reached the church path before turning. He heard it finally return and stop a few metres shy of the same gate he'd climbed over. Callum waited, fingers teasing the button on his knife, but it was another minute before he spotted movement on the far side of the gate. He held steady, observing as, first, the figure tested the gate and then, when he found it seized shut, he followed Callum's lead and scaled it. The figure jumped down, taking the landing in the bend of his knees and arms spread for balance: Perlman was a stocky build, but athletic with it.

Perlman paused where he'd settled. He scanned the grounds before turning his attention to the house, giving the impression it might not be his first time sneaking on to somebody else's property. He finally moved, and instead of heading for the back of the house, he approached the front. Tentatively he peeped in through one of the front windows, but Callum knew from experience that he'd see nothing important. Next, he approached Toby's Range Rover. He immediately went to the rear and checked inside: he hadn't arrived in time to see Josie and Danni ushered into the house, and probably hoped to find them tied up on the back seat, where a swift rescue could take place.

'Foiled again,' Callum whispered, and laughed nastily under his breath when Perlman's search came up short. Perlman looked across the garden to the gate. He lifted his cupped palms. Callum followed the gesture and spotted a second figure beyond the bars. It was the woman from the car. She pushed a hand between the bars and jabbed a finger, directing him towards the back. When he thought about it, Callum couldn't recall Steph locking the back door after she'd let him inside earlier. The woman moved from the opening, going towards the front entrance. The hedge was taller than her, completely concealing her from view; but it worked both ways, because she wouldn't spot Callum either. As Perlman headed around the far side of the house, Callum emerged from hiding and darted along the line of rhododendron bushes to go round to the opposite side.

He had been at the back of the house previously, but then it had been in daylight. Now darkness had fully descended, and if there was any ambient light from the moon or stars it was blocked by the thick crown of trees crowding the back garden. Some light shone through a window on an upper floor, but it made only an elongated oblong on the back lawn: as long as he didn't move through it, he was invisible. He took out his knife, and instead of flicking it open, he gently depressed the button while controlling the blade with his other thumb. Shame, because the sound of it snicking out always gave him pleasure, but under the circumstances it might alert his prey.

There were a few outbuildings. Plus the house had been added to over the centuries, with extensions forming nooks and niches in which it was easy to hide. He caught no sign of Perlman but doubted he was concealed in any of those spaces; he was simply slow to complete his approach. Callum moved swiftly to the paved path to the rear door. He settled between two large wheelie bins, crouching, knees flexed and ready to spring the ambush.

Raised voices emanated from within the house, and he wondered fleetingly what was happening. Whatever was going on, it was for his *superiors* to handle; he couldn't allow any distraction to derail him. Separate to, and louder in his hearing, he could hear the scrape of Perlman's shoes on the pavement, and his rapid, shallow exhalations. Callum held his own breath in response.

Perlman hove into view. He was bigger and stockier than he'd seemed from a distance. He was taller than Callum by several inches, probably outweighed him by half again, and his bulk was with muscle rather than fat. Toe-to-toe, fist-to-fist, it would be an unfair fight, but Callum didn't go in for the Queensberry rules or any of that Eastern martial arts honourable shit. As Perlman stepped past, craning for a look inside through the back door, Callum sprang, his left arm looping around Perlman's neck and his knife sinking between his ribs.

JOSIE

Josie blinked in astonishment at the sight of Pete, who moved towards them along the hallway. He held his arms to the sides, palms showing empty, unthreatening. He almost looked as if he was about to welcome them all home, as if Steph and Toby were a couple of old family friends. But his attention slipped from them, to Danni, and then to her, and she could see the war being fought within him. He was at first relieved to see them alive, and returned to their rightful place, but also terrified by the circumstances. Toby didn't help to soothe his nerves by taking out his pistol and aiming it at him.

'Pleathe, therth's no need for a gun,' Pete lisped, 'I did exthactly as I was warned and never called the polithe, or anyone else.'

He shot Josie an apologetic grimace, thinking she must believe him the worst coward. There had been points during the day when she had thought badly towards him, but her ire was unfounded. If their positions had been reversed and she had been the one warned not to call for help, or the hostages would die, she wouldn't have either. She couldn't tell him that, but tried to soothe his conscience by aiming a sad smile and gentle nod at him.

Steph's jaw set rigid as she stared at him. Toby set Danni to one side, with a warning not to move, while he ducked one way and then the other, checking that the rooms flanking them were empty.

'I sthwear there's nobody else here,' Pete said. He wiped his mouth with the back of his bandaged hand: the bandage was dark red with blood; the freshest glistened on it. 'Thorry,' he added, and his eyes shone with tears at how pathetic he sounded. He swallowed hard, and ensured that he had more control of his voice. 'You don't have to worry. You said you'd bring Josie and Danni home, safe from harm, if I did as I was told. They're what are important to me. I swear to you. I did not call the police.'

'Watch them,' said Steph.

She stabbed a finger at Pete, and then at the foot of the stairs. 'Sit down, and do not move.'

Pete did as instructed. He again looked up at Josie, trying to project his love, his shame, through the expressions on his face. She sent a silent question back at him. He misunderstood, only opened his mouth to touch trembling fingertips to an open slit at the end of his tongue. He nodded several times, barely detectable movements of his head, meaning he was in pain but otherwise all right.

Steph went to the kitchen. Franklin toddled ahead, sniffing semi-familiar territory.

In the hall, Josie and Pete watched each other, while Danni stood knock-kneed, and touching a finger to the end of her own tongue. 'Does it hurt?' she wondered.

Pete said, 'Only a little.'

'You sound like Daffy Duck,' she said, with a complete lack of sarcasm.

Pete grunted, and even Josie, her emotions all over the place, allowed a chuckle.

'All right, that's enough talking,' Toby said. The scratches Josie had gouged in his face were livid under the hall light.

'What happens now?' Pete asked.

'You shut up, that's what happens,' Toby said. He pointed the gun at Pete. 'Unless you want me to shut you up permanently.'

'Sorry,' said Pete.

'Fuck him,' said Josie, and caught a yelp of astonishment from Danni at her coarse words.

'Mrs Lockwood,' said Toby, 'I've tried keeping things as amicable as possible, but you keep on testing my patience. Would you rather I acted like Callum, and maybe beat in Pete's head with my gun barrel, before you'll show me any respect?'

'It's hard to respect anyone threatening my family.'

'Then don't make me do it.'

'Fuck you,' she said, and would've spat in his face if not for Steph's abrupt return.

'How did you get out of the pantry?' she demanded.

Obviously she was talking to Pete, but she still brought Josie around.

The pale woman was shivering. It wasn't through fear, but a flush of adrenalin.

'I worked my hands free,' said Pete. 'Then after that—'

'No. You are lying!'

'I'm not lying, honest I—'

Steph's face grew livid. 'There are garden ties all over the floor, cut by a knife, and the gag was also cut with a knife.'

'Yeah,' Pete agreed. 'I worked one hand free and got my hands on a knife. I used it to cut myself free. I wasn't lying, you just didn't give me a chance to finish.'

'Oh, you just happened to get your hands on a knife?'

'You've seen the junk in there, there could be ten knives, if you looked for them.'

She shook her head, unconvinced.

'Where is it?'

'Where's—'

'The bloody knife! Where is it?'

'I . . . I don't know. I think I maybe left it in the kitchen. I went to the sink to wash out my mouth.'

Steph shook her head, this time at Toby.

She stepped forward. Beside her the little dog wiggled, greeting Pete, expecting a belly rub perhaps. Rather than its master, Pete met the gaze of the dog. He was unaware that the woman had lifted her hand until it slashed across his cheek. Josie jumped at the effect of the slap, more by Pete's cry of dismay than how much it must've hurt.

'Lie to me again and I swear . . .'

'I'm not lying,' Pete croaked. A fresh dribble of blood rolled from his lips.

'You were so resourceful that you found a knife and freed your-self?' Steph glanced across at Toby, checking he understood there was more to reveal about his escape from the pantry. 'Explain to me how you were able to then remove the wedge jamming the door shut.'

Pete mimed jabbing with a knife. 'I did it with the knife. Put it under the door and forced the wedge free.'

It was a feasible explanation, and it gave Steph a moment's pause. Pete flicked a look at her, and it was his undoing. She must have read the deceit in his face, the way that Josie could often read him when he was telling a fib.

'No! Somebody else let you out,' Steph yelled, 'and you will tell me who.'

'I swear to you—'

A second slash of Steph's hand turned Pete's head sideways. Spittle flecked with blood sprayed from him.

'That's enough!' Josie yelled, and she lunged at Steph.

Toby was ready for her. He didn't shoot; rather he pivoted, extended a leg, and swept her feet from beneath her. Josie thumped down painfully on her backside. White-hot pain flared from her coccyx to the top of her skull. Toby curled a lip. 'Didn't we just go over the subject of your constant belligerence?'

Josie seethed – or she appeared to. Inside she was happy that her words and actions had both drawn the attention off Pete, and also off the subject of who released him. The last thing she wanted was for her captors to guess her sister was the one following, otherwise they might use her or Danni against Grace and draw her into a trap. She swore at Toby a final time, then rolled over on to her knees. Danni was fine, if not concerned for her mum, but Pete looked the worse for being slapped. She moved towards him, but Toby grabbed the back of her sweatshirt and dragged her to her feet.

'Bring them to the kitchen,' Steph commanded.

Toby rounded up his trio of prisoners, then ushered them forward with a jerk of his pistol.

By the time they entered the kitchen, Steph had already discovered where a large kitchen knife had been deposited in the bloody sink. Several cloths and tea towels were stained red. Steph ignored them, instead tearing off a sheet of kitchen paper from a roll on the counter. She used the wadded paper to wrap around the knife and pick it up to inspect it. She held it so that Pete could get a clear view of it. 'Is this the knife you found?'

He nodded; there was no other recourse.

'And you found it where?' asked Steph.

He flicked a look past her, indicating the vestibule leading to the cluttered pantry where he'd been held.

'Oh?' said Steph, and a cruel smile of victory writhed at the corners of her mouth. 'So you didn't find it here?'

She slid the knife into the single vacant slot in a wooden knife block. The knife's handle was a match to the others that formed the set. He was undone, in Josie's opinion, but Pete must continue the lie.

'I don't know how it ended up in the pantry, but it did.'

Without warning, Toby struck Pete a sharp rap with the barrel of his pistol. Josie could swear she felt the noise it made go through her teeth. Who knew how painful it must've been to Pete, but it sent him to his knees, hands cupping his torn scalp.

Steph ignored her downed partner, and instead glared directly at Josie. 'I'm no fool. I know somebody else has been here. We've been followed for hours now, and I believe it's by the same person that released *him*. Your computer is still unplugged, and so is the landline, I see, but it's safe to bet they weren't minutes before we arrived. I wonder what I'll find in the computer's search history if I choose to look, or who that call would go through to if I hit the redial on your phone.' She switched target, aiming her next words at Pete. 'Is there anything you'd like to confess before I have it beaten out of you?'

Toby stepped forward.

He halted in his tracks, Pete momentarily forgotten.

Josie, Danni, Steph – even the dog – all jumped in surprise and turned towards the back door.

It swung inward, cracking loudly against the vestibule wall, and feet slapped and drummed towards the kitchen door. For a second, it was as if the home had been breached by a hostage rescue squad, but then a familiar figure appeared in the doorway, his narrow shoulders and long legs still swathed in his off-the-rack suit, but his previously off-white shirt was now dotted with splotches, almost as dark in colour as his skinny neck tie. Callum Grieves still carried his flick knife, but his left hand was clamped tight to his face. From under it, more blood dripped on to his shirt.

Dazed, Callum stumbled into the kitchen. His one visible eye was bright with shock, but there was very little lucidity in his gaze as he snapped it over each of them. He said something, and it was a strained groan at best, and then his left knee folded, and he collapsed against the counter. Franklin scrambled to escape, while Steph stood transfixed a moment longer, wondering how, or if, she should help her lackey. Callum didn't give her a chance to decide: he slid off the counter, turning sideways in the air and slammed flat on his back on the floor. His hand fell away from his face, and it didn't matter how much Josie hated the sight of him, she still winced at how badly he'd been disfigured. His cheek was split open, a gaping wound where the underlying bone had collapsed, as had the lower edge of his left eye socket. The lids were already swelling around an eyeball full of blood and twice its normal size.

After her initial dismay, Josie allowed herself a second or two to silently cheer at Callum's downfall, but a celebration couldn't last longer than that when she had no idea where the turn of events might lead: probably not for the best.

GRACE

*C*all the police, Grace thought.

Call the police and let them handle things. Now that Josie and Danni are back home, time is against them, and you must call the police.

She left her phone in her pocket.

Instead she flitted along, staying close to the hedge so its shadow would help conceal her from anyone looking out of a window.

Adjacent to the front of the house, she paused, settled into the alcove in which the old gate once gave access on to the road. She couldn't see where Kyle had got to, but the last time he'd been in sight, he'd headed towards the back of the house, where he was more likely to see or hear what was going on.

She trembled.

She was fearful, yes, but she also shivered in anticipation of what she must do.

You know what to do!

For God's sake, just call the police, every fibre of her being screeched, but still she didn't take out her phone. She told herself it was because she would have to put away Kyle's revolver in order to make the call, and it would leave her unprotected. Other parts of her reasoned that the police wouldn't arrive in time to save her sister and niece, or if they did get there before they were executed, Josie and Danni would be used as human shields and die in the crossfire anyway. Their only hope was as she'd convinced Kyle only minutes earlier: he must cause a distraction, while she crept inside and helped spirit the hostages to freedom. It would only be once she had Josie and the others – she mustn't forget that Pete was inside too, and party to their plan – that they could safely call the police.

She had called ahead to warn Pete of the impending arrival of the Range Rover and its occupants. It gave Pete only minutes to try hiding the fact that he'd been freed by her, and that he'd been subsequently assisting her search for their loved ones. Pete, a blubbering wreck when first she found him tied up and bleeding in the pantry, had shown there was more steel in his spine than she'd originally credited him with. He could have fled the house, ensuring he was out of further harm's way, but he hadn't given it a second's thought when Grace said she'd need his help. He had agreed, and even sworn to her that, this time, nobody would lay a hand on either Josie or Danni while he still lived. She'd asked him to be careful, and play along with the abductors' demands until it was time to help her free the hostages. She told him that Kyle would cause a distraction, while she would enter the house, and to be ready when it came time for them to run.

'There are only two of them,' she'd reminded him. 'Between us and Kyle, we should be able to handle them with surprise on our side.'

Pete had croaked, 'Only two of them? What about the third one, the bastard who cut me?'

'There are only two of them in the car,' she'd said. 'The woman and a muscular, dark-haired guy.'

'He's the gunman . . . but what about the one with the knife, the evil bastard?'

'We've never seen a third one.'

'He was definitely here, do you think I invented him?'

'Of course not, it's just we've never seen him, and we've never noticed anyone following us. Maybe once the abduction took place earlier, he left, and went about whatever other fucked-up business he's into, but—'

Pete had cried, 'You have to believe me, he's there and he's a threat to us all! Please, Grace, don't underestimate him – be very, very careful.'

She would be a fool to ignore his warning, so every step she had taken was with the expectation of the previously undetected knifeman leaping out at her, but really, it was the thought about going up against the gunman indoors that gave her most pause. Kyle had shown her how to shoot, but without allowing her to waste a round. Dry-firing the revolver had given her the sense that when the thunder-crack and flames accompanied it, it'd be a different experience entirely, and not one she was prepared for.

'It's there mainly for show,' he'd reminded her, 'but you have to be ready to shoot. If it comes down to you or this gunman's life, who do you prefer gets shot?'

If anyone had posed the same question twenty-four hours earlier,

she wouldn't have been able to give an honest answer. She'd have
lied, said the right thing about not wanting to take another life, but
who was she kidding? Faced by certain death, she'd blow the head
off her would-be murderer first. Undoubtedly, he wouldn't pause to
shoot her.

Suspecting that the abductors would control the front-door
access, Grace had no intention of entering via it. Instead, she'd
asked Pete to leave one of the windows in an adjoining room open.
She was unsure if he had done as requested, and it took a swift
check at each window, gently pulling at the frames to see if any
would give. None did. The house was old, and building restrictions
demanded that a certain style of window had to be adhered to during
any renovations. The windows at ground level were in the sash style,
and required the use of a counter-pulley system indoors to open
them; thinking ahead, Pete must've chosen to leave another window
open for her ease. She moved further around the front of the building,
took the corner and found the window he'd chosen: it was to a
ground-floor toilet, used for convenience when Josie was at work.
The window at first looked shut, but a simple pull at one corner
opened it. Inside Pete had laid the latch atop its fastener, so that
during the briefest of inspections it would appear secure.

Grace teased the window as wide as possible, wincing when the
hinges squeaked through lack of use. She needn't have worried
about the slight noises, because they were nothing compared to
what was going on indoors. She heard shouts and scrapes, and more
irate conversation. Dreading that her loved ones were already being
murdered, she scrambled to get inside. She paused: Kyle had yet
to launch whatever distraction he had in mind, so she was probably
entering too soon. No! She must get inside, get close to where the
hostages were being held, and be ready to spring into action in an
instant.

More speed, she cautioned, *but less haste*. She'd be of help to
nobody if she fell head first into the bloody toilet bowl, knocked
herself unconscious and drowned. After securing the gun in her
pocket, she took care squirming inside, using one hand on the
window ledge to control her descent until she could fit through a
bent leg. She contorted her body, rising up, while feeling for solid
footing. She found the top of the cistern, but it had a pot lid prone
to easily being slid off. She reached for the lid, picked it up and
eased it out through the window. She allowed it to drop on to the

dirt nearest the wall, and was gratified when it didn't smash to pieces. She then used the corner edge of the cistern nearest the wall to support her weight. She drew in her other leg and then was able to step down on to the bowl, and then to the floor. Other than a few soft scrapes and grunts, she'd managed the precarious climb while avoiding alerting the bad guys. From the sounds of things, they had other concerns to deal with.

She took out the revolver, gripping it tightly in a two-fisted grip.

There was no way of figuring out what had happened but, by all accounts, Kyle had come through with his distraction tactic. From what she could tell, something had gone badly wrong for the abductors. A woman bleated expletives, and it wasn't Josie's voice. A man, sounding calmer, but still ruffled, shouted something that was almost a challenge. Unless the knifeman had returned ahead of the others, it was doubtful he was the one she could hear, so it was probably the dark-haired gunman. His voice diminished a little as she moved along the hall towards the back of the house, and she guessed it was because he'd left the kitchen. His muffled voice suggested he was either in the utility corridor, or outside.

Any second she expected to hear the sounds of gunfire, but it didn't occur. She made it to the kitchen, but couldn't enter blindly. She placed her back to the wall next to the door, holding the revolver up alongside her jaw like she was the star in a Hollywood action movie: did those heroes in the movies shake so hard they felt they were about to fall apart, did they sweat, did they smell their own terror rising from them in waves?

Before she lost all courage, she peeped around the doorjamb. It was a quick glance at most, but she saw enough to paint a close enough picture in her mind. Surprisingly, Pete, Josie and Danni were nearest to her. Next, the blonde woman she'd seen briefly at the motorway services, with her little white dog straining at the end of its lead to hide under the table. Another person lay on the floor, head towards her, feet towards the back door, and it was immediately apparent that it wasn't the dark-haired gunman. It was the other; the evil one who'd delighted in hurting Pete before. He was unmoving, while the blonde crouched over him, jabbing his shoulder to get a response.

She could only guess that Kyle was as tough as his reputation, and he'd dealt the knifeman an injury that had temporarily put him out of the game. The gunman, witnessing the knifeman's downfall, must have gone out for a reckoning with Kyle. For now, with no sound of gunfire, the chase must still be on. She darted another look into the kitchen. The tableau had shifted, but only subtly. Danni was now nearest her, and Josie only a step further beyond. Pete had positioned himself between them and the blonde woman: the woman, with her back to them, had no idea her hostages were on the point of running.

Still fearing that everything could end in disaster, Grace stepped silently through the door, and shut off a squeak of surprise from Danni with the flat of her hand. She drew Danni to her, even as Josie's eyes widened in disbelief at the gun her sister held. Pete was unaware that the escape plan was under way, and still held his position, blocking them from the woman. The little dog watched them though, his eyes bright coals in the dimness under the table. It'd be just like the yappy little thing to give the game away, Grace thought. But then she had pulled Danni into the hallway, and Josie followed quickly. They hadn't abandoned Pete; he knew they were on the move and would follow the instant he believed them safe: he was earning kudos for his bravery with Grace that she wouldn't have believed earlier.

Josie went to grab her in a hug, but there was no time. She shook her head, and used the gun to gesture her sister to run for the front door. With nobody in the hall, it was the quickest way out of the house. She leaned close to Danni's ear and whispered, 'Look after your mum, get her out of here, yeah?'

Danni's face lit up, and she turned to the task with a new sense of determination. She grabbed Josie's hand, and urged her to speed. Josie looked back over her shoulder, staring at Grace.

'I'm coming,' Grace mouthed, but it should also be apparent she didn't mean before she'd ensured Pete was out of immediate harm's way too. Before Josie could do the big-sisterly thing, and return to protect *her*, Grace adjusted her grip on the revolver and entered the kitchen.

KYLE

Pressing his back to the wall, he touched fingers to his side. They came away wet, and glistened under the weakest of starlight. Kyle grunted, and forced his hand over the wound, hoping that direct pressure would do the trick. If he survived, he was going to demand a couple of grand on top of his usual fee, to cover his loss of earnings while recuperating from his injuries – or to go towards his funeral if he perished. It was a ridiculous notion, and it held less water than his hand stemmed the blood from pouring down his side.

The wound to his ribs hurt like hell.

The pierced intercostal muscle had contracted, making breathing difficult and painful.

Luckily for him, it wasn't a fatal stab. Not yet. If he couldn't stop the bleeding, it would weaken and slow him down; he could even pass out. Blood loss wasn't his first concern, though; he was more interested in avoiding a bullet through his head.

It was a good job that Pete had reminded them about the third abductor. Grace had earlier mentioned the group was composed of a woman and two men, but they hadn't given much thought to where he'd gone when they hadn't seen the knifeman. Until Pete had brought him up again, Kyle had more or less dismissed him, and it had been a stupid mistake. Either the knifeman had waited here at the house all these hours, setting up an ambush, or he'd stayed in the background, following them even as they followed the Range Rover. Kyle didn't know the facts, only that the sneaky bastard had been in position to jump him.

As the knifeman sprang, looping an arm around his throat to drag him off balance on to his stabbing blade, Kyle hadn't been totally off-guard. A split-second after the bloke pounced, he reacted, trusting to thousands upon thousands of hours of training. He'd spun and battered back with an elbow at the same time. Turning away from the blade meant that it had barely pierced his hide when he yanked free. His elbow rammed his attacker in the gut, winding him, and slowing down a follow-up stab of the knife.

His opponent's face was a pale blur in the darkness. His fist –
augmented by brass – struck a single blow that landed on the left-
hand side of the man's face. The crunch confirmed to Kyle that
the punch had caused serious damage, but how much he couldn't
say. As the man reeled away, Kyle kicked at him, and caught him
somewhere between his knee and hip, preferably his balls, but it
was too dark to tell.

The entrance to the house was behind him.

Kyle could have smashed the knifeman again, put him down
cold on the ground, but what then? Should he enter the house with
only his brass knuckles and invite a bullet from the gunman? That
wasn't part of the plan: he was only supposed to cause a diversion,
to allow Grace to get inside undetected. He grabbed the knifeman
instead, and dragged him bodily around, and threw him towards
the back door. He shoulder-charged the wheeled rubbish bins,
causing enough of a racket to wake the neighbourhood, then raced
for the nearby outbuildings. He avoided a patch of light thrown
from one of the upper-floor windows, sticking instead to the thickest
clots of shadow. He made it almost to the temporary safety of a
garden shed when the pain hit, and he understood that the knife
had scored him deeper than he'd first thought.

He again tested for blood.

Yeah, he still bled like a bloody stuck pig.

He teased aside his jacket, pulled up his sopping shirt and craned
to see where the knife had gone in. It was awkward, especially in
the darkness, to inspect his injury. With his fingertips he could feel
something reminiscent of a tiny mouth, a couple of centimetres
wide, but complete with puckered lips. From its angle of entry, he
had to assume that the steel had nicked one, or perhaps two, ribs,
but also that he was very lucky not to have been injured worse: a
little deeper and his lung would have been punctured. If he hadn't
reacted as violently as he had, the knifeman could have opened him
front to back within another few seconds. For that reason, he felt
no remorse whatsoever at breaking the scumbag's face.

As he'd retreated, he had heard sounds indicative of the knifeman
stumbling indoors. A chorus of muffled sounds followed, none he
could make much sense out of, but then other sounds chased him,
not least the slap of feet along the paved walkway at the rear of the
house. He doubted his pursuer was the woman, intending setting
her little mutt on him, so it had to be the gunman. Back at the

service station, the bloke had appeared fit and strong. Kyle had been around fighters most of his adult life, and knew their type couldn't be pigeon-holed to a sole body shape – he'd known obese guys who were as fast and agile as hell, and skinny lads that were as strong as bulls – but the gunman had the look of a professional about him. Not necessarily a pro-boxer or martial artist, his look reminded Kyle more of a soldier, a professional killer.

But Kyle had also been around soldiers before, some of them the most professional of killers to be found anywhere. Up until a decade ago, he had been one of them.

If the gunman was ex-forces, or hell, even currently employed as a mercenary, then it was highly likely that he'd kept up his training to stay on top of his game. It was a decade since Kyle had left the army and, despite keeping his hand in at the gym, his training hadn't been as intense as it had been back in the day. He was rusty: attesting to the fact was the dripping wound in his side. If he'd kept a hold of the Webley instead of handing it over to Grace, he would feel a tad better about taking on the gunman *mano a mano*, but he'd be fucked if he was going to try some sort of bullshit ninja move and try to liberate the weapon from him. His best bet was to avoid being a target, whilst drawing away the gunman to give Grace a chance.

Once the gunman left the pavement, his footfalls fell silent, and Kyle had no idea where he was. He assumed that the man wasn't going to be easily lured into an ambush, but with his pistol would probably fancy his chances. His knuckleduster had worked its magic on the skanky-looking bloke, had knocked him three-cornered, and witnessing its result on his pal, it might give the gunman slight pause. To be fair though, if the pistol was in his hand, he wouldn't worry too much about his opponent getting within punching range before he finished him.

The outbuildings didn't offer safety. They formed a temporary bulwark between him and his pursuer, but once the gunman closed in, he would be done for. He could find access to one or the other, but what then? The buildings were small, and he'd be trapped inside: the phrase 'as easy as shooting fish in a barrel' came to mind. He looked for another way.

The gardens to the front and sides of the house were expansive, and no different at the back. The difference was that the hedge and the rhododendron bushes that dominated the front were conspicuous by their absence. Instead, a thorny row of hawthorn and bramble knitted an ancient metal fence; beyond that was some sort of drainage ditch, or stream. Trees on this side of the fence were few and sporadic, but were denser on the far side of the ditch. Whoever looked after the grounds, they had mowed the lawn but allowed a strip a couple of metres wide to run wild, allowing for the brambles and hawthorn to take over. The snaggles of thorns would ordinarily be uninviting, but could prove a lifeline to him. He immediately ran, clutching his side. He went down on his backside the instant he reached the taller grass, and squirmed to find a hiding spot under the spiny branches. Now that he was among them, he saw how brittle and dried the grass was, and how spindly the branches around his intended den. It was the best he could hope for under the circumstances. He wormed backwards on his belly, watching intently, gaze skipping from one outbuilding to the other, because he'd no idea where the gunman would emerge. He'd made it far enough that his heels met the old fence. He took care not to catch his feet between the bars, but splayed his knees so he could reverse in further.

The gunman edged out from beyond the shed, gun leading the way, as he cleared the very space where Kyle had crouched less than a minute ago. Finding the spot bare, the gunman turned towards the rear garden. Kyle snapped his head down, and instantly regretted his kneejerk response. Rapid movement, even in darkness, could catch the eye more easily than a slow, smooth movement. He tilted his head, checking if he'd been spotted. The gunman moved away at an angle, to get a wider view of the other small outbuildings: for now Kyle could breathe and try to consolidate his position. He dug his bloody fingers in his pocket, seeking his mobile phone.

Before they had left the car, they'd concocted a way to keep in touch with a pre-typed message ready to send from Grace's phone to his. Once she had her family safe out of harm's way, she had agreed to hit the send button: once he received the all-clear, he would go to ground and call for police reinforcements. For now, his message inbox was empty.

He had no way of knowing what was going on inside the house, and could only hope that his diversion had been enough to get Grace in undetected. Armed with his revolver, it should be deterrent enough to stop the blonde bitch from trying to stop her. Perhaps Grace had freed her family, but wasn't yet in a position to dig out her phone. He was seriously tempted to go for it and call the police, but what if he was wrong, and the captives were still under control? If the police arrived, would the criminals try fighting their way to freedom, murdering their hostages in an act of brutality? Would they perhaps realize that the game was over, and come out with their hands up, sparing the hostages? He couldn't be certain; under circumstances like these, people couldn't be trusted to react logically.

He slid away his phone, ensuring that if Grace called him, the screen's glow wouldn't give away his position but he'd feel it vibrate.

The gunman was on the move. Having cleared the sheds and outbuildings, he extended his search to the garden once more. He moved back towards his initial position on the paved walkway, then crouched. Kyle understood what he was up to: using the lower elevation, and the darker shadows cast by the starlight, he could probably spot the faintest indentations in the lawn. He was seeking where Kyle had run: Kyle's only saving grace was that the lawn was trampled in several places, dotted with footprints, probably made by Danni using the space as her playground.

After a few seconds, the man came out of his crouch and stood, scanning the garden, and Kyle understood he was allowing his peripheral vision to do most of the work: the faintest movement was easiest spotted from the corner of the eye rather than directly. Kyle held steady.

Some sound from within the house alerted him, and the gunman immediately spun on his heel and tracked back the way he'd come. He paused on the paved walkway, again looking out across the back garden. For one terrible moment Kyle thought that he'd been spotted, because the gunman's gaze came to rest on his hiding place. But another second or two after and the man had discarded finding him as being less important than what was happening indoors. He jogged for the path to the door where Kyle had earlier pushed his semi-conscious victim. Then the man was out of sight.

Kyle remained still.

The man's disappearance could all be a ploy to draw him out of concealment. Perhaps the gunman was giving him a few seconds to come out of hiding before springing out again and gunning him down.

From a distance, Kyle heard voices.

There was no way to separate the babble, so he couldn't tell who was talking, except that all the voices sounded female.

Kyle waited for a little longer, and when the gunman was a no-show, he felt more confident about leaving his hiding place. He began a slow crawl forward, feeling the thorns snag in his clothing, as if they were trying to hold him prisoner. He halted, tried freeing his clothing from the grasp of a tendril of brambles, and concluded that he was better off continuing reversing to the fence. He backed up until his heels once more touched the iron railings, and then drew up to a crouch. The majority of branches and thorns bowed over him, though there were plenty more entwined through the bars. He could see a clear passage though, and could move along it under cover of the thorny shrubs. Ten or fifteen feet along, he paused to check for movement at the back of the house. There was none, but his position now allowed him a view down the side of the house. Three figures ran for the gate he'd scaled on his way in to the garden. By their sizes and shapes, he guessed he was looking at Grace, Josie and Danni: there was no hint of Pete. As much as he meant the bloke no harm, Pete would just have to look after himself. It was on Kyle to help the women and the kid first.

He tested the fence. The bars, ancient and rusty, still formed a sturdy barrier. However, when he continued another few metres, he found where a couple had rusted enough to become unstable in their moorings. He forced the bars aside, forming a gap wide enough to squeeze through: he'd lose a layer of skin, but it'd be worth it.

Hurriedly he forced his way through, finding the hawthorn barbs loosening their grip on him as he tumbled on to the bank of the drainage ditch beyond. He allowed gravity to take him, and his body slid into the ditch with ease. On all fours he crawled to the top and peered below the thorny hedgerow. He'd made it into concealment in time to avoid discovery, because the gunman was outside once more, scanning the grounds. This time though, it appeared he wasn't the gunman's priority. The man started and moved at a tangent, heading for the side garden, and the gate where the women were still clambering over. Once he was around the house, he'd spot them, and was fleet enough on his feet to chase and pull down Grace, the last to attempt the climb.

Yeah, well, Kyle wasn't about to allow the fucker to have his way with her.

He shouted wordlessly, and immediately ducked low, so that the gunman wouldn't spot him, but would be slowed down by the sudden yell.

After a few seconds, Kyle raised his head with care.

The gunman had halted, and again scoured the grounds with his gaze, but obviously the surroundings had played with the acoustics and he hadn't pinpointed Kyle's location. During those few seconds of distraction, Grace made it over the gate. But not without being seen. From the front of the house, a figure bolted across the lawn, closely pursued by another.

The knifeman was back on his feet. Kyle's punch had left him injured and weak though, and he had little chance of catching Pete while stumbling after him like a B-movie zombie.

However, Pete wasn't proving too agile either, and wouldn't make it over the gate before the gunman joined the chase. The sisters and the girl beckoned Pete from beyond the gate: Kyle wished they'd run for his car – a prearranged manoeuvre planned with Grace – and get the hell out of there.

Grace was still yet to give him the go-ahead, but it didn't matter. They were clear for now, and it was time for reinforcements. He dug out his phone and hit 999.

Before his call could be answered, he heard a car engine, and its headlights washed across the lawn, causing Pete and the knifeman to stand out as dense silhouettes Hopefully Grace had taken the initiative and called for reinforcements.

JOSIE

t was too soon for Josie to believe they had made it to safety, certainly far too soon for any form of celebration other than relief. She wanted to throw her arms open and scoop up both Danni and Gracie and spirit them to another place, but her sister especially wasn't for leaving, not while Pete was still in danger too. Throughout the day and into the evening, Josie's opinion of her partner had swung with the regularity of a pendulum. One moment she despised his weaknesses, the next she admired his flashes of bravery, then she'd recall how much she cherished him, and in the next moment reflect on how never seeing him again might not be the worst thing that could happen. Her negative thoughts shamed her, and no amount of positives she aimed at him would negate them if she turned away when he was at his most vulnerable.

Pete had reached the other side of the gate, but he was gasping for oxygen and in his fear he couldn't seem to make his injured hand support him in the climb. Rather than scramble over the gate as the women and Danni had, he sank at the knees, and fell with one shoulder against it, while pawing pitifully through the gaps. Grace and Danni exhorted him to climb for his life, while all Josie could do was stare open-mouthed as Callum Grieves stumbled towards them. He was hurt, with blood pouring down his cheek and neck, but the agony and blood loss seemed to galvanize him, to stir his own need to inflict pain and draw blood. He could barely support his weight without stumbling, but his grasp on his knife was remorseless. He was senseless of the gun that Grace aimed at him or, if he was aware of it, he didn't care. He knew from her actions inside the house that Grace was reluctant to shoot, and probably believed he could take down Pete before she plucked up the nerve. By then he probably thought the sight of Pete gurgling on a slit throat would be enough to rob the fight from the rest of them.

A minute ago, when she'd had the chance, Grace should have gunned him down. She hadn't, choosing instead to try dragging Pete to freedom rather than blast the people threatening him. After Callum crumpled indoors, he'd been unconscious for less than a minute. He'd started awake, and almost came to his feet before recalling the situation he was embroiled in. His first instinct had been to search for where he'd dropped his knife, his next to touch his swollen eye, and thirdly to spin around with a snarl and slash at the person nearest him. Steph took a nick to her forearm, but she lunged aside, and immediately Callum sprang at Pete. Rapid slashes and darting stabs made ribbons out of Pete's forearms, but thankfully he avoided having his throat cut open. He didn't back away; he blocked the knifeman from chasing Josie and Danni down the hall. Danni tugged Josie's hand, exhorting her to get out, but Josie couldn't abandon Pete, or her sister.

She took a step back towards the kitchen, watching the two men jostle for a second or less before Grace intervened. She should've shot Callum, but instead she only forced the barrel of her revolver under his chin, screaming at him to back off. At the same time she yanked Pete away, and they both backed into the hall. Callum didn't initially follow: he seethed. Josie had no idea where Steph had got to, but she wouldn't risk the woman racing out the back and round the house to cut off their escape. And where had Toby gone?

With Grace and Pete following, she allowed Danni to urge her towards the front door. Josie took the lead, pressing Danni against the wall, protecting her with her body as she fumbled at the latches and handles. She must have opened and closed that front door a thousand times or more in the past year, and yet the task had thwarted her for longer than she liked. She found the correct combination of twist and pull at the same instant that Callum exited the kitchen. Before she'd thought of him as some kind of living scarecrow, now she imagined he was a scarecrow possessed by a demon from hell. His injured eye was so swollen it was solid red with blood and fit to pop, adding to the devilish imagery. He came at them, heedless of Grace's gun and her holler to back off: having not shot him the first time, he probably believed her threats were empty.

Danni helped Josie yank the door open, and all three women backed out, while Pete again set his feet for a fight. As injured as Callum was, it was a fight that Pete couldn't win: Josie knew it, Grace knew it. But it was her sister who again hauled Pete after them, then – once they were fleeing across the lawn – she released him so that she could run alongside Josie and Danni, encouraging them to run for the side gate, and the promise of a car parked beyond it.

The three of them had scaled the gate in seconds, but not so Pete. He was slower to follow, still torn between fight and flight, and it was obvious that Callum would spit him on his blade before Pete climbed the gate. He reached for Josie between the bars, and she clutched his hands, trying to impart love for him in a look she knew must be more of sympathy than anything. His fingers were slick with blood, and they plucked out of her grasp. He turned half on, trying to shoulder open the gate again, maybe thinking he could overcome decades of corrosion and overlaid layers of paint. It would take a battering ram to force it open.

Callum came on.

His deck shoes sank deep in the lawn. Each step was difficult for him, but despite that, his rage carried him forward, and he was seconds from launching on to Pete's back. Josie pushed Danni aside, so that the hedge obscured her view: she didn't want Pete's murder to be burned into her daughter's memory, not when she'd already witnessed enough trauma to make most adults crumble. Josie reached through the gate, prepared to try fending off Callum's stabs even as she knew that she couldn't save Pete.

Grace hollered warnings, but again she didn't shoot.

Josie was tempted to snatch the gun and blast Callum to death. Before this she wouldn't have believed it was in her to shoot another human being, but she'd make an exception for him. She'd sure as hell try clawing his one good eye out of its socket if she could get close enough.

Pete turned and faced his would-be killer. Palms up, he curled his fingers, inviting Callum to try him.

Callum halted, but not through concern over Pete's sudden show of bravery. Stark light washed the grounds.

Perhaps the knifeman thought the cops had arrived.

Josie glanced at Grace and saw a look of hope on her face too, but Josie had overheard what Grace hadn't. She knew that Steph had requested volunteers and that she'd arranged to meet them here at the house before continuing their search for the loot tomorrow. Not for the first time that day, Josie's guts turned sour as a large van sped up the drive, kicking up gravel. Her briefest impression of the van was that it was of a deep blue colour, with windows tinted for privacy. A sliding door on the side, probably double doors to the back but she couldn't see. The van was large enough to disgorge a dozen people.

If that wasn't bad enough, a second vehicle arrived. This one didn't enter the grounds as the van had, but continued on, and Josie understood that either Steph or Toby, both conspicuous by their absences, were probably guiding the reinforcements to assist in their recapture.

'Run,' she yowled, 'get to the car!'

Without another thought for anyone except Danni, Josie reacted. She spurred her daughter towards the Nissan Qashqai that Grace had followed them in, not knowing whether it was locked, its driver was onboard, or anything else.

When Grace didn't move to follow, Josie returned a few steps and clutched her sister's shoulder. She tugged Grace to follow.

'We can't leave Pete,' Grace said.

True, they shouldn't leave him alone, but Josie understood this was Pete's way of redeeming what must've felt like his earlier failures to protect them. 'He's giving us the chance we need to get Danni away,' said Josie. 'Let's not waste it.'

Pete looked back at them, and said, 'Just go. Get Danni some-where safe.'

'Pete,' Josie said, 'I promise you I *will*.'

He nodded and turned back to confront Callum.

The knifeman stood in indecision, uncertain who the new arrivals were and not ready to condemn himself by slitting open Pete in front of hostile witnesses.

Josie turned to chase after Danni towards the Nissan.

A figure stepped out of the darkness about ten metres to their left. Josie took a misstep, but only faltered for a second. Finding her balance, she ignored the man blocking the route to the path alongside the graveyard, determined to get Danni in the car and away in the opposite direction. However, the driver of the second vehicle had other ideas. After initially slowing down, the car sped up and Josie screeched a warning. The car would hit Danni before ramming into the Nissan.

Danni jumped and leapt aside, landing hard on her knees and palms. She cried out in pain as her flesh was abraded by gravel. She scrambled, coming back to her feet, and lunged for the far grassy verge. Beyond it was a wire fence, and regularly interspersed trees surrounding a ploughed field, and maybe a quarter-mile distant was the Welsh border. It was tempting to encourage her daughter to keep on fleeing; as if the border offered an insurmountable barrier that the bad guys couldn't cross. Danni turned and stared at the car, which hadn't come close to flattening her: it had halted a good five metres short of her.

The driver's door swung open, and disgorged a figure wholly too massive to have fitted comfortably inside. In the dark behind its headlights, Josie could only make out a huge hulking shape of sloping shoulders, and a head as big and cylindrical as a propane gas bottle. Danni took a step towards the stranger, bent quizzically at the waist, as if the extra few inches would help discern his features beyond the headlights.

Josie had halted mid-stride when screaming the warning at Danni. She began sidestepping towards the verge, stretching a hand to Danni. The big man moved from his car, taking confident strides, and covering the ground alarmingly fast. Josie darted glances at him and her daughter.

'Run, Danni. Run!'

It was Grace who had shouted.

Josie also ran, but it was towards Danni.

Her daughter had a look of wonderment on her face. As Josie grabbed her, and tried scooping her in her arms, Danni twisted free and set her feet on the ground again. She took a step towards the giant, her eyes diamond-bright, grinning her gap-toothed grin at Josie. 'Mum, it's OK. It's only Coal Axe. He's my friend.'

Danni avoided another snatch by Josie, and took a step towards him.

'No, Danni, don't. He isn't your friend. He's—'

The one who Josie recalled was named Kolacz proved in the next instant exactly *what* he was.

He lunged, and a hand twice the size of Josie's circled Danni's throat. He lifted effortlessly and Danni was plucked off the ground and she slumped over his opposite elbow.

Josie screeched a war cry, and Grace threatened to shoot, but the giant was unmoved by their threats. He held Danni, bent backwards over his arm, as he returned to the car. The sisters pursued him, but there was nothing they could do for fear of hitting Danni, or before he could crush Danni's throat or snap her spine.

He tilted his head on one side, smiling in victory, and Josie got the message as soundly as Grace. His unspoken instruction said, 'Give up, or the girl dies.'

KYLE

The instant the car accelerated towards the trio of females, Kyle darted beyond the cones of its headlights, to crouch again at the edge of the road, this time on the side nearest the ploughed field. He suspected that the new arrivals weren't rescuers, rather reinforcements summoned by the criminals. As he observed, bearing his weight equally over each heel, he remained still, and his silhouette merged with the other dense shadows at the roadside. He didn't move even as the car came to a halt, and Danni, who'd at first been rushing to his Nissan, went down on her knees. The girl scrambled for the grassy verge, but then the car door opened and she made the mistake of stopping.

A figure emerged, an inkblot expanding on water. How he'd fitted in the front of the car was a mystery because he was huge. Kyle was known for supplying door staff to the rougher bars and night-clubs in town, and some of those were imposing people, but they'd be like kids standing before this bruiser. For a second, Kyle tested the weight of the knuckleduster in his hand, thinking it could be wholly ineffective against that brute: it'd be like trying to crack granite with a toffee hammer. Going up against that man gave Kyle pause.

He wasn't a coward, just a pragmatist.

He needed a weapon more powerful than half a kilo of metal. He wished again he'd given Grace the knuckleduster and kept the revolver instead. She sure as shit wasn't putting it to the use for which it was designed. The brute took no heed of the Webley, or of Josie's screams, when he grabbed Danni and carried her towards his car. The women danced futilely, feet drumming the tarmac, moving at first towards and then retreating a few steps. Grace held out the revolver, and she must've been commanded to drop it, because she tossed it away as if it was burning hot.

It was a stupid reaction to the threat the man must have made, but one that might benefit them all in the long run. Next, he watched as every effort the women had made to escape was negated by them sidestepping towards the gate they'd recently clambered over. From his angle, Kyle couldn't see what was going on beyond the hedge, but by the sound of things, Pete wasn't able to put up much of a fight against the knifeman. Kyle was tempted to spring to action, but at what cost? He'd lost sight of the gunman, and for all he knew he could be back in his sights the second he moved. Voices filtered from beyond the sounds of Pete's beating, a woman, and more than one male jabbered excitedly. Any of the closest neighbours over-hearing could be forgiven for believing Josie was throwing a garden party.

The sisters put up their hands.

The giant shook Danni, and the little girl squawked in alarm, or was it disappointment? She must have fallen into a swoon from the pressure around her throat, because she suddenly bucked and twisted in the man's grasp. The sisters grasped at each other, unsure whether to attack or stay their ground. The girl was held aloft, while the giant made a shooing motion with his spare hand. The sisters hurried to comply with his instruction: they didn't climb back over the gate, they followed the hedge to the front of the property, no doubt with orders to present themselves as prisoners once more of the blonde woman and gunman. The giant watched them, and while his back was turned, Kyle took a moment longer to check he was unobserved. Once the women had disappeared beyond the curve of the hedge, and approached the entrance gate, Kyle slowly straightened. He stood again, mouth open to sharpen his hearing, eyes still to benefit from his peripheral vision: he was confident that he wasn't being watched. He began a steady trot forward, keeping to the verge so that his footfalls were deadened.

The giant took Danni the shorter route, handing her over the gate into somebody else's hands. Once unburdened by his hostage, he walked after the women, ensuring they behaved exactly as he'd warned them. He had no idea Kyle was behind him, and therefore no reason to look back. Judging where Grace had slung the Webley, Kyle rooted around in the grass. He'd misjudged its trajectory. The gun wasn't where he'd expected, so he had to widen the search. He spotted it, partly buried under longer grass. He crouched to retrieve it, grimacing at the dirt he saw clogged the barrel: shooting the gun before it was cleaned could prove hazardous. But if push came to shove, he'd risk an eye or even a hand rather than give his life without fighting back.

So much for being pragmatic, he thought.

He glanced to the gap in the hedge. Through it he could see Pete, lying on the lawn. He lay without moving, a curled foetus, his head wrapped in his arms. His clothing was dark with blood. Standing over him was the knifeman, his blade glistening darkly. The darkness otherwise conspired against Kyle, so he still couldn't tell how badly he'd injured the man: not enough by half, because the bastard was still standing and capable of hurting Pete. Kyle expected it to have been him that took Danni from the giant, but it wasn't. She was not in view, but he could hear her weeping.

Contemplating shooting the knifeman, then going over the gate to confront the others, Kyle began to move for the gap in the hedge. He made it only a couple of steps before caution caught at his heels and drew him to a halt. He was now armed better than before, but he was still outnumbered, and probably stood more chance of getting the hostages killed than freeing them. He moved aside, put his back to the hedge and took out his mobile phone again. He hit 999, and as his call was answered, he was short and to the point. He ended the brief call, but pulled up another function, then stuck the phone in his shirt pocket; only the top edge peeked above the material.

Taking several deep breaths, he held the revolver with his right hand against his sternum, while his left fingertips plucked out the dirt clogging the barrel. He was about to move when a voice addressed him: he was yet to hear the gunman, but Kyle believed it had to be his voice.

'Kyle Perlman,' the gunman called. 'We know it's you out there. Yes, *Kyle Perlman*, we know your name. We know it was you who hurt our friend, and we know you are probably looking for an opportunity to come to your friends' aid. You can't help them, so here's what you are going to do instead. You are going to surrender, show yourself and come out with your hands above your head.'

Kyle said nothing. How had they discovered his name? He couldn't imagine how they'd learned it, unless perhaps from Pete, but it was unlikely, seeing as Pete was so still he must be a dead man. No, the knifeman had been hiding, ready to spring an ambush, so was probably aware that he and Grace were following his pals: they probably had contacts who'd identified him from his car ownership details. So what? They knew his name: he'd brand it on to each of their fucking foreheads, given a chance.

'I know you can hear me, Kyle,' the gunman went on. 'Come

out, surrender, and we promise we won't make your family suffer. That's right, we know about your ex-wife. We know about your boys. We know where they live. Whose life is most important to you, Kyle Perlman; the lives of your sons or of a little girl you barely know?'

Kyle chewed his bottom lip.

Earlier that afternoon, he'd told Grace that he'd kill anyone who threatened his children. At the time she'd probably believed his words were bravado, but no. It had not been an idle boast.

'I'm coming out,' he called, and stepped into the gap in the hedge.

The knifeman stared back at him, one side of his malformed face twisting into a pained grin. But then his one good eye rested on the gun in Kyle's hand and he loosed a croak of dismay,

Kyle squeezed the trigger and the revolver barked.

DANNI

The few fond memories Danni had recalled from her time before the accident mostly revolved around Coal Axe. Back then, he'd treated her with kindness, affection even, and he had shared his sweets with her, where nobody else got a look at them. Even as a small child, Danni had thought that Coal Axe could be scary – never towards her, though. He used to sit her on his knee and tease or curl her hair between his sausage fingers, and he'd sometimes stroke her knees or gently pat her bottom, and in her innocence she hadn't sensed anything wrong, other than that he liked her. Her mam didn't like it when Coal Axe petted her, but she couldn't say or do anything, except be called the horrible C-word, and sent away. Mel needn't have worried, Danni had thought in her simplicity, because Coal Axe was her friend. But now her mum, her *real mum* Josie, had warned her that he was nothing of the sort, and as usual her mum was right. Mel had also been right.

What kind of friend would squeeze her neck till she went unconscious and then hand her back to the awful people she had just escaped from? She had run towards Coal Axe, expecting him to wrap her in a comforting embrace, to protect her from further harm, but he'd shown he was as bad as all the others. He was as bad even as Barker, and that was tough for her to accept.

Toby held her, his fingers entwined in the collar of her sweatshirt. He had his gun out, but it was pointed at the ground. He'd looked nice the first time she'd seen him, like a handsome celebrity, but faster than some kids should, she'd learned that beauty was only skin deep. She thought that if she could peer inside Toby, Coal Axe, and especially Creepy Callum, she would find dirt, and pus and venom, and all sorts of nasty stuff. Steph, for all she was pretty in a cold and aloof way, was as filled with nastiness as the men; there was a time when she'd fancifully imagined Steph as a vampire queen, but Danni had reassessed, and now thought of her as a different kind of blood-sucker: an albino leech. She moved in a wriggly, squirmy way as she stood in front of another man who had been disgorged from the van. He sat in a large electric wheelchair. He could propel himself by way of a small lever on one of the arm rests, but still his ever-present companion stood directly behind him. Earlier, Danni couldn't recall the nurse, and it was little wonder, because the tall, skinny man looked like a skeleton in need of the chair more than Freda. His features were bland, with thin lips and watery eyes, his hair short and colourless, and his skinny neck protruded from the collar of his tunic like a spoon handle from a cereal bowl. Danni believed if she saw him again, she would remember him, but not if he was stumbling along in a pack of brain-eating zombies.

Freda looked frailer than she remembered. Back when she was a little kid, he'd towered over her in his chair, his square, underslung jaw like the blade of a bulldozer as he'd glared down at her. Now she was taller than he was when seated, and not much skinnier. Freda was wasting away, diminishing before her eyes, and he couldn't disappear quickly enough for her. No, she mustn't discount him so easily. Of all those horrible people, Freda was the worst. He was the one who'd sent Steph, Toby and Callum in search of her, and been behind all of the hurt those three had dished out. He was the one who had turned Coal Axe against her. No, Freda's hulking bodyguard had never felt any affection for her, only an unwholesome liking. Danni was a kid, but she wasn't a little kid any more: she knew and understood more about adult stuff than she sometimes let on to her mum. She knew what Mum and Pete got up to in the privacy of their bedroom, and she knew also that there were some weirdo men that liked to do stuff like that with little girls and boys. She'd had the 'stranger danger' warning drummed into her by her mum, and not only to protect her identity, but to keep her out of the clutches of a filthy-minded man like Coal Axe.

She sneaked a glance up at Toby. His attention was fully on Freda, only he kept on calling the wheelchair-bound man Leonard, like the actor that played Spock in the oldest version of *Star Trek*. Freda, or Leonard, or whatever, didn't pay Toby much attention, choosing instead to direct his questions at Steph. Steph wriggled and squirmed again, but nothing she said appeared to satisfy her boss. Freda jabbed a finger and, following his gesture, Danni turned to where Callum stood over Pete. Pete was the person that Danni had closest to a father; not that she could think of him as Dad without knowing it was untrue, but she loved him all the same. She didn't like to see him like this, beaten up, bleeding, kicked while he was down. The others all seemed to think it was OK, though, because not a single one of them thought to help him. Danni feared he was dying. Surely all of the blood she could see glimmering wetly in the dark hadn't come from one person?

A clatter of footsteps in gravel, and they all turned to observe the entrance to the drive. Her mum and Aunt Grace entered the grounds, holding each other in mutual support and fear. Within a few seconds, Coal Axe appeared beyond them, walking nonchalantly, confident they'd do exactly as they'd been instructed. Danni's stomach knotted at the sight. Her mum and aunt had an air of total despair about them, and she knew it was because of her stupidity, and how she'd run into Coal Axe's hands. Before, Aunt Grace had waved around a gun. She'd lost it, but apparently Coal Axe hadn't found it, or else he'd stuck it down the back of his trousers or somewhere.

Danni dropped her gaze and spotted Franklin. The little dog was the only friendly face among those surrounding her. His ears and eyebrows danced, and his tongue hung out. He panted, the noise like a distant steam train. She'd heard that small children and dogs could sense evil – it was something to do with being innocent and nearer to God – so the poor little dog's life must've been *interminable*, constantly being so close to all those monsters.

Danni thought, *I'll rescue you from them, Franklin.*

In truth, she meant to first save her mum and aunt, herself, and Pete, and even whoever it was who had helped Grace follow them, but Franklin was right there before her, the catalyst for her promise.

She winked at him, blew a tiny kiss, and she would swear later that his panting grew quicker, as if excited by the prospect of freedom.

She turned towards Toby.

A gun barked, the flash lighting the scene. Callum almost fell on his backside, before regaining balance. Toby jerked in surprise, but then straightened, bringing up his pistol.

He held her collar, but had mostly forgotten about her, while he'd joined Steph in explaining to Leonard/Freda how they were confident that his money could be found at the train museum, but that they needed more hands and more time, to avoid drawing attention to the hunt. Now he was on high alert, seeking the source of the gunshot. Mistakenly, he deemed her less of a concern than he should have: Danni was tall for her age, but despite being gangly and awkward, she was stronger than she looked, and also more flexible. She drove the tip of her knee between his legs.

The wind gusted from Toby, and he jerked forward at the waist, his knees nipping together. His eyelids crunched tight, and a groan of abject torment leaked from between his gritted teeth. The grip on her collar didn't lessen; if anything it tightened. But that was OK, because Danni dropped low, twisting and pulling, and she yanked free of her sweatshirt, leaving it hanging, partly inside out, in his grasp.

She didn't shout instructions at her mum or aunt, because it should be apparent what to do. They took her lead and ran. Coal Axe might very well be a monstrous figure, a man capable of beating most men to a pulp in a fight, but he lacked the women's agility. They danced around him with little trouble, while he ineffectively swept his big arms about, and hurtled out of the front gate they'd recently come through. There was nothing Danni could do for Pete, but hopefully if she were chased, the others would leave him alone, and if he was able he could maybe hide. She checked to see, and yes! Creepy Callum was on her trail, though he was limping and wincing in pain with each step. She ran directly for the side gate, and launched over it with very little effort: determination had added wings to her heels. She absorbed the landing with bent knees, and then bounded away. Callum's groping hands missed her by a fair distance, but she heard his hissing curse and the impact of his chest against the gate. Another man shouted something, and she knew without looking that it was Toby, despite the pitch of his voice being sharper than before. She grinned, a rictus grin, because fear still gripped her.

Her mum and Aunt Grace raced towards her. She headed for the parked Nissan, but this time Mum shouted and lashed her hand back and forward, warning her to ignore the car this time. Danni understood; before they all could get inside and the engine started, Callum and Toby would be upon them. Danni swerved, and headed for the path beside the village graveyard.

She glanced back. Seeing was difficult out beyond the headlights and dull gleam cast from the house, but she spotted her mum and aunt once more. They kept to the far side of the road; clear of the gate over which Callum attempted to scramble. The horrible man shouted curses at them, or maybe they were aimed at his frustration.

Toby's shouts mingled with his: Toby wanted to be first over the gate. Danni kept running, conscious that she'd given both men reason to hurt her.

A figure crouched at the roadside.

Danni balked. She scrambled for balance, her breath caught in her chest. But the man made no attempt to grab her, and in a blink she understood that he was Grace's friend. He was the source of the gunshot that had given her the opportunity to take Toby by surprise. He held up his left palm to her. She didn't stop, but that was not his intention. It was to show he meant her no harm: his hand looked darker than it should have, even in the darkness. He returned it to where he clutched his side. He must've also been the one who had smacked Callum in the head, but he hadn't come out of the scrap unhurt. His own blood smeared his hand.

Reaching the entrance to the path, Danni halted. On previous occasions she'd only ever walked the path in daylight. Now that it was dark, she wasn't so keen on wandering about so close to a graveyard: she was old enough to know what adults got up to in bed, but not old enough yet to have shed an uncanny terror of the dark and of what went on in graveyards after the lights went out. She danced from one foot to the other, her fingers flexing open and closed, while she waited. Her Aunt Grace was first to materialize out of the darkness. For a dread-filled moment, she thought her mum had sacrificed her freedom to allow Danni and Grace to escape. But that wasn't it: Mum appeared seconds later, huffing and puffing at the extra strain. Grace was several years younger than her mum, and a whole lot physically fitter.

Danni ran into Grace's embrace, but she didn't linger before running instead to her mum. Josie held her tightly, and all three headed for the graveyard path. Danni checked for pursuit. The friendly gunman was in sight, still bent over, but retreating slowly after them. The bad guys couldn't be too far behind.

'Here,' her aunt said, and indicated a place where the wall had partially collapsed. 'Danni, climb over first.'

Danni peered over the fallen stonework. Rows of ancient headstones filled the space, some of them crooked, others fallen down altogether, some still standing resolutely against the decades and perhaps centuries. They looked like the decaying snaggle teeth of an elderly but gigantic man-eating ogre. She shook her head at the suggestion.

'They'll catch us in minutes if we keep running,' Grace said. 'It's best we hide, and where better than in there?'

'It's too scary,' Danni whimpered.

'I'd rather face a ghoul than those two chasing us,' Grace said.

Danni wouldn't. The last thing she wanted was for a vengeful ghost to drag her to hell.

Her mum took any decision to continue running from her. Josie grabbed her hand and went first, gently but firmly tugging Danni to follow. Once in the graveyard, Danni wasn't as perturbed, but the skin crawled between her shoulder blades when she thought about the number of spectral eyes observing them. It was silly kid stuff to believe in ghosts, wasn't it? Surely if the dead could come back to torment the living, then Barker would have haunted her, seeing as Mel was no longer around? Maybe he did haunt her, and it was he who had somehow sent the message to Steph where she could be found living. No, that was a plainly daft notion. Steph must've found out by a source other than the supernatural.

Several rows in, Mum pulled Danni close and they crouched behind a large sandstone headstone; her aunt hid behind the next marker along. Grace's friend, the stockily built man with the gun, hadn't followed them into the graveyard. When Danni checked, she thought she spotted movement next to the perimeter wall, a lowered head darting towards a fresh hiding place further along the path.

'Kyle's trying to draw them away from us,' said Grace, as if reading Danni's mind.

'Hasn't worked,' her mum groaned, as another figure materialized at the collapsed portion of wall. Even in the darkness, it was apparent that it was Callum Grieves. His spiky hair caught the tiniest glimmers of starlight, and made it look as if he was wearing a crown of ice-crystals as he stepped over the tumbled stones. He clutched his ever-present knife in his right hand, the steel also flashing as if coated with hoarfrost. A second figure flitted past the gap, Toby hot on Kyle's heels.

Callum paused at the edge of the graveyard.

He didn't move for several seconds. Danni wondered if he contained so much evil that the holy place repelled him, the way a crucifix could chase off a demon. In the next moment he proved that the hallowed grounds held no fear for him. He stepped forward, and bent down to touch fingertips to the grass, testing for freshly broken blades. Some of the graves were ancient and overgrown, untended by descendants too distantly separated from their ancestors to care. Fleetingly, Danni thought of how few times she had been to her first adoptive dad's grave, but for all she knew, it was a regular visit made by her mum while Danni was at school. She made herself a promise that if any of them failed to get out of this alive, she would never forget them, and she would visit their graves every Sunday without fail.

Why was she so interested in burial places, while under such duress? She studied the headstone they hid behind. It was worn by age, the name of the deceased all but scoured by wind and rain. She recalled sitting next to a similar gravestone once, and Mel was there too, her hands dusty. She tugged on Mum's wrist, and gestured. Josie said 'Mmm', as she sometimes did when her mind was busy elsewhere.

As if he heard, Callum stood erect. His gaze swept the grounds. Danni couldn't see his features, but knew that one side was as swollen as a balloon, and the eye on that side was as good as useless. His one eye wasn't enough to pick them out where she crouched with her mum. But his first steps took him directly towards them. Danni tensed, preparing to run, but her mum held her down. 'Don't move,' Josie whispered.

Callum stopped, peered all around, and then turned ninety degrees, and began a faster walk between the graves in the direction of the church. Grace crept up her head to observe him go. She held out a cautioning palm to them, and once Callum was distant enough, she held up her thumb. Danni and her mum bunny-hopped across to join her.

'Little bitches, little bitches, come out, come out wherever you are,' Callum sang in a creepy taunt that carried over the rows of headstones.

'Not by the hair on my friggin' chinny-chin-chin,' Grace wheezed sourly.

Danni couldn't resist a quick check to confirm Grace hadn't cultivated any facial hair since last she'd seen her. Grace's chin was as hairless as Danni's.

Callum continued to move away, twirling his knife.

From elsewhere there were other noises, a brief scuffling and thudding sound, and then a gun fired. Kyle and Toby. Whoever had got off the first shot, Danni had no way of knowing. A different gun replied: Crack! Crack! Crack!

Mum and Grace held on to each other, with Danni between them, encircled by both their arms. Their reaction was natural, but pretty pointless, because she doubted that their bodies would stop a bullet reaching her. Even she knew that distance – and as many headstones as they could put between them and the guns – was the best defence. Danni ducked out of their embrace, and headed away, running at a crouch to each successive row of graves. The adults followed. Sadly, their en-masse flight to escape the gunfight was noisier than intended, and Callum's shout of victory rang out like the hunting cry of a nocturnal beast. Danni sought him, and could see a blur of movement at the rear of the church. He was running parallel to them, trying to find a way to cut them off. Danni was familiar with what lay beyond the graveyard on that side, and it was open fields sweeping down to the River Dee. If they could keep ahead of Callum, they could possibly jump in the river and let it carry them beyond his grasp: stupid idea. There'd been little rain in weeks, and the river was barely knee-deep there.

Besides, Mum and Grace had other ideas to trusting to a river to whisk them to safety. They turned to face Callum, standing apart so he had only one target at a time.

'Danni,' said her mum, and her voice was brimming with conviction. 'Get over the wall and keep running. Don't stop until you find a house with lights on inside. Get help. Ask for the police.'

Grace dipped her hand into a pocket and came out with her mobile phone. 'You know how to work one of these, yeah,' she asked with a wry twist of her mouth. 'Soon as you're safe, you can call the cops yourself.'

Danni took the phone. It was a smart phone. She didn't own one, not yet, but she'd seen plenty, and she was fairly sure she could find her way around it better than either of the adults. On the screen, it showed that Grace had already tapped in a contact number, and she guessed it was probably Kyle's. Best she avoid calling him by accident, when the ringing phone might make him a target for Toby. She cancelled the call and began tapping out 999.

'Go, Danni, go now!' her mum insisted.

Danni backed up, but she wasn't going to run away like a frightened little rabbit. Not when there wasn't any need.

Callum advanced towards them.

His working eye darted from Grace to her mum, then to her, and he snarled at the phone in her hand.

'I'd better make this quick, huh?' he sneered.

The adults moved apart, placing headstones between them and Callum. It looked for a moment as if they were opening a gap in their defences so he could get at Danni. She didn't hang around. She darted back and then turned towards the perimeter wall. It was still several metres away when Danni stopped. Callum also stopped. Both women were beyond his reach, and he was trying to decide who to go for first. Apart from following her at a distance, he was unfamiliar with Grace, but Josie had attracted his ire on several occasions already. He angled towards her, with her mum sidestepping in time to keep gravestones between them. Her mum darted a glance to check on Danni. Danni was safe for the moment, with time enough to hit the call button.

Callum yelled and lurched after her mum.

STEPH

'You have a lot of explaining to do, Whizzer. How is it one of my most competent people has managed to make a mess of such a simple task?' Freda snorted in annoyance. 'I'm indebted to you for finding Daniele, but I should have sent Volos sooner, and had him squeeze the answers out of the little brat.'

Steph didn't immediately have the answers that Freda demanded. She had requested extra people to assist with the search for the stolen money, expecting paid monkeys, not the organ grinder himself. Of all those who might have arrived, the last people Steph had expected at the Lockwood home were her boss, Leonard Freda, and his henchman, Volos Kolacz.

'I had everything under control,' she reassured him. 'I have a location for the money, but staying there, trying to search the area in darkness could have attracted unwanted attention.'

'Tell me again how you had everything under control.' Freda flicked a hand at where Pete lay on the lawn. After his heroic stand, the man had taken a hellish beating from Grieves and Toby, and was unconscious: if not for his noisy laboured breathing, she'd have suspected him dead already. 'How do you plan on covering this up? How do you intend shutting up the others involved? I take it they have learned my name by now, and what my interest in Daniele is?'

'Davis and Grieves will silence them.'

'Will they? By all accounts, neither of your boys has managed any better than you have to contain a troublesome woman and a little girl. It's fortunate I was in the area on other business and could come and take over before you ensure we all end up in jail.'

'Until now we needed to keep Daniele and Josie amenable. We needed them to find your money, Freda. We don't any longer.'

'The money is not back in my hands yet,' he reminded her. He looked again at Pete. 'Jakub,' he said, and his nurse stirred at the summons. 'Go see to him.'

'You want me to help him?'

'No, I wish him silenced.'

'Of course.' Despite his answer, Steph spotted the reluctance in the nurse's demeanour. It had nothing to do with having taken a Hippocratic oath, nor any other morality in practice, only that Jakub had never been – to Steph's knowledge – asked to murder anyone before. Perhaps this was a test set by Freda, but one to trick a negative reaction from her. Steph hid her unease well enough, or perhaps not, because one corner of Freda's mouth twitched.

'On second thoughts,' and he waved over Kolacz. 'Perhaps we should leave it to a professional, eh, Volos?'

Since his mishandling of the women prisoners, Kolacz's reluctance to get too close had been noted by Steph. Volos, whose name aptly meant 'ox-like', unless she was mistaken, was a terrifying individual, but not without having a wary fear of his employer. He knew he'd fucked up, as much as Steph had in many respects, and might expect some form of punishment in due course. He moved with more alacrity than normal, keen to show Freda he could still be relied upon.

Her dog cowered away from the giant. Steph pulled Franklin to order, using the few seconds to manhandle the little dog to conceal her emotions. She hadn't balked at violence in the past, not much, but when Kolacz was involved, it always brought to mind Barker's fate when he'd displeased their boss. She wondered if Freda had already put in an order for some steel oil drums, and couldn't help worrying that he'd requested enough to sink all involved to the bottom of the English Channel.

Pete mewled in fear.

Maybe he had not been as sound asleep as he'd made out. As Kolacz strode towards him, Pete pulled up to his hands and knees, and he began a slow, pained crawl away. He didn't make it more than a few metres before Kolacz grabbed him. Steph avoided watching, but she heard the big man grunt, and then there was the whistle of clothing rubbing against clothing, and Pete made a gargling sound.

From perhaps a hundred metres away, a gun fired.

They all flinched.

When another gun returned fire with a close grouping of three shots, Steph danced in place, looking for somewhere nearby to take cover. Kolacz dropped Pete in surprise. The giant wasn't immune to bullets: he covered his head with his forearms and backed towards Freda. Their boss was blasé when ordering the deaths of others, but showed his true colours when under personal threat: swearing, he hit the controls on his wheelchair, and reversed towards the van. The electric wheelchair was an all-terrain brute, and yet it didn't move as quickly as he'd like across the deep, mossy grass. His nurse grasped the handles and helped pull the chair out of the line of fire.

Leaving Pete lying on the lawn again, Kolacz backed up, intent on protecting Freda but not at the expense of taking a bullet.

'We have to get out of here,' Freda called, and Steph was unsure if he included her in his assessment. Directly to Kolacz he said, 'Go get your car. Those gunshots are going to wake the neighbourhood, and the Old Bill won't be far away.'

His words proved too prophetic. Before he could speed up the ramp, allowing access to the rear of the van once more, and before Kolacz had made it halfway to the exit, blue lights lit up the night.

A police car pulled directly into the grounds, and continued up the drive. Effectively it blocked the van from reversing: it had parked too close to Toby's Range Rover, for Jakub, the nurse-cum-driver, to manoeuvre around it, too.

Freda exchanged a grimace with Steph. 'Deal with this,' he said, 'or I swear I'll have Volos snap your neck and hand your skull over to the coppers.'

Steph clutched the dog's lead tightly, and affected a terrified expression. Perhaps she could pose as Josie and fool the police until she could make her escape while the others were rounded up. No, the cops would have to be naïve fools to believe her. The gunfire hadn't summonsed the police; they had arrived within minutes of the first shot happening, so they had been called earlier, perhaps by Pete even, as they'd arrived back at the house, or maybe by the tough guy, Perlman, between almost beating Callum's face in and shooting to distract Toby so Danni could escape. She couldn't be certain that the police already had her description as the ringleader of Danni and Josie Lockwood's abductors, but it was possible. Secretly she'd be relieved to be recognized and arrested, because she understood that there was only one alternative after this royal mess-up. If she escaped while Freda was arrested, she'd never be safe again: he was so well connected he could sentence her to death as easily from behind bars as anywhere else.

The police car disgorged a single officer, a young man, whose uniform was too pristine for him to have been more than a few months into service. He approached, his gaze never resting as he surveyed the odd-looking collection of people greeting him. He had one hand on his chest-mounted radio, the other with his thumb tucked into the armhole in his stab-proof vest. He tried to exude a look of calm confidence, but to Steph he looked more like he was about to break into a barn dance.

'Would somebody mind explaining what's happening here, or shall we all go down to the nick?'

Steph winced at the young officer's pathetic opening: she wondered how many crime dramas he'd watched on TV, and how many times he'd practised his tough-guy delivery in front of a mirror before being let loose on the mean streets of Cheshire.

Freda had brought his wheelchair to a stop, and behind him, Jakub stood stock-still and silent. Kolacz, spotting the lone, and probably inexperienced cop, had wandered back within a few metres of their boss. Steph realized that – being the only woman, and maybe the only one with a right to be there, considering she was in charge of a cute dog – his question had been aimed at her as the probable householder. She dropped the frightened expression, and instead turned a quizzical one to him. 'Is there something the matter?'

'That's what I'd like to know,' said the police constable. He coughed, and said, in a voice an octave deeper, 'We received an aborted emergency call from this location. It's standard practice to investigate, just in case—'

'Just in case of what? Oh, in case I'm in danger and being coerced into silence? Well, as you can see, that isn't the case. I'm just seeing off some friends who were kind enough to visit. I can't imagine who rang the emergency services.' She feigned a silent question to Freda, and he shrugged it off. 'I can assure you that it wasn't any of us.'

The officer stood a second or two in contemplation. He nodded to himself, and reached to depress the send button on his radio.

From the darkness, Pete moaned in alarm.

'Who was that?' asked the officer. He took a step forward, passing Steph as he searched for the source of the sound. Out of his immediate line of sight, she frowned darkly at Freda, who had no intention of allowing this young cop to take him in. Freda made a single gesture with his hand.

The cop spotted Pete curled like a foetus on the lawn. His instinct was to turn back to Steph, questions spilling from his mind to his tongue. They remained unspoken, because Kolacz rushed him, and one hand plastered his face, sealing in his cry of alarm, even as the other hand caught him between his legs. Kolacz heaved the young man in the air, and slammed him down with his spine bent over his knee. Releasing him, Kolacz dumped him on the gravel. He picked up a heel, and aimed it at the constable's throat. The actions were so sudden and shockingly brutal that Steph had been unable to avert her gaze. As the young cop's life was snatched from him, she knew his killing would be forever etched in her brain. Unbeknown to her, her fingers had fallen lax at sight of the murder, and Franklin's lead dropped at her feet.

'How in god's name are we going to explain this?' she croaked.

'I don't care what you do, Whizzer,' said Freda. 'As far as anyone learns, I was never here. If your boys deal with the others, and Volos finishes the husband off, you could stage it to look like a house invasion gone wrong. Simply, I don't care what you do. But I want my money, and I want my girl.'

'Why, though? Why the little girl?'

'Because she is *mine*,' he said, and that was as much of an explanation as was needed as far as he was concerned.

Steph understood that Danni had been on temporary loan to Barker, a prop along with her birth mother, Mel, to assist his disguise as a dad on an outing with his young family: a car containing a mother and child was less likely to draw suspicion than one containing a single man. Statistically fewer family groups were randomly pulled over by the cops than solo drivers or groups comprising only men. At the conclusion of Barker's job to deliver payment to their Glaswegian suppliers, he was supposed to return Mel and her illegitimate daughter to Freda. When he claimed that Danni was his, Steph had to wonder if he meant literally, or that she was simply a chattel to greedily hold on to until she proved useful in some other manner. If Freda was indeed Danni's biological father, that made allowing her to be a plaything of some of his important clients too despicable to stomach.

'What is wrong, Whizzer?' Freda sneered. 'I've said something that offends you?'

Kolacz lingered nearby.

'I'm only worried that we've gone too far,' she said. 'I mean, killing a copper is a huge mistake. The police won't rest until they find who's responsible, and—'

'Then make sure that they don't, or we might have to set a few dead ends and red herrings in their way to the truth.'

A shiver rode the length of her spine. By dead ends he wasn't mincing his words; she, and her two male helpers, would be fed to the cops, but only once they were dead and unable to answer any questions.

'I suggest you'd best get a move on,' Freda said, with a nod at the dead constable. 'I assume he's already given his location, and when he fails to follow up with his control room, other officers will be sent to find him. And don't forget those gunshots. Around here the locals probably hear farmers shooting crows or whatever, but not with automatic pistols.' He didn't expound. 'Volos, Jakub, let's be going, shall we?'

From the darkness a voice snapped, 'You murdering bastards aren't going anywhere.'

CALLUM

C allum taunted her as he chased Josie. He swiped his knife several times, even though there was no chance of it cutting her, but the action was about intimidation and keeping her off balance and on the move. He hoped to corral her between some taller monuments and the wall, where she'd be at his mercy. She knew what he was up to, and kept on the move. She once even vaulted on to a tomb, and used the advantage of its height to spot a path past him. He grinned maliciously, and lurched at her. She launched away, and this time his blade fell within a hand's span of cutting her. She jogged along a narrow gravel path between the graves, and then found some taller markers to set between them.

Callum swore at her.

She swore at him. He found the back-and-forth exchange of profanity amusing, as if it were a challenge to come up with the most inventive put down.

He wasn't laughing after the younger woman hurled a memorial vase still containing some brittle flowers and it bounced painfully off his shoulder. He viewed her attack as good enough reason to drop his pursuit of Josie for the time being and chase her instead.

He pursued her for only a few seconds before realizing he'd fallen into their ploy to wear him down. He went after Josie again, confident that he could reach her before she could scale the wall. Once he had her, he'd bet the younger bitch would rush to her assistance and then he'd pay her back for chucking the vase at him. The bloody thing was heavy sandstone, and sharp cornered, and had put a dent in his back that he was certain was bleeding beneath his clothes.

The younger woman threw something else, but it wasn't of concern; from the light impact it made off his thigh, he guessed it was one of the less expensive plastic flower holders she'd thrown.

He bared his teeth at Josie.

She was holding something aloft.

It looked square and solid . . . and heavy.

'Shit,' he said.

'Shit head,' she replied, and hurled it at him, and it was all he could do to dodge the missile. It smashed a gravestone, knocking a chunk of sandstone flying. Smaller bits of stone pelted his face like hail. He grimaced, turning aside to avoid his one decent eye being blinded.

There was noise, a brief *scrat-scrit-scrat*.

He snapped around, seeking her.

The move was too fast, and his brain reminded him that he'd taken one hell of a smack to his face. His brain swirled, thoughts caught in a kaleidoscopic whirl. He staggered, off balance and on the verge of passing out. He grabbed for support with his left hand, missed the gravestone he'd groped for and went down on one knee.

The noise changed: *scrit-scrat-scriiiittt* . . .

'My fuggun head,' he groaned.

His hand went to the side of his face. Beneath his fingertips, the entire left side of his head felt spongy, and sore. His eyelid was puffed up to the size of an apple. Fluid leaked from between the lashes, too viscous to be tears alone.

Perlman had done a bloody number on him.

Perlman wouldn't have been there to smash in his face if not for the younger bitch.

She wouldn't have been there if not for her relationship to Josie, and to the goofy little shit, Danni.

Each of the three little bitches was responsible for Perlman pounding his head to mush.

'I swear to you, I'm going to gut you all and hang your puddings between these gravestones like fuckin' bunting.'

His words were issued from his mouth, and yet they sounded alien to him, as if someone other than he – somebody who actually had the strength and resolve to go through with the threat – had uttered them. Physically he felt too weak to push up from his knee, let alone commit the savagery in his mind.

Scrit-scrat-scraaatttcccchhh!

Fingernails down a chalkboard, wet fingertips on a balloon, a dentist's drill, any of those cringe-inducing sounds would've been preferable to whatever actually sent red-hot needles into his brain.

He launched up, shouting in anger. His knife whipped in wide arcs.

A hurled object glanced off his back.

Callum spun and almost lost control of his feet. He darted out his blade to stab the younger woman, but she was well beyond his reach.

She showed her teeth in a feral snarl.

She picked up another object and over-armed it as if bowling a cricket ball. He couldn't tell what she'd thrown, but – by fuck! – it hurt when it him directly on his pubis. A couple of inches lower and the bloody thing would've got him in the balls.

Something else struck him. This missile had come from else-where. He cringed, turning, trying to anticipate and ward off another stone. He spotted Danni, looking pleased with her aim as she stood atop the wall. The weirdo kid crouched to worm loose another smaller stone from the wall.

'I should have done you the second you'd outgrown your useful-ness,' he barked.

'You've threatened my daughter once too often, you bastard!' Josie's voice sounded as if she was standing at his left shoulder.

Callum whipped his knife around, stabbing for her abdomen.

Once he had his blade in her, he'd give it a twist, wrench upwards to her breastbone and open her like he was unzipping a suitcase. Except his knife blade grated against stone.

Standing astride the monument he'd struck, Josie heaved her shoulder against the statue of an angel. This time, galvanized by anger at his threat towards her daughter, she rammed the thing off its stand. The *scrit-scrat* sounds had been her working it loose, the heavy object scraping loose of its base. Silence followed its topple . . .

He was the proverbial rabbit in headlights. Reflex should have caused him to leap for his life, but for reasons unknown, his mind and body weren't in sync. When he tried to jerk back, it was as if his feet were mired in the earth. His knife was no defence against the weathered statue: it wasn't as tall as him, and it outweighed him by a good twenty-five kilos. His left hand shoved against the statue, but his elbow only folded, and then the face of an archangel came at him, and St Michael was as happy to headbutt a servant of the devil as he was to spear Satan with his sword.

The punch landed on his face by Perlman, augmented with metal, had crushed his eye-socket and cheekbone. The statue crashing down, headfirst into his, finished the job Perlman had started. After the initial impact, and the scarlet flash that swept through him subsided, Callum found that having his cranium crushed wasn't as bad as he would have previously imagined.

He lay on his back, the statue atop him, wrapped in his arms as if he hugged the angel in an act of contrition. The weight of the stone made breathing almost impossible. But it was OK. His head didn't hurt any more, and who needed to breathe anyway?

'Is he . . . Josie, is he . . .?'

The voice sounded hushed, musical, as if it was the voice of the angel singing a soothing lullaby.

'Dead?' Josie answered, equally as musical. 'I . . . I think so.'

'*I'm not dead,*' Callum said.

Neither of the women heard him, but how could they when the words were spoken inside what was left of his mushed brain.

'Did he just move?'

'I don't know. I think it was only the statue settling.'

'Maybe we should . . .'

'No, he got what he deserved. Let's just leave him like that, Grace.'

Grace?

Her name sounded ironic under the circumstances.

Callum laughed, a soft, reed-thin chuckle.

'Where's Danni?' It was unknown to him which of the women asked the question; he couldn't even tell if perhaps it was he who had made the enquiry.

'I'm here,' said Danni.

Callum tried turning his head towards her, to see the gawky-looking kid one last time, but neither his head nor eye obeyed him.

'*I s'pose you'll be happy you won't hafta pay me my expenses now, eh, Tobe?*'

He loosened his hug on the statue, and his arms flopped wide. His flick knife sat cupped in his palm. The weighty stone settled on him, forcing out a noisy exhalation.

'If he wasn't dead before, he is now.'

KYLE

There was more chance of the women escaping the knifeman than dodging the more capable, and less physically disabled gunman, hence his reason for drawing the latter into a cat-and-mouse chase. Kyle didn't consider himself any more bullet-proof than Grace or her sister, but if the gunman went after them then they were finished. He'd already softened up the knifeman for them, and knew from the injured man's staggering approach to the grave-yard that he was a long way off recovering from the blow that Kyle had dealt him. The women had a fighting chance, and from what he'd witnessed of them both, they weren't going to give in against the creep: he'd put his money on the women coming out victorious any day of the week.

He adjusted his phone in his breast pocket.

After firing the shot into the air, and distracting the gunman long enough for Danni to break free, Kyle had considered his next move. Out on the road, he'd ushered the women and Danni to use the cover of the graveyard, while he'd continued on along the path. He deliberately made enough noise to ensure that the gunman knew where he'd gone. Kyle didn't think he was about to pay back the little girl for kneeing him in the nuts but, sure as shit, he'd try kicking Kyle's bollocks up his back given half a chance. Kyle had no intention of giving him any chance.

The gunman progressed quickly, and on steady feet. He'd shaken off the knee to the testicles, but held on to the cold rage of being made to look a fool by a child. He carried his pistol held close to his chest, while he scanned the deepest shadows, seeking Kyle's hiding spot. The man's head moved by small increments, but likely his eyes were wide against the gloom and he was using his peripheral vision to spot the tiniest of move-ments. Kyle had a better view of him as he approached than the other way around. Kyle was stationary, whereas the gunman was on the move, and constrained on two sides by the graveyard wall, and the adjoining property's fence. The overhanging tree boughs formed a thatched ceiling, through which faint starlight fell on the gunman, painting his dark hair and shoulders the colour of hoarfrost.

More than a decade ago, Kyle had been drilled on weapon handling to such a degree that shooting became second nature to him. But that was then. He hadn't so much as put a bullet down a range in years, never mind into a living, breathing human being. To operate as a Special Forces soldier, he had been able to detach from reality, and dehumanize his targets, so that killing his enemies was no different than mowing down avatars in a video game. Somehow he thought that he'd be able to drop this guy with impunity, but since his days in the forces, Kyle had become a different person. He'd become a dad, and being a murderous bastard wasn't the type of role model he hoped to present to his boys.

From only metres away, he fired, and the instant he did, he knew he was wrong to aim only to wound. His bullet struck the gunman, but it didn't drop him, and if anything it stung him into action. The gunman loosed a flurry of three bullets in rapid succession, each aimed in the direction of the Webley's muzzle flash. How Kyle didn't die under fire was a miracle, and a relief, but it was outstanding luck that none of the other's bullets had found their mark, and he wasn't about to test the gunman's aim a second time. He drove up from both bent knees and launched into a grapple for control of the pistol. His Webley was used to bludgeon rather than shoot. The barrel struck the gunman's left arm, but it saved the man's head, and then fingers furled around the gun's butt, digging into the trigger guard as the man tried to wrench away his weapon. Kyle more or less did the same, contesting for control of the pistol by bearing down on the barrel and trying to use leverage to break the gunman's trigger finger, forcing him to drop the gun.

Neither man wasted bullets. Kyle reeled a few seconds, vision flashing in starbursts of red and white after taking a butt from the man's forehead. He repaid the discomfort with a knee that missed the sweet spot by inches, but it was close enough on the thigh that it brought on residual agony from the knee that Danni had served the gunman. They crashed from one side of the path to the other, rebounding off the graveyard wall, almost crashing through the flimsier fence on the opposite side. Each grasping the other's gun hand, they almost waltzed a few metres down the path, and then they spun around and retraced their steps. Kyle headbutted the gunman. His forehead smacked painfully against the man's ear and temple, missing the bridge of the nose he'd intended, but the force of the blow sent the man staggering. His back caromed off the graveyard wall. Small stones toppled off the top, clattering between their feet. The man gave up on Kyle's revolver. He understood that Kyle was reluctant to fire, and sought to punish him for his stupidity. The fingers of his left hand dug at Kyle's side, seeking where the knife had pierced him earlier. The pain was intense.

Kyle swore at his temerity for using the dirty trick.

Right back at you, he thought, and batted at the man's face with the gun's butt.

The gunman stepped back and threw a kick. Kyle had not let go of his right wrist, so the distance wasn't ideal for generating full power, but the boot still sank into Kyle's gut. Kyle though had been training in mixed martial arts long enough that his body was conditioned against the probing kicks of an opponent, and it would take something more powerful than a front kick to finish him.

'You made a big mistake thinking you can take me on,' the gunman said. It wasn't a boast to him but basic fact, and he was confident in his summation.

'Nah, mate,' Kyle growled. 'You maybe look the part, but you aren't all you think you are.'

Their positions allowed Kyle a line of attack. He folded his right arm, and stabbed at the gunman's chest with the point of his elbow. Bone on bone made for pain and it didn't matter how conditioned the body. The gunman snapped out a curse, and Kyle sensed as much as saw the way the man's shoulders rounded inward, in an effort to protect his abused sternum. Kyle rammed him again. The pistol fell from spasming fingers. Kyle let it go, heard it clatter on the path. As they scuffled, they kicked the pistol and it spun away into a clot of shadows – for the moment out of sight and mind. He didn't relinquish his gun, he jabbed it into the man's face. Already Josie, he assumed, had torn his face with her nails. The front sight on the revolver tore another bloody furrow in the man's cheek.

A hand cut at Kyle's throat.

Shit!

A knee drove deep into his gut.

A flurry of punches set Kyle back on his heels.

The guy was defter at hand-to-hand combat than Kyle had first thought.

Time to end things then, and somehow that decision changed his thought processes away from sparing life to saving his own. He caught the next punch on his upraised forearm, and drove in with the revolver; at the same time he hooked his heel around the back of the man's lead leg, and drew it to him. The leg was ripped from under the man and they both went down hard on the path, with Kyle on top. Later he'd have to convince the cops that he didn't deliberately shoot, but that the gun fired due to the impact of their bodies. However, Kyle knew his version of events would be challenged, considering he'd crushed his left palm over the man's mouth, jammed the muzzle deep in his abdomen and gently squeezed the trigger. The compression of their bodies muffled the retort, but not the result of a bullet ploughing through flesh and organs.

His opponent didn't die immediately.

Kyle sat astride him, hand sealing his mouth and nostrils, holding him down as his heart slowed and the feral lights dimmed in his eyes. All the while, Kyle made frantic noises, begging the man to rise, acting as if he was trying to revive him, not assist him to cross over. Once he was confident he'd done enough to sway a jury in his favour, he let go of his opponent and slowly stood. It hurt to stand, and walking was an effort, but it was simply through a cramping of his muscles. With each step he loosened a little, until he was jogging without too much discomfort back towards the top end of the graveyard.

He met Grace, Josie and Danni at the collapsed section of wall. They looked worn but otherwise unhurt. Actually, on deeper study, he thought that all three were riding on waves of adrenalin, and would collapse very soon, but for now victory over their aggressor made them high. They looked determined to end the fight, but he wasn't about to allow them to fall back into the hands of the bad guys, not after all he'd done to free them. He tried corralling them and urging them down the path, to where he'd spotted an Audi car abandoned at the far end. He'd wondered if the car belonged to a late-night dog walker, who might have returned to their car in the meantime, who could help get them safely away. Another part of him warned that the knifeman had got back to the house ready to ambush them, so it was very possible the car was his. He told them that they would come across the gunman on the path, but not to worry, because he was beyond harming them. He was surprised to note that Danni barely flickered an emotion, the poor kid had grown inured to violence and death in such a short period of time, it wouldn't surprise him if she weren't slipping into a second bout of trauma-induced amnesia.

'We can't just run away,' Josie told him. 'Not while Pete's back there, all alone, and suffering god knows what punishment.'

Kyle sighed, thought about it for no more than a second.

'OK, you lot stay behind me and try not to show your faces. I'll go and get him.'

Minutes later he stood, facing the real villains of the piece, whose disregard for life had been extended beyond Pete to a young police constable who looked no older than some of the schoolboys that attended Kyle's martial arts sessions. He tasted stomach bile.

'Volos, Jakub, let's be going, shall we?' an elderly man seated in a wheelchair announced.

Kyle snarled, 'You murdering bastards aren't going anywhere.'

JOSIE

The sisters obeyed Kyle's instruction no longer than it took for him to confront the group of criminals. They stood next to the gate he'd clambered over, with Josie physically restraining Danni so that the girl didn't follow him. Danni had shown rare bravery in the fight to stop Callum, and seemingly she was up for more. Josie understood, because she also was still alight with outrage brought on by those horrible people. She could tell that Grace itched to climb the gate too, to go and help her new friend. In that moment Josie wondered how close her sister had grown to him in the hours they'd spent in such proximity. She didn't detect a hint that there was anything romantic about her feelings for him, but Grace showed an almost fierce loyalty: when you fight together, you fight the hardest. For Grace, and especially for Danni, Josie had just crushed a man to death, so she understood how far that bond could incite violence. Sadly, she was sickened that there wasn't much more she could've done to help Pete.

She sought her partner.

He lay several metres from where she'd last seen him. Bundled foetus-like, he didn't stir, even when Kyle hollered at the bad men who were preparing to leave. Fresh tears stung Josie's eyes. Previously they'd been fed by ignominy, now they were by genuine grief. Nearby was another figure and it took Josie seconds, and a dash of her wrist to clear her vision, before she could make out who it was: a police constable! She noted the police car then, parked at the rear of the van that'd disgorged Leonard Freda, hoping upon hope that the constable had called for assistance before being beaten – or killed, because he was as unresponsive as Pete, and there was something unnatural about the odd way his torso was twisted.

She couldn't focus on the wounded, but on those still capable of harming them further. Freda wasn't a physical threat, and the nurse looked as if a stiff breeze would knock him over, and somehow any fear that Steph had instilled in Josie throughout that long day had diminished to a point where she appeared pathetic in the company of the others. Especially when she considered Coal Axe, or Kolacz as she'd heard Danni corrected earlier, who loomed large and fearsome. He squeezed and unfurled his fingers a number of times, breathing deeply as he appraised the revolver pointed at them. He was like a bull, and Josie almost expected him to begin digging at the ground as he built up to a charge.

For the moment, Freda kept him in check.

The disabled man showed he'd nurtured an attitude where he felt himself above all others: what Freda wanted, Freda got. He must've thought himself bulletproof, because he disregarded the command to stop, and flapped a hand at his nurse/driver to assist him into his carriage.

Kyle moved forward, aiming the revolver directly at Freda, only for the seated man to disregard him with a toss of his head.

Kyle adjusted his aim.

To the nurse, he said, 'Try to help him, I'll shoot you.'

The man balked, his skeletal face turning ashen.

'It isn't him you should fear, Jakub,' Freda crowed. 'If you don't help me, then it means I must sever our relationship.'

There was enough unspoken threat in Freda's words to ensure that the nurse reached to grab the rear handles and help guide the wheelchair on to the ramp.

'Stop right there.' Kyle fired a bullet.

It buried itself in the turf.

His warning shot actually had the opposite effect.

'See,' Freda said with a victorious snarl, 'he isn't going to shoot you. He's too afraid to shoot.'

'Tell your other friend that,' Kyle replied. 'You know, the arsehole with the pistol. Oh, hang on, you can't, because he's dead.'

'You killed Toby?'

Kyle allowed his silence to answer.

Josie saw Steph almost fold inside herself at the news.

'Don't look for that other shitbag, either,' Kyle went on, meaning Callum Grieves. 'Because he's as dead as his buddy.'

Nobody appeared that bothered by Callum's demise, but apparently Toby had been a valued member of the team.

'Get him, Volos,' Freda hissed.

Working up to confront him, Kolacz suddenly bellowed and rushed at Kyle.

Kyle was already wounded, bleeding from his ribs, and had apparently fought a tough battle with Toby. He was no match for the charging brute. Kyle steadied the gun, and squeezed the trigger.

The bullet hit Kolacz dead centre.

The giant seemingly brushed off the bullet to his chest, barely slowing in his charge.

Kyle fired again.

This bullet struck Kolacz in the throat, and his reaction belied his indestructible appearance. He slapped both big hands over the wound, gagging on the blood that rushed into his throat, and folded at the knees. His momentum caused him to slide on the lawn, his knees digging deep furrows, and then his upper torso flopped forward and he lay face down, dying at Kyle's feet.

Coolly, Kyle turned the revolver on the others.

'I didn't want to do that. His death is your fault,' he told Freda as he slipped out his mobile phone from his shirt pocket. 'I warned you, and I warned you again, but you had him attack me and I had to shoot in defence.'

Freda understood then, and so did Josie. Kyle had been filming the goings-on for evidence, or maybe he was even live-streaming them direct to the police. She wondered how long he'd had the camera function on his phone running, and how close the police reinforcements were to arriving.

'This is your final warning,' Kyle said, and he dabbed his fingertips over the phone screen, and Josie, even twenty or so metres distance, realized he had stopped the record function. It was a weightier threat than shooting into the lawn again.

'You won't shoot me, a cripple in a wheelchair,' Freda said, but he lacked the confidence in his invulnerability of before. Behind him, the nurse Jakub held up his hands, fingers wiggling to indicate he'd loosened his grip on the chair. He stepped back a few feet and Kyle allowed him to. Steph also backed away, watching the gun the entire time, before she knew that Kyle had no intention of moving it away from his prime target. She turned and fled.

Freda croaked, 'I'm just a disabled old man, I'm no threat to you.'

'No, you aren't a threat to me. But you threatened to kill my ex-wife and kids,' Kyle said calmly. 'I can't risk you ordering a hit from your jail cell.'

Kyle's revolver barked one last time.

Freda clasped a hand over his chest, looking down at the spot where the bullet had entered him. He held that pose, lacking the strength to raise his head ever again.

The killings of Kolacz and Freda had been swift and final, and Josie felt no pity for them. Kyle had been right to kill them, because for as long as they lived, none of them, from Danni to Kyle's children, would be safe from the gang boss's retribution.

The nurse, Jakub, stood with his hands in the air, and was no threat to them. Whatever agreement he had with Freda, Kyle's bullet had freed him from it, and he seemed relieved in his own way. Without asking permission, he sat down on the grass, and laced his fingers behind his neck.

Grace clambered over the gate and rushed to Kyle's side.

Josie ignored whatever went on between them for the moment; she helped Danni up and over and then followed, and they both jogged to where Pete lay.

'Pete, darling, can you hear me?' Josie said and dropped to her knees. Danni held on to her while she gently shook his shoulder.

Pete rolled over and flattened out on his back. His face was bloodied, and the tip of his slitted tongue protruded slightly between swollen lips. His eyes also were swollen, but there was lucidity in them. He blinked up at Josie as he said, 'Ith it all over?'

Josie cried in relief.

Danni said, 'You still sound like Daffy Duck.'

'Are you OK, babe?' Josie asked.

He held out his bandaged hand. 'It still hurts like a bugger to point.'

Danni laughed uproariously and, after a few seconds, so did Pete. Josie's voice cracked in a cry of joy, and she bent down to kiss him better.

Franklin snuffled them.

Josie raised her head from Pete, and then looked at Danni. Danni took the lead in her fingers and gently urged the dog away.

'This isn't over with yet,' Josie told Pete. 'Steph isn't getting away from this scot-free. Not after bringing these people here to our home and causing all of this hurt.'

She stood, looked down at the tiny dog and then offered it a smile of encouragement. 'Where's your mummy, Franklin? Yes, there's a good doggie,' she purred, 'show us where your mummy is hiding.'

Franklin grinned and his button eyes twinkled, delighted by the idea of a game of hide-and-seek.

'Find your mum, Franklin.' Danni encouraged the dog with a flick of the lead, and he dashed to comply.

Halfway past the house, Josie saw Grace approaching. There was no need for explanation, and while Kyle watched the nurse, Grace had decided to help her sister to find the final bad guy.

Franklin led them around the house. He skipped from side to side, nose to the ground, working over time. He chuffed excitedly, his breaths quickening as he brought them closer to where Steph had hidden. She had made it to the same perimeter as Kyle had earlier while being stalked by Toby, but whereas he'd had no qualms about using the thorny hedge for cover, Steph saw it as an insurmountable barrier. She tried running one way and then the other, seeking a way through, but beyond the hawthorn and brambles, the old iron railings blocked any route.

Finally, she took a leaf out of Jakub's book and sank down on her backside on the lawn. She struggled to catch her breath.

Josie, Grace and even Danni stood over the woman, while Franklin rushed back and forth, his loyalties divided, and unsure who he should expect praise from for finding his mum.

Nobody spoke.

Recrimination was pointless and wouldn't change anything.

They simply waited, while the sirens and flashing lights of converging emergency vehicles descended on the house and grounds.

Finally, Steph looked up at them and there was genuine regret in her pale eyes. 'I never meant Danni any harm,' she promised. 'You might not know it, but I was like her once. I was the little girl growing up surrounded by those evil men. I'm glad Danni escaped, even as I know there was never any hope of escape for me.' She grunted at the absurdity of her position, and the grunt became a chuckle. 'The good thing is, because Danni escaped, she has helped me to escape too. Yes, it led to *this* and those evil men can't hurt me ever again.' She spoke directly to Danni: 'You've grown into quite the amazing young lady, Danni. You're clever, the way your birth mum was. You know as well as I that Freda's money isn't within miles of the train museum you led us to.' She held up her hand to stay any rebuttal. 'If you do know where to find it, the money's yours, and, well, it looks as if Franklin's yours too. I can't take him with me where I'm going, so please look after him, and love him as much as I know you will.'

''Course I'll love him,' Danni said, and she crouched to tickle the dog under its forearms. 'He'll have the best home ever with me.'

Despite owing the woman nothing but hatred, Josie had no objection to the idea.

EPILOGUE

Bareback Mountain – or, more accurately, Farleton Knott – loomed over them as if the prow of a great ocean-going liner had been sculpted from the limestone ridge. In more recent years, some of the bareness had disappeared, and plants and shrubs had begun to colonize the once scoured rock so that it didn't fit the sisters' jokey moniker as much any more. Nevertheless, huge swathes of bare stone still showed through, pale shades of pink and yellow in the morning sunlight. The rush of works traffic on the nearby motorway played a backing track, sounding almost like a tidal sea washing the foot of the hill.

Josie and Grace stood shoulder to shoulder, while Pete and Kyle hunkered down behind a dry-stone wall. Danni moved around the four adults, tugged erratically about by Franklin, as he sniffed out rabbits, or rodents, or even imagined creatures. Danni found excitement in Franklin's hunt for his elusive prey, more so than she did the buried treasure.

Weeks had passed since Danni and Josie had been taken hostage. In the interim, Stephanie Wyszogrodzki had been remanded to jail awaiting trial, as had Jakub Holstein, while the others had all gone to the morgue. Kyle's actions were under suspicion, despite him being very selective about the footage he'd recorded on his phone, but it was unlikely that any jury would condemn him for slaying the worst kinds of humanity represented by Leonard Freda, Volos Kolacz or Toby Davis – considering their deaths had all been seen as desperate acts of self-defence or in order to save the lives of two innocent sisters and a child. He claimed that Callum Grieves had brought the revolver to the fight and, seeing as he was no longer around to argue, it appeared that the police had bought Kyle's explanation of how he'd come into contact with it. In Callum's abandoned Audi, they'd found tiny droplets and smears of blood, and DNA tests matched them to the brutal murder of Danni's saviour, the truck driver Robert 'Bobby' Charters. There wasn't a person in the country who would claim that Josie and Grace had been wrong to kill the monster now preying on their little girl. They admitted that Freda's people had targeted them in search of money stolen by Mel, but that Danni simply had no other memories of the fateful day between abandoning Barker at the service station, stopping at the railway heritage museum and the pile-up further north on the M6 hours later; it was generally assumed that the bag and its contents had been burnt to cinders in the conflagration following the collision; in the aftermath of the crash, nobody was looking for bags of cash, and any evidence of Barker's burnt-out car was now long gone. Surprisingly, throughout the legal proceedings, neither Steph nor Jakub had tried to contradict Kyle or Josie's version of events. It now seemed safe enough to try recovering the money without fear of being under surveillance from either the police or rival gangsters.

At first Josie had been loath to chase the money any further. It was cash earned through the pain and suffering of others, allegedly an upfront payment to Freda's Scottish business associates to supply him freshly trafficked immigrant girls to the sex industry. Mel, they discovered, had been trafficked from an Eastern European country in a similar fashion, the reason why her charred remains had gone unidentified. Morally Josie wanted no part of the dirty money, but Grace and her new partner, Kyle, had reminded her that Mel had died for taking the money she'd intended to buy Danni's freedom with: it was Danni's inheritance, and should be used to give the girl the life she deserved. There was the matter that she and Pete were struggling to make ends meet, and required more income than theirs to continue living in the big house that had almost become an anchor around their necks. With the money they could move away, leave behind the terrible memories the house held, and begin afresh in a new home. In the end, Josie relented, but only after a promise that some of the money should go to Kyle and to Grace in setting up a more fitting permanent home for her and her boys: or their boys combined, depending on how committed the adults became.

She'd suffered a minor wobble, wondering if they were attracting other hyenas to come sniffing around, but nobody beyond those closely involved in the case learned what Freda's interest was in the Lockwood family, and certainly it was never raised that Danni and 'the Girl in the Smoke' were one and the same: the Scottish gangsters remained under the impression that the money en route to them had burned up alongside the thief who'd tried denying them.

Besides, a young constable barely two months out of his probation period had been brutally murdered, and no criminal in their right mind would want involvement in the murder inquiry and the cops shifting their focus on them.

Back in the graveyard when Callum was hunting them, Josie and Danni had shared a moment of epiphany, and due to the earlier one shared when passing Farleton Nott, it had given Josie the idea where they might find Mel's hidden stash. At the base of the hill sat an ancient burial ground and adjoining chapel, used – she supposed – by farmers and villagers of old. She'd fancied that Mel had come across an open grave that had been prepared to accept a recently deceased body into the earth, and had dropped the bag into it, perhaps covering it with a fine layer of dirt. Coming back would be akin to grave robbing, and it had given her more pause even than the thought that other gangsters might join the chase. Yet, Pete and Kyle had only laughed at the notion, and had refused to bring with them the requisite spades and crowbars depicted as the tools of ghouls in horror movies. It stood to reason that Mel must've known she didn't have the wherewithal to excavate a grave unnoticed, so it wouldn't be her choice of hiding place. Not in a freshly dug grave, at any rate.

The sisters stood watch while the men searched the graveyard, seeking any sign where one of the older graves had been disturbed, where perhaps Mel had dug a hole just deep enough in which to dump the bag, before covering it up again with turf. Twice now the men had returned to them shaking their heads softly, and Josie knew that all involved were fostering doubts that she was on to something there.

Josie watched Danni roam.

Her daughter and the Bichon Frisé had become inseparable: at the beginning Danni had attempted to change his name to something a little more catchy like Button or Snowball – Snowy for short – but the dog had refused to respond to anything except Franklin, so Franklin he'd stayed.

Franklin picked his own route among the headstones, sniffing and rummaging.

But more than once, the girl had unerringly pulled him to her and headed towards the back left corner of the yard where a small outbuilding stood. The men had already made a thorough examination of the shed, without any results, but something about it subconsciously attracted the girl. Josie observed her as Danni allowed Franklin a little freedom by playing out the lead, but it was so she could crouch and rub her fingertips through the grass.

'Something's going on over there,' said Josie.

Grace followed her nod, and she crinkled her forehead in contemplation. 'D'you think she's having another recollection?'

'She once told me she could remember everything. I think she did experience a tidal wave of memories last time we were here, but they were all mixed up in her mind. Something about the ground next to that shed has definitely piqued her interest.'

'Let's take a look then.'

Josie grasped her sister's arm, holding her back for a few seconds. 'If we do find the bag, it means it changes our lives, and maybe not all of those changes will be for the better. Maybe we should just forget about it and drive away and never look back.'

Grace considered her words. She shook her head. 'Nah, sis, let's not do that, eh?'

They walked to where Danni still scrabbled about on the ground.

Pete and Kyle, sensing the change in the sisters' demeanour, stood and watched them from across the graveyard. Kyle, the more alert of the two, also took a lingering check of the nearby road, ensuring they were not being observed: should they attract attention, he'd come up with a cover story that his folks originated from the nearby village of Burton-in-Kendal – a complete fabrication – and he was checking if any of his ancestors were buried in the plot. Nobody had approached in the twenty minutes they'd been searching, so it was unlikely they'd be disturbed anytime soon.

'What are you doing?' Josie asked.

Danni had dropped to her knees, heedless of the green stains on her jeans. She patted and probed and plucked at the ground. 'I'm sure it was—'

Danni halted all movement.

Josie placed a hand on her shoulder and gently squeezed in support.

Danni tilted her head on its side, offering a grin, while she formed a fist and gave it a swift rap on the earth. The sound of her knuckles on stone was unmistakable.

'What have we here?' Grace joined them, crouching low. She fed her fingers into the grass and traced the edge of something, even while Josie performed a similar act. They both looked at each other.

'A paving stone?' Grace surmised.

'No. Think about where we are. It's a fallen headstone. And by the way that the grass has partly grown over it, it has been here for ages.'

'My mam used a big stick to lift it up last time,' Danni announced.

The headstone was buried half an inch or more in the earth, and it was not easy to move. Mel had shown some initiative in levering the headstone up, but the sisters didn't need a big stick when they had Kyle and Pete to call on. Grace stood and waved them over while Josie and Danni continued to peel away layers of grass; it had overgrown the headstone and formed a thick wad of interwoven stalks that Mel could easily have rearranged over the top once she'd re-laid the stone in the ground.

Without instruction, Pete and Kyle took up positions on each side, and then they dug their fingers under the stone and hauled it up.

A cavity was dug from the earth below, and filling it was an old nylon holdall. The bag was stained with age, covered in cobwebs and the dried silvery trails of slugs. The zip had been fully closed, so whatever was inside remained a mystery. But not for longer than the second it took for Danni to whoop in delight and tug back the zipper. The adults crowded around her, with Josie shivering in a mixture of excitement and anxiety, allowing Danni to be the first to unpack her inheritance.

END